# EVIL ALWAYS FINDS A WAY

## TED TAYLER

Vinci Books

vinci-books.com

Published by Vinci Books Ltd in 2026

1

Copyright © Ted Tayler 2017

The author has asserted their moral right to be identified as the author of this work in accordance with the Copyright, Designs and Patents Act 1988. This work is a work of fiction. Names, characters, places and incidents are the product of the author's imagination or are used fictitiously. Any resemblance to actual persons, living or dead, places and incidents is entirely coincidental.

All rights reserved. No part of this publication may be copied, reproduced, distributed, stored in any retrieval system, or transmitted in any form or by any means, including photocopying, recording, or other electronic or mechanical methods, nor used as a source for any form of machine learning including AI datasets, without the prior written permission of the publisher.

The publisher and the author have made every effort to obtain permissions for any third party material used in this book and to comply with copyright law. Any queries in this respect should be brought to the attention of the publisher and any omissions will be corrected in future editions.

A CIP catalogue record for this book is available from the British Library.

Paperback ISBN: 9781036700560

The EU GPSR authorised representative is Logos Europe, 9 rue Nicolas Poussion, 17000 La Rochelle, France
contact@logoseurope.eu

## By Ted Tayler

### The Phoenix

*The Olympus Project*
*Gold, Silver and Bombs*
*Nothing Is Ever Forever*
*In the Lap of the Gods*
*The Price of Treachery*
*A New Dawn*
*Something Wicked Draws Near*
*Evil Always Finds A Way*
*Revenge Comes in Many Colours*
*Three Weeks in September*
*A Frequent Peal of Bells*
*Larcombe Manor*

### The Freeman Files

*Fatal Decision*
*Last Orders*
*Pressure Point*
*Deadly Formula*
*Final Deal*
*Barking Mad*
*Creature Discomforts*

*Silent Terror*

*Night Train*

*All Things Bright*

*Buried Secrets*

*A Genuine Mistake*

*Strange Beginnings*

*Dead Reckoning*

*A Normal November*

*Into the Sunlight*

*Tame the Storm*

*One True Friend*

*Whispered Truths*

*A Morning Murder*

*Quick to Anger*

*Red Herring Season*

*Gathering Clouds*

*Still Standing*

## Chapter One

***Monday, 26th May 2014***

The cellar walls were dark and damp. Her metal chair sat in the centre of the room, bolted to the concrete floor. They had strapped her feet to the legs of the chair with gaffer tape, and no matter how much she struggled against them, they didn't budge an inch.

They had secured her hands behind her, and the stress on her shoulders only eased when she passed out. Either from the nagging pain or the cocktail of drugs that they gave her. In a few minutes, she was lucid enough to assess her surroundings; she could not see a thing. Her underground prison was in total darkness.

If only she could get her hands free and cover her ears. As she sat there, hour after hour, alone in the pitch-black room, the sounds drove her mad. A constant drip from a pipe, somewhere high up on the wall behind her. The staccato movements of mice, or worse, when they skittered across the floor, heading for holes in the walls.

As much as those sounds preyed on her sanity, there was the ever-present fear of her captors' return.

The woman knew the exact moment her nightmare began.

She left her colleagues at five on Friday evening to drive the short distance home. After a busy week, she wanted a long soak in the bath, a pizza, and a cold beer. The others were going to a local bar before making a Tube journey to the capital's outskirts or a train trip back to the country.

Why didn't she listen to their cries as she headed to the underground car park?

"Aw, come on, don't be such a wuss," Brandi shouted.

"It'll be a laugh, babe. I'll get us Sex on the Beach," Selina offered, which brought squeals of laughter from the rest.

She had waved a hand in their direction, smiled a weak smile in reply, and carried on taking the stairs to the lower level.

Why did she prefer solitude to the heady social whirl of a raucous wine bar on a warm summer's evening? Memories of her past life shaped her present attitude; those places had been the building bricks of the lifestyle she led in her twenties. They had been the slippery slope into addiction and prostitution. These days she shunned every invitation that might tempt her back into her old ways.

Her drive home posed a few problems. Instead of making for Holland Park Avenue as she did nine times out of ten, she cut up Kensington High Street. Big mistake. Traffic was at a standstill. The roadworks she had forgotten to read about caused her to spend the next fifteen minutes in her hot little car, with no air-con, as hundreds of drivers negotiated the temporary traffic lights. Patience was at a premium. At last, she turned onto Abbotsbury Road. She endured a brief battle with pedestrians on Holland Park Avenue and reached a calmer spot where a red light stopped her progress near the Gate cinema.

Almost there now, she had thought; her flat lay just around the corner. The streets nearby were home to various stores, restaurants, and cafés, plus more specialist shops that dealt in rare records and antiques. It was the neighbourhood where she settled a year after leaving University.

The Gate, a Grade II listed building, had stood here since Edwardian times. She often visited the far more beautiful place on the inside than the façade through her windscreen might suggest. Several bars and clubs were dotted about, too, in the vicinity. Those weren't on her radar any longer. Despite their temptations, she was happy with her choice of where she lived and wouldn't change it regardless of her financial situation.

That thought drifted away in seconds as she experienced spasms of pain in her shoulders and lower back. On earlier occasions, she had screamed or cried for help. This time she laughed, and the more she thought how ridiculous this reaction was, given her current predicament, the more she laughed.

Why didn't the bastards come and dose her up again? She craved the release the needle would give. To be knocked out for hours, to not feel a thing, or to spend what felt like a day on a multi-coloured drug-fuelled trip was preferable to sitting here wide-awake, losing her grip on reality.

Nobody came.

Friday, at five pm, yes, that had been the start of this nightmare. Thirty-five minutes later, she reached her street. Then she parked the car and climbed the four steps to the front door of the Victorian terraced house she shared with five other flat owners. Her ground-floor flat was in the shade in the afternoons. She had opened a window and flopped onto the sofa. The stuffy atmosphere from the flat being shut up all day soon went. She relaxed in the fresh air, flicking through TV channel menus to find something to watch that evening.

Ten minutes later, with the pizza ordered, the bath filling, and a clean glass on the worktop by the fridge, she could relax. She entered the bathroom at six o'clock, just as the theme music for the news bulletin started. It struck her as strange that she could remember everything she had done during those sixty minutes.

How many hours had passed since then? How many days?

A cramp in her left calf replaced the aches and pains in her arms and back. But, no, if she concentrated hard, she could isolate five separate individual areas of pain. Her calf was now nine out of ten; her shoulders and back had subsided to eight apiece — the cramp in the toes of her right foot a mere six. The fifth remaining niggle came from her bladder.

As she leant over to turn off the taps back in her flat, however long ago, she had heard the doorbell. She cursed Domino's every stride she took away from the luxurious bath that awaited. At seven o'clock, she told the muppet on the phone; it wasn't a problem if they couldn't get there until a quarter-past, half-past seven even. But not before. She had wrapped her dressing gown tight around her and stood behind the door, with the chain on, as she opened it to give the delivery boy a volley of abuse.

The heavy wooden door hit her squarely in the face, cracking into her nose as it flew open. She had been stunned and fallen back onto the stripped wooden floor, unable to protect herself when the intruders burst into her flat. She tried to clear her head, to get back onto her feet. It was no use; she felt the point of a needle pierce the skin on her neck below her right ear.

That was when the passage of time got away from her. She drifted in and out of consciousness several times while her attackers prepared to leave. It was clear they were taking her with them; they placed a canvas hood over her head, and her hands and feet were bound. They collected items from her medicine cabinet and checked drawers and cupboards. Then she remembered nothing until she woke up here, in this room. Whatever they injected her with had taken effect, at last.

When she awoke, she had been seated where she sat now. The hood had gone, but it changed nothing. There was no light whatsoever — no amount of screaming, crying, or struggling made any difference to her situation. Her nose throbbed like crazy.

She felt vulnerable. She was naked under her flimsy dressing gown. Her early thoughts centred on why they broke into her flat. Was it a burglary gone wrong? Had she been kidnapped? Did they intend to rape her? Who were they? Where were they?

Her captor's first visit told her everything she needed to know.

A door opposite her chair opened, and lights in the corridor outside blinded her. She hung her head on her chest to shield her eyes from the glare. There were three voices. Guttural. East European accents, perhaps. Men in their thirties or forties, not kids. She had no clue how long she sat there, but her bladder betrayed the fear she felt. She wet herself.

The man closest to her grabbed her chin and lifted her head. Then he slapped her cheek with his open hand, cursing her in his native language. Was that Bulgarian? Hungarian? She must have peed on his shoes; it served the bastard right.

Another man now stood behind her. He pulled her hair away from her neck, and she felt another sharp prick. He whispered into her ear in English, this time, but heavily accented: -

"It would have been better for you to do as ordered," he said, "now we will use you as a guinea pig."

A chill had run down her spine. Dawn Prentice knew at that moment who had taken her and why.

These days she worked for a charity helping recovering addicts. Eight years had passed since she escaped her old life under the yoke of addiction. The wealth she inherited from her late parents went to good causes over the past year. Brandi, Selina, and the others she worked alongside battled daily in the fight to stop the spread of drugs. It was an evil that always found its way into every level of society. Their battle against that evil was relentless, but the forces they faced were brutal and almost overwhelming.

Dawn's past life was public knowledge. The press made great play of it soon after her parents died. The charity didn't shy away from her offer of financial help. They recognised there's no such thing as bad publicity. A former addict donating vast sums hoping she could help make a difference, gave the charity a boost.

The feel-good factor didn't last; her colleagues noticed a change in her attitude. Dawn became withdrawn and less engaged. There had been similar occasions to last Friday evening when Dawn rushed away rather than mix with them socially. Something troubled her or someone.

Dawn said nothing to her friends. Then, one Saturday morning, a man approached her in the street as she walked to the nearby deli to pick up something for lunch. He walked beside her, close enough to intimidate her but never laying a hand on her. She didn't recognise him, but he knew her name, where she lived and worked, and the car number of her little Fiat. He knew the things from her past she tried to keep hidden for eight long years.

The man mentioned a name. He said his boss wanted to get in touch. Dawn shuddered at the memories the name brought back. Adam Kovacs had been the last in a long line of dealers to have supplied her with the drugs she craved. Finally, they reached the door to the deli. Dawn waited for someone to exit the shop before entering. She realised no one was behind her when she pushed the door open. The man had disappeared.

Minutes later, with her sandwich, and smoothie in her oversized shoulder bag, Dawn stepped back onto the street, looking both ways. Dozens of faces streamed past, but she saw no sign of her old dealer's errand boy. Dawn thrust her hands into her coat pockets and hurried back to the flat. When she withdrew her house keys from her right-hand pocket, a piece of paper fluttered to the hallway floor.

Dawn grabbed it and ran inside, locking the door behind her. She emptied her purchases onto the kitchen table and threw her coat over the back of the sofa. Dawn imagined the slip of paper as a receipt or a shopping list of a few necessary items to buy several weeks ago. Dawn was on the point of screwing it up and throwing it in the bin when she saw the handwritten note.

'It's been too long, Dawn. Ring me in the next twenty-four hours if you want your little secret to stay hidden.'

The note was signed 'AK', and the mobile number scribbled underneath was unchanged from the old days. Adam Kovacs threatened to uncover her sordid secret.

Dawn had been desperate for a fix, flat-broke and too ashamed to ask her family for money. She turned to prostitution. Adam had been her first customer, and then he pimped her out to his colleagues. It had only been for six or eight weeks, but realising she had reached rock-bottom was the spur she needed to break free of Adam's clutches and try to get clean. If she continued, her outlook would have been bleak, and an overdose, accidental or otherwise, lay in wait.

For the rest of that Saturday, Dawn stared at the slip of paper and wrestled with her conscience. If she rang Adam, it could lead her back into the life she now donated tens of thousands of pounds to help conquer. If Dawn didn't call him, she would read of those horrid days in the media. It was bad enough that the world and his wife learned she was an ex-addict. Dawn dreaded the exposure of what she did to pay for those drugs at her lowest ebb.

It had been an awful weekend. On Sunday evening, Dawn rang the number she hadn't dialled for eight years. The mere sound of Adam's voice made her skin crawl. She asked him what he wanted her to do for him.

In return for his silence on her past, Adam told Dawn he imported designer drugs from Central Europe these days. Their potency meant small, easily transported packages could slip through customs. Dawn learned Adam wasn't working alone. He was part of a gang operating on both sides of the Channel.

Adam forced her to finance the import of those raw materials. His suppliers then manufactured and packaged the final product. Finally, when the drugs reached him, he and his fellow dealers got them to the consumer.

Dawn knew how damaging it could be to the charity if word got out that she financed the very trade against which she campaigned. That was why she distanced herself from her friends. It pained her to do it, but they must never discover the truth concerning her past, nor how she intended to protect it.

After a while, it became easier to cope. Adam gave her details of an anonymous-sounding bank account his fellow gang members had provided. She set up a monthly bank transfer, and thankfully, she heard nothing further from Kovacs while the money kept getting transferred. Neither did his errand boy happen to bump into her on the streets of Notting Hill Gate.

Dawn pushed thoughts of the matter deep into a dark corner of her mind. Something she had grown accustomed to doing with unwanted memories.

At the end of April, she arrived home one evening to discover a note shoved into her letterbox. It was from Adam Kovacs.

'We're having a party this weekend. You should come. I have friends who wish to meet you.'

Dawn hadn't called him on his mobile. She didn't want to hear his voice; she sent him a text.

'What's in the past stays in the past. You're getting the hush money, nothing more.'

She waited and waited for a response. After a day or two, Adam sent his reply: -

'OK. Sorry that you can't be available.'

Dawn heard nothing more. Although she continued to keep her distance from her colleagues, she hadn't anticipated the events of that Friday evening. As the days and weeks ticked by, she thought Adam was happy to take her money, which would be the extent of her involvement in the filthy trade.

She had learned of these new designer drugs through

her work with the charity. When she started using, she had taken the traditional route to the gutter; a little weed at parties, a few uppers and downers. Then a gradual but inevitable slide into heroin and cocaine.

In the days, or was it weeks, that they had strapped her to this chair, she came to know a new cocktail of products that hadn't been on the charity's radar when they kidnapped her. Her punishment for not attending Adam's party as a plaything for his foreign friends was to be a human lab rat.

The spasms in her shoulders were back. She tried to move her position slightly to ease the stress. The movement kicked off another bout of cramps in her toes. The urge to pee grew greater. That niggle fast became a necessity. After their first visit, her captors brought a metal bucket and placed it between her feet. With a few painful presses of her hips, she could get far enough forward to relieve the pressure on her bladder.

Dawn dragged herself back into the chair and tried to forget the aches and pains in her calves and toes. She fantasised about that hot bath she had run and how wonderful it would be to immerse her aching body in water. Her captors provided her with very few creature comforts.

The raid on her medicine cabinet allowed them to keep her on active birth-control pills so far, which was one less worry for her; also, it was one less problem for them to handle. When she needed to do more than pee, she held on until they brought her scraps of food and water. She imagined this was daily, in the mornings, but couldn't be sure. When she fell asleep through pain, exhaustion, or the effects of the designer drugs, she had no idea whether she slept for an hour or half a day.

The routine for the visits she received was simple. The

three men entered the room, and one released the bindings on her hands. She received a bowl of odd scraps of fruit, cold vegetables, and chicken to scoop into her mouth with her hand. A plastic cup of water helped her swallow her pill and whatever else they wanted to try out on her.

If she begged to squat over the bucket, they re-tied her hands and then released one leg from the chair. The first time, they laughed as she tried to sit, but the strength had gone from her legs, and she and the metal bucket toppled over.

Dawn received another open-handed slap that loosened a filling for that misdemeanour. She had needed the bucket only three times so far. Maybe that meant she had been here for between six and eight days? Who knew?

The last thing they did before they left each time was to wash her, which was further humiliation. One man drenched a sponge in cold water from the container they used to fill her plastic drinking cup. Then with her hands and feet securely tied once more, he wiped her face under her arms, and they took turns to stroke her breasts and between her legs.

The last two stages seemed to take forever. The conversation was limited. Each time Dawn thought they would rape her, but so far, they had gone no further.

When they were satisfied that she was clean or humiliated enough for one day, they laughed and prepared to leave. Her daily 'special' injection followed if a pill wasn't tested on her on that occasion. Then, after exchanging a few words in their native language, they left her alone in the dark.

Dawn knew what to expect after swallowing a pill or receiving an injection. Her only hope was she would get one dose of different synthetic drugs rather than successive hits of the same base synthetic. These new drugs could destroy life by triggering psychotic episodes of hallucinations, aggression, paranoia, suicidal thoughts and destructive tendencies.

Alone in her dark prison, Dawn had no way of controlling these symptoms. She twisted and turned on her chair, trying to break free, to run away from people she imagined were chasing her. She sweated profusely, saw flashes of colour, and experienced prolonged, dull headaches.

Almost everything they fed her produced a negative or negligible reaction. Her heart raced one minute and was normal the next. She was confused. One trip left her seeing Adam's face on all three men who next visited the room. She vomited as soon as the cold sponge brushed against her face. She was punched hard in the face. If her nose hadn't broken before, it did then.

Dawn assessed the pain in her nose at ten that morning. It registered only a six or seven now; she supposed it would need to be re-broken and set straight when she got out of here. If she ever got out. Dawn pushed that negative thought into the same dark corner as the bank transfer.

The wait for a visit seemed longer this time. Her bladder emptied maybe three hours ago. They didn't feed her much, but her hunger wasn't so great that she was desperate for food or water. Dawn wondered whether the next thing they tried on her would be a happy pill. She could suggest the men played with her a little longer in return for a real buzz that gave her several hours of grinning at the blackness surrounding her.

"I'm losing it," she said as the tears came unbidden and ran down her cheeks.

The door opened. One man stood silhouetted against the brightly lit corridor.

It was Adam Kovacs.

He walked across the room and stood in front of her.

Adam looked as if he had arrived from a company board meeting. He wore a well-tailored dark suit, a light blue shirt with a burgundy tie, and highly polished shoes. Dawn spotted the diamond stud in his left earlobe and remembered how it had felt against her inner thigh. The bile in her throat threatened to make her former drug dealer clean those smart leather shoes.

"We have a problem, Dawn," said Kovacs.

Dawn swallowed hard. Kovacs continued: -

"The bank transfer that should have arrived in our account this morning was stopped. We queried this matter. Your work colleagues were worried when you didn't visit the charity offices where you volunteered. Everyone knew of the money left to you by your parents. Two of your friends called your landlord and asked to be allowed access to your flat. They were concerned something may have happened to you. My boys forgot to tidy up after they collected you, and the landlord found the door unlocked. Inside, your friends found the number for your solicitor. You instructed him weeks ago to freeze your credit cards and bank accounts should you go missing."

"Your errand boy made me nervous," said Dawn. "I sat and fretted all weekend over that note you sent with him. I talked with my solicitor at once after I visited my bank to set up the transfer. I'd forgotten I'd done it. I'm sorry."

"Until you are seen in person by your solicitor to sign various documents, there will be no more money," said Kovacs. "This means, as helpful as you have been as a guinea pig over the past three weeks, I now have no further use for you."

Dawn struggled against her bonds; panic gripped her as

she realised what the drug dealer had said. Her kidnapping was not for ransom. There would never be any cosmetic surgery on her broken nose.

"Goodbye, Dawn. Sweet dreams," Kovacs said as he turned and strode out of the room.

Her three tormentors appeared in the doorway. Only one of them entered. The other two watched impassively as he approached her chair. He waited long enough for her to thrash around until she was exhausted. But, as always, it was to no effect, and the limp figure now slumped in front of him registered acceptance.

He gently lifted the hair from Dawn's neck, and the needle performed its final task.

Without a word, the three men left the room. Dawn was plunged into darkness once more.

Minutes passed, and she noted tiny flutters of her heart and subtle changes in her blood pressure. This euphoria was what she dreamed of, that intense excitement of well-being that nothing had given her in the past three weeks.

Dawn Prentice found she could relax despite her restraints. The pain levels dropped. Seven. Six. Five. Dawn understood what lay ahead and wanted it more than anything she had enjoyed in her life.

A few short breaths away stood oblivion.

## Chapter Two

***Wednesday, 28th May 2014***

Colleen O'Riordan signed the forms the solicitor spread on the large oak desk in front of her. Apart from cards of celebration or condolence she scribbled on over the years, she hadn't done as much writing since she left school.

Tommy was the man of the house.

Colleen prepared and cooked his meals, poured his drinks, gave him what he wanted in the bedroom, and produced an heir and a spare. She had known it best to hold her tongue for the rest of the time. He required little else of her. She never needed to get involved with the household budget, school fees, or anything remotely financial.

In the gangland world Tommy inhabited, cash was still king. Colleen might have graduated to having a credit card in their domestic lives instead of a fistful of notes thrust into her hands if she asked for something. Still, she had no idea how much lay in the account she used to pay for her weekly shop or her few personal luxuries. It was none of her business.

Times had changed; Tommy was in Belmarsh nick. Colleen was visiting him this afternoon. They had things to discuss. First, he would want to know how Tyrone and Rosie were doing. Did they miss their Dad? Were they ashamed of him? When were they flying in from Marbella to visit?

Colleen hoped to keep him away from that subject for a few weeks. The ink was hardly dry on those forms she signed. She tried to recall the last time she held a proper fountain pen in her hand, with ink as blue as the Caribbean rather than a bloody black biro, but she couldn't recall it.

Maybe when they signed the register in the vestry on their wedding day?

Colleen wasn't one for looking over her shoulder at the past, not these days. She was determined to move forward. Colleen shook the limp, bony hand of the solicitor and stared at the top of his head. She thanked him for everything he had done and smiled as she turned away.

Colleen paid him enough to re-arrange the O'Riordan family affairs in double-quick time. She could afford to let him stare at her tits without reproach and dream.

Her brother Sean had his hands full with Hugo Hanigan and Grid's business. Seamus McConnell was being eased gently into a role as Sean's number two. A job for which he was unsuited as far as Colleen could tell. No matter, it meant she had a clear road to do what was required. It would be a done deal before Sean or Tommy realised and tried to put a spanner in the works.

As soon as Colleen noticed Sean was otherwise engaged, she started with the cars. Tommy didn't need one, and she was happy not to drive herself around town. Time to get rid. The cash could come in handy.

The Mercedes and the SUV went to auction. Colleen knew nothing about cars and cared less; it was a fire sale. Two lucky punters picked up decent motors for chump change. Colleen treated herself to a new dress and stashed the balance in the bedroom wall-safe.

As she had closed the door and spun the dials, she allowed herself another smug grin. Tommy thought himself so clever. He always forgot the combination. He wrote it on a playing card, the ace of spades, and tucked it into a drawer under piles of his socks and pants. Tommy didn't think she'd find it or realise what it meant.

When Colleen opened it for the first time, the day after the trial, she was stunned by what she had discovered. His gun and ammunition lay inside, which was no surprise. Instead, the rolls of notes, secured by elastic bands, made Colleen gasp and sit back on the bed with a bump.

"You bastard, Tommy," she muttered, "you had this much cash lying around. Yet you moaned every time I held my hand out for a few quid."

Colleen had spent an hour counting out the cash. Eighty-five thousand in English money and thirty-five thousand in euros. The sixteen and a half thousand she deposited from the car auction was peanuts, but it would find a home in time.

After her first trip to visit Tommy in Belmarsh on Wednesday, the seventh of May, Colleen called Tyrone. He and Rosie had lived the high life at their father's expense for long enough. She told him the apartment they shared must go on the market. Their nearly new open-top sports cars would return to the dealer. She'd try to salvage enough from the proceeds of the sale to give them the deposit on a modest place they could finance themselves.

Tyrone was apoplectic. Rosie, listening in the background, was in tears. Colleen had no sympathy for them. It was time for the spongers to stand on their own two feet. The bank of Mum and Dad had closed.

"What's this rubbish," stormed Tyrone, "where's the money going?"

"Where do you think?" snapped Colleen. "I visited your father yesterday, and he's hellbent on appealing. It doesn't matter that they had him bang to rights. Of course, it will be money down the drain, but there's no telling him. You know what he's like, Tyrone."

"What happened to the rest of his money, though, stuff that's not tied up in property and that?"

"While he ran the show, he had plenty of money," said Colleen, "but Uncle Sean is the big man now. Gang leaders don't keep the inmates of Belmarsh on the payroll, not when they're unlikely to work again for thirty years. Gangsters don't get benefits, Tyrone. It stands to reason. No, you two must stop messing around and get stuck into proper jobs. The private school education your Dad paid for has given you the tools. It's time you used them."

Colleen had ended the call. Tyrone and Rosie needed that reality check. Tommy never dreamt of questioning the way they wasted their money. Rosie was his princess; the Spanish sun shone out of her backside. Tyrone was intelligent and hard-working when it suited him. He knew damn well criminal operations were where the money came from and had been happy to take it, but he kept a million miles from the career path his father and grandfather had chosen.

The Marbella apartment should sell for seven hundred thousand euros. Colleen made up her mind on Wednesday afternoon as she sat in the taxi en route to Belmarsh prison. It went on the market within five days of the conversation with Tyrone. Tommy paid around three hundred thousand pounds for it, although he never told her exactly how much. They would make a decent profit.

The trip took her ninety minutes, there and back, on Wednesday afternoons. It wasn't for the stimulating conversation. Tommy expected her to visit him, week in and week out, on time, and look beautiful. Not for him; it was for appearance's sake. His status as one of London's leading gangsters demanded his wife keep up the standards expected. He couldn't have her turning up in jeans and a hoodie to let the warders and other inmates' wives think she'd let herself go.

Of course, it was rubbish, but Colleen dressed up for her prison visits to put on a show. She looked good when she made an effort. It didn't take long, and she knew what a mouthful she'd get if Tommy thought she disrespected him and his perceived importance. But, of course, her cleavage had to be covered, so Tommy and the warders didn't get excited. It was the little things you missed on the inside.

As the miles ticked by, she recapped what she had to tell him, what was safe to mention, and what subjects to avoid. The taxi driver dropped her outside the prison at two forty-five. He headed off towards Woolwich for a cup of tea. He was under orders to pick Colleen up at four twenty on the dot. As soon as visiting time ended, she wanted to be in the car and back home as quickly as possible.

Once Colleen booked in at the Visitors' Centre, she put everything not allowed in the Visit Room in a locker. She kept her visitor's ID badge, a small amount of cash and the locker key. She then went to the prison to go through the security process.

Tommy was a Category A prisoner, so, as well as a thorough search by a female warder, the hand geometry system recorded a 3D image of her hand on her first visit and stored it on a barcode recognition purposes against a photograph of her face. All this got checked as she went in and out of the visit.

Then after a short wait with the others in the waiting room, they were called through to the visit hall. Tommy sat at the table, waiting for her.

"Hello, darling," he said, "it's good to see you."

"Hello, Tommy," said Colleen, "how's life treating you?"

She listened as he gave her a blow-by-blow account of the past seven days. Prison life wasn't all people cracked it up to be. Boredom had become his worst enemy.

Tell me about it, thought Colleen, who listened to the same string of complaints last week. She heard something different today and concentrated on what Tommy said.

"Belmarsh maximum security is a jihadi training camp. The bloody extremists brainwash young prisoners and spread their terror message across the whole prison system."

"How can they do that, Tommy?" she asked.

"A group of jihadists who call themselves the Akhi have got the run of the place. The screws and the governor know what's happening but aren't doing a thing. The problem is Belmarsh is a holding prison and a home for blokes like me and young guys who get indoctrinated then move on in the prison system and create wider Akhi networks."

"The authorities are letting a whole heap of trouble pile up then," asked Colleen. "Has there been any violence here? Are you in any danger?"

Tommy shook his head.

"They don't bother me. I keep myself to myself. I try to

be positive and pray the appeal is successful. What's the latest on that, Colleen? When did you talk to the solicitor?"

Here comes the first hurdle, Colleen thought. I need to get my story straight. One slip from what I told him on my last visit, and he'll be sending a message to one of his mates on the outside to visit me.

"I dropped in to talk to him only this morning, Tommy. I wanted you to have the most up-to-date news. The old codger was keen to keep me abreast of his progress. Because they convicted you in the Crown Court, you must first apply for permission to appeal. A judge will examine your application and decide whether to permit you to appeal. There must be proper grounds for making an appeal and strict time limits within which we can get it done."

"Yeah, I get that," said Tommy impatiently, "so where are we then?"

"He sent off the form last Wednesday. Applications to appeal and leave to appeal against decisions made by the Crown Court are dealt with by the Court of Appeal Criminal Division. You got sentenced on the twenty-eighth of April, and you had to apply within twenty-eight days of the date you were convicted if you're appealing against your conviction. Or the same length of time from the date you got sentenced if you're appealing against the length of sentence."

Colleen could see Tommy struggling with the long words.

"It's complicated, isn't it?" asked Tommy. "Did he get the forms in on time?"

Colleen nodded.

"Think about it, Tommy. If the judge rejects your plea

to challenge the conviction, you might still get a shot at reducing the sentence."

"I want that solicitor to earn his bloody money, have the conviction quashed, and get me out of here. How long's this going to take, anyhow?"

"If we're successful, you'll get a letter before the hearing to tell you when and where it'll take place. Our case will go before the judges. Because you're appealing the conviction, representatives from the prosecution will present the case against you. The prosecution doesn't necessarily get a look-in if we use the sentence appeal path. Still, let's stay positive. First, get the go-ahead for the appeal; then, get the conviction overturned. Then, you'll be walking the streets of Kilburn a free man again."

"Have you heard from the kids?" asked Tommy.

"I had a quick chat with Tyrone shortly after you went to prison. He and Rosie were agitated. I should give them another ring to see whether they can take time off work."

"I haven't had a peep out of your Sean either for a while. I suppose he's too busy to spare an hour for his brother-in-law?"

"I assume so," said Colleen.

"What, you haven't talked to him either?"

"I expect Hugo Hanigan keeps him busy, and he must keep tabs on Seamus McConnell now he's his second-in-command."

"You are joking? That eejit couldn't tie his shoelaces until he was fifteen. Portmarnock's finest. What was Sean thinking, picking him as his right-hand man?"

"Maybe he hopes you will be back before long. Sean was always happier being your lieutenant; he's never a born leader. Seamus was probably the candidate who would be least pissed off with you taking back your natural role."

"You might have a point there, Colleen," said Tommy, "you're not just a pretty face, are you?"

No, thought Colleen, I'm not. A pity it's taken you twenty-odd years to notice. She glanced at the clock on the wall. What were they going to say to each other for the next half-hour?

"Fancy a few refreshments?" Colleen asked. Tommy nodded, and Colleen wandered over to the vending machines. Two cups of tea, a packet of biscuits, and two chocolate bars punched a sizeable hole in the loose cash she had in her pockets, but it helped pass the time.

Tommy blew on his cuppa.

"I can't believe they get away with calling this tea. We used to call this 'love by the river,' didn't we?"

Colleen laughed.

"Yeah, I remember. Love by the river is the cleaned-up version. So, there's no other gossip from the inside you've picked up, then?"

Tommy attacked his chocolate bar and stared at the ceiling, trying to remember if anything significant had surfaced in the past seven days.

"Oh," he said, sitting up straighter in his chair, "when I told you about the Akhi mob and prisoners moving on from Belmarsh. I forgot I heard a whisper concerning Durham. I can't see it happening because you only live twenty miles away. This bloke reckoned prisoners like me might get transferred to Durham. I can't see it. First, it inconveniences my family visiting; second, I'll be free as a bird when my appeal comes through. No point moving me three hundred miles, is it?"

Colleen had a sudden surge of hope. Despite Sean saying nobody ever escaped from Belmarsh, she insisted that if Tommy's appeal didn't materialise, they needed to make plans to help him escape.

"We can't let him rot in there, Sean," she told him. "Tommy will expect nothing less. Do you want to tell him we're abandoning him without at least trying?"

Colleen leant forward.

"If they did want to move you to Durham, Tommy, it might be our best chance of breaking you out."

Tommy's face lit up. In case the guards overheard, he didn't say a word, but he felt happier than when he took his place in the visiting room at a quarter past two.

"Let me know next week if something further surfaces on that rumour," said Colleen.

"Is it time to go already?" asked Tommy. Then he looked at the table. "Are you going to eat those biscuits?"

Colleen shoved the packet of custard creams across the table.

Visiting time was at an end.

Colleen and Tommy said their goodbyes. Tommy sat and watched his wife leave. Once she was outside, Colleen looked for her taxi. Her driver stood by the open passenger door, smoking his last fag on the first rank of the car park. Poised for a sharp exit. Excellent, with luck and only slightly manic traffic on the way back to the city, she should be home by six.

Her driver wasn't the talkative type. Colleen was glad. She had plenty to think over on the drive back to Kilburn.

She had convinced Tommy everything was on track with the appeals process. However, her solicitor had grave doubts they would grant an appeal against the conviction, which was why he delayed sending it until the last minute. He was happy to add the costs to his bill, but he preferred to advise his next potential client his firm just secured a good win, not be laughed out of court.

As for the sentence option, the wily old bird had a few cards to play. Colleen's solicitor thought they stood a chance of arguing thirty years excessive when weighed against other similar cases. There were enough cases in the media highlighting lenient sentencing by a limp-wristed judiciary.

Colleen hadn't told Tommy the solicitor warned her that often the judges re-affirmed the length of the sentence and ordered it to recommence from the date of the appeal hearing. So if it took a year to reach court, Tommy could be looking at thirty-one summers inside those high walls.

She had steered around the problem of talking about the kids and deflected attention on her, avoiding contact with Sean. Tommy wasn't mad keen on cars. They were just a convenient way of getting around town, so she wasn't surprised he never mentioned them.

Colleen O'Riordan's face wore a smile a mile wide the whole way back to the capital. The news her solicitor gave her this morning had been the icing on the cake. There was no way Tommy raised that subject during one of her visits.

'Have you checked our bank balance, sweetheart?' 'Will you find out how my stocks and shares are performing?' 'Did I ever tell you I have Cayman and Channel Islands accounts?'

No, Colleen thought, you always told me not to worry my pretty head about how much we had in the bank. If I plucked up the courage to ask outright, you always said, 'Enough.'

As for stocks and shares, or off-shore accounts, fair enough, she wouldn't have understood how they worked, but she could learn. Who said crime didn't pay?

It was just as well she was seated when the solicitor told

her this morning the overall sum Tommy salted away after laundering it through Hugo Hanigan's private bank. Her hand had still been shaking when she completed the paperwork. There wasn't a chance that Colleen would tell Tommy that access to all of his bank accounts was now in joint names. With him inside for the foreseeable future, she controlled the purse strings.

Her taxi driver glanced in his rear-view mirror. Mrs O'Riordan was a regular pickup for his firm. He wouldn't mind putting his name forward for being available every week. She would soon get lonely, and she was fit. He idly wondered whether he might get lucky today.

At that moment, Colleen pondered the inconvenience Tommy's move to Durham might cause. If Sean and the other gang members managed to disrupt the transfer and get Tommy away to a place of safety, she needed to act quickly to protect her newly acquired fortune. The steely look in her eye the driver saw when she caught his eye made his blood run cold. Ah, well, it might be best to share the job with the rest of the lads. He kept his eyes on the road and the heavy commuter traffic for the last few miles.

It was ten past six when Colleen walked into the house she, Tommy, and the kids had shared for so long. There were happy memories amongst the fiery arguments and bruises. It was a toss-up which had a higher number. Colleen would be glad to see the back of it. What use did she have for a four-bedroomed detached house in a desirable district, kicking around in it alone?

Colleen prepared herself a meal and then relaxed for the evening. None of her favourite soaps was on TV, so she searched for a new place. Tyrone and Rosie had been well into computers for their work and playing games. They taught her the basics when they still lived at home. Tommy never trusted technology unless it involved weapons and ammunition. There was a laptop in the spare bedroom. Tyrone had left her idiot notes to help her find her way around before he moved out to Spain.

She decided to search online to gauge what price she might get for the house, then browse the local estate agents for something suitable for a single woman of means. How difficult could it be?

After the odd false start, Colleen found the information she wanted. Once again, her eyes lit up when she saw prices asked for similar houses. She was smart enough to appreciate London prices were off the scale compared to other parts of the country. Yet, the news that these prices applied to the area they lived in came as a surprise.

When she and Tommy first got together, they lived with Orla, Tommy's mother. Tommy Senior spent more time in prison than he did at home, and Orla needed the company; and his contribution to the housekeeping. Tommy had bought this property on the edge of the borough of Kilburn for eighty-five thousand pounds.

It was close enough to his roots on the South Kilburn estate to keep tight control of the business but far enough away that he didn't have to smell the poverty when he sat on the patio with a beer.

Colleen got up, wandered around upstairs, and then went downstairs to her lounge diner and kitchen. Tommy made sure they had a downstairs cloakroom and a utility room when they moved out of Orla's terraced house. It was a huge step up from the living accommodation on the seven streets back in Dublin that their parents rented. Tommy wanted the wider community to know he had moved up in the world, no matter that he had blood on his hands in getting there.

She retraced her steps and sat back at the table with the laptop.

"One point one million quid," she grinned, "bring it on."

The following site she browsed was the estate agency whose 'For Sale' signs littered the capital. Something she had noticed, but not considered important until now, was how soon the 'Sold; subject to contract' sign appeared. The quicker she could get the sale agreed upon and move to her new bolt-hole, the happier she would be.

There were plenty of apartments from which to choose. But, for a simple Irish girl, the idea of a one-bedroomed penthouse to come home to after a hard day's work sounded too good to be true. Yet she could afford two of the damn things with a fighting fund from the Marbella apartment, the family home, the cars, and the cash Tommy had stashed in the wall-safe.

It gave her such a great buzz she ran downstairs and poured herself a large glass of Prosecco before carrying on with the pursuit of her dream pad. As night fell, she looked out of her first-floor window at the garden beneath. Tommy was no gardener. Everything was low-maintenance beds or grass and paving slabs.

Over the fence, the panorama showed other gardens and houses whose owners had much the same outlook on life. They sweated their guts for their wages during the week, played hard at the weekend, and then did it all again.

Once, or maybe twice a year, if they were lucky, they flew off to the sun to escape the rat race and the little boxes they called home.

Colleen cursed, not bringing the bottle upstairs with her.

She looked back at the screen: -

*'Residents enjoy the services of a twenty-four-hour concierge. In addition, they benefit from secure underground parking, and each property has stunning views over the City.'*

*'London's financial hub and its cosmopolitan surroundings are on your doorstep. You will live in an area that has become a sought-after London address. The eclectic mix of chic restaurants, stylish bars, cosy cafés and cool clubs across your near-neighbourhood accentuates the apartment building's fashionable reputation.'*

Colleen drained her glass and resisted the urge to pinch herself.

"Perfect," she purred, checking the distance between her choice and other prominent sites in and around The City.

Colleen closed the laptop and returned to the kitchen for a top-up of her glass. She sat on her sofa, leaned her head back, and gazed at the ceiling. Colleen had marked today's date on the calendar by the fridge when coming past. She mentally ticked off the days she thought it might take to be savouring a glass of wine in her fashionable new apartment.

A place that didn't have views over gardens and little boxes but of the historical financial centre of the capital. An apartment only a hundred yards, as the crow flies, from the one occupied by Hugo Hanigan.

"Let the Games begin," said Colleen.

## Chapter Three

***Thursday, 29th May 2014***

Henry Case sat in his quarters at Larcombe Manor. The month of May had delivered a wide variety of tasks which were a mix of the pleasant and the unpleasant, as was often the case with Olympus matters.

This morning he received news from the Reverend Sarah Gough in the form of a hand-written letter. A letter was a novelty for Henry. He received text messages and emails by the dozen every day, but an addressed personal missive was rare.

Henry slit open the cream envelope with his FS Commando knife and extracted several sheets of cream writing paper. That was encouraging. Henry lifted the letter to his nose and inhaled. He convinced himself Sarah's scent remained on the paper and reminisced before reading the letter's contents.

As head of security at Larcombe, Henry had a role that gave little chance of developing social relationships. He moved to the West Country from Hereford after leaving the SAS. The opportunity to work with the Olympus Project had been too attractive to miss. His interview with Erebus had been brief. The old gentleman recognised a kindred spirit.

When there was a job to do, it needed to get done quickly and efficiently. There should be no hesitation if the task demanded an opponent's termination with extreme prejudice. Henry prided himself on managing all aspects of his role.

The security of Athena, Phoenix, and the other senior Olympus members was paramount. The estate's boundaries were well-protected by personnel from the stable block where he sat twenty-four hours a day. An array of motion sensor floodlighting supported the human guards, and booby-trapped areas discouraged the unwelcome intruder.

Henry referred to this work as Border Control. His views on the ever-changing version that protected the nation's borders were scathing. He deemed them not fit for purpose.

In the first week of May, he received Dean Laker and Adam Dosumu. Henry never 'welcomed' anyone delivered to the ice-house for interrogation. There was never any social element to conversations, or the treatment meted out. If you reached the lower level of the underground bunker, then you had committed more than a misdemeanour.

Dosumu was responsible for the death of Awusi Debrah, the nineteen-year-old Ghanaian girl forced into prostitution in Birmingham.

Dean Laker was the weasel who stalked Amy Grant in Reading and attempted to disfigure her with acid thrown at her face. Orion and his colleague dealt with that issue and suggested Olympus could decide the appropriate punishment. Dosumu and Laker got collected by local agents who then drove them to Bath.

Both prisoners found their way to Thomas and Longdon. The two former SAS sergeants now spent most of their working hours above ground. Two older agents, now retired from active duty, replaced them in the armoury and the shooting gallery.

Thommo and Bazza escorted Dosumu and Laker to Level Three and handcuffed them to a chair in Interrogation Rooms One and Two. They then removed the hood covering their head. Neither man had any idea in which part of the country they were now held. They may have registered the distinctive sound of a cattle grid when the van entered the Manor grounds, but the location of the room in which they now sat would forever be a mystery.

Laker looked around him. He was a frightened man. Opposite him sat a military type in his mid-forties, tall, well-built and with a face made for radio. He had a file on the desk in front of him, and he hadn't looked up since removing the blindfold.

"Where is this place? Who the hell are you? You can't hold me here. We're not living in a police state. I demand to see a lawyer."

Henry Case didn't answer. He was reading Laker's file; Dean Laker had a criminal record. Amy Grant was not his first victim. The level of abuse was escalating with each young lady. Henry hated men who hit women. His father tended to give his mother a cuff around the head when the mood took him.

Henry's father served in the British Army for over thirty years. Henry's early life involved moving from country to country, married quarters to married quarters, and school to school. No sooner than he made friends with a few chaps at school, he would start again elsewhere in the world.

Little wonder he joined the army himself as soon as he left university. Little wonder, too, that he never got married. The camaraderie in his regiment, and the SAS when he transferred, was a cocoon. They trained together, fought side-by-side, and socialised in large groups. He met women occasionally, but his physical appearance left him way down the list of likely candidates when those women paired off with his mates.

Dosumu had beaten a woman to death because she was pregnant and could no longer earn money for him.

Henry imagined Laker meeting Sarah Gough and smooth-talking her like he had Tina Fowler and Amy Grant.

The lengths these animals were prepared to go to suggest only one course of action.

He visited each prisoner and asked the same question: -

"Can you hazard a guess why they blindfolded you?"

Neither man offered a reply.

"We take the precaution with every guest," Henry had said. "You are nothing special. Indeed, you are one of the most despicable toads I've ever met. The reason is simple. I'll leave you to work it out."

Henry stood up, switched off the lights and left Interrogation Rooms One and Two. Once the door closed, the music blasted out from speakers mounted high-up in each corner. Not long after Phoenix's arrival, the genre of music changed. It proved most effective. Adam Dosumu and Dean Laker could sit and have their eardrums assaulted by heavy metal music for the next eight hours.

Then he would return.

In the present, Henry snapped out of his reverie and examined Sarah's letter.

She apologised for not writing sooner. The odd text and email had passed between them since the wedding at Larcombe, but they weren't an appropriate medium for the amount she needed to report. But, first, she had sad news. Her beloved VW camper van, 'Maggie', finally ground to a complete halt. Sarah told him she shed a tear when 'Maggie' went to the scrap yard.

Sarah made her visits to her parishioners on her bicycle. She assured Henry she always wore her safety helmet and had only suffered one mishap. That was when two of her kittens played chase and shot across her front wheel as Sarah left the house one morning. She avoided hitting either of them but landed unceremoniously in a heap among the cabbages in her vegetable garden.

There were other stories, too, concerning a churchwarden and a lady who did the flowers in her church. They had both been in their early eighties and passed away. Sarah officiated at their funerals.

Henry found this fascinating. It was terrific to learn more about Sarah and the work she did. The time they spent together on her first visit to Larcombe and over the wedding weekend had been far too brief.

The news he hoped for arrived on page three of the letter. Sarah had arranged a stand-in for the August Bank Holiday weekend. As a result, she was free to travel to Larcombe to christen Hope in the tiny estate church. Henry's heart filled with joy. He couldn't wait to see Sarah again. It seemed a lifetime ago when they shared their first kiss under the Rock of Ages at Burrington Combe.

He glanced at the wall calendar. Good Friday; gosh, that was less than two months ago; how things had changed for them both. Sarah's next tale was about Annabelle Fox and the high jinks they enjoyed at Cambridge University. Henry wasn't sure she should share this, but he still read on. As a carefree undergraduate, Athena was a different character to the calm, meticulous leader of Olympus at the Project's HQ at Larcombe Manor.

Something dramatic and life-changing brought her here to work with Erebus. She left the world she inhabited behind to commit her future to an organisation that promised to redress the balance between good and evil.

Evil such as that perpetrated by Dosumu and Laker; Henry waited twelve hours before coming to his final decision; his conscience was clear. Neither man could ever be set free. The risk was too high. Henry opened the door to Interrogation Room One; the music died at once. Dean Laker's head lay on his chest. Judas Priest and the rest had played their part.

They walked along the corridor on Level Three, moving from one pool of light to another, the darkness filling in behind their steps as each successive ceiling light dimmed behind them.

Their destination was that final door — the one called Hotel California.

Laker had his arms secured behind him, and the chain they were attached to was raised. Straps on the floor pinned his ankles; his body angled at forty-five degrees. He never uttered a word in protest. Henry withdrew his SAS-issue FS Commando knife from the leather holder at his waist and cut Laker's throat with one swift slash.

The Olympus head of security watched for a few seconds. Over ninety per cent of the blood would collect in the drain beneath his prisoner. He turned and headed back to collect Adam Dosumu.

A work detail would remove the bodies for burial in the pet cemetery in the morning and return to Hotel California for clean-up duties.

Henry wondered how long his secrets could remain hidden from Sarah. Death was a regular occurrence in her parish. She accepted it as inevitable, just as night followed day. But could she care for a man who chose whether another human being lived or died?

The guests who ended their days in Hotel California were evil. Henry never dispatched anyone who didn't deserve to die. Could Sarah agree with the Olympus philosophy that the ends justified the means? Or might the padre refuse to have anything more to do with him if she uncovered the truth?

Henry read through to the end of the letter. The news items and memories of university life with Annabelle Fox were complete. In the final pages, Sarah told him how much she looked forward to seeing him in August. If only they could meet before.

Henry reread that part several times. The padre invited him to stay at the pub in the village in early July. It was the weekend of the village fete, and she would love to see him. If he could come, she could book the room. 'The locals will gossip more than enough if we're seen together at various functions,' she wrote. 'I should prefer to invite you to the vicarage, but the scandal would be too great.'

Steady on, old girl, Henry had thought. Things are moving fast. He studied the two kisses after her name at the foot of the final page. Why not? August was a long way away. He must ask Athena for weekend leave at tomorrow morning's meeting. Henry replaced the letter in the envelope and put it away in his desk drawer. He had work to do. He would reread it later.

His Border Control duties were over for the day. There were no perceived threats to security at Larcombe. His next task was to oversee the progress of their latest batch of trainees.

Athena and Phoenix had returned from London and the last Olympus meeting with news that around one hundred agents were being brought home from overseas. The threat level was low enough for numbers now to decrease. After a brief period of assessment and retraining, they would increase the current figures available for direct actions against The Grid in the UK.

Thomas and Longdon started the retraining two weeks ago in batches of twelve. Henry assisted in the assessment to pass the older agents mentally fit for the task. The former armoury personnel now took them through the rigorous training process. As each batch completed the course, Henry had to check their progress with the two trainers and confirm their move out into the field or look for administrative posts within the organisation to use their experience if they didn't meet the required standard.

Next week, the first intake of twelve brand recruits arrived at Larcombe. These ex-servicemen would be under the supervision of Kelly Dexter and Hayden Vincent. The aim was to have these men and women in the field by September. The twelve-week course would be gruelling. Henry planned to keep an eye on their progress and offer advice to Rusty Scott on updates to the training manuals.

It promised to be a tough summer ahead. A few lighter moments spent with the Reverend Sarah Gough would be most welcome.

The ongoing struggle against The Grid might put a spanner in the works. Events during May didn't offer hope that they were cutting back on their aim to increase their criminal network's stranglehold over the country. Phoenix and Rusty struck telling blows, but the imbalance of numbers was evident.

Henry left his quarters and checked how Thommo and Bazza thought things were progressing with this first set of agents.

### *Friday, 30th May 2014*

"I won't be sorry to see the back of this month," said Athena, "let's get to this final meeting of the week."

"Life's hard, and then you die," replied Phoenix as he bounced Hope on his knee.

Athena gave him a stare. Phoenix stopped bouncing their five-month-old daughter.

"Daddy said something silly,"

Hope's expression suggested she wanted to know why he had stopped playing with her.

"Sorry, darling, that was insensitive. I've spent little enough of these past four weeks at home. We must stay positive. Our efforts have taken many criminals out of the game in the missions we've undertaken."

"We've lost three good agents in the process," said Athena, joining her husband and daughter on the sofa, "notifying families of the death of a husband, or a son, doesn't get any easier."

"Neither of us will be comfortable with that task," said Phoenix, "but we must remind ourselves that our cause is. Erebus always stressed that fact when times were tough. When we suffer casualties, we should measure the loss of a colleague against the damage we've done to the enemy. So far, Olympus has consistently inflicted more harm to the opposition than they have to us."

There was a knock at the door. It was Maria Elena, their nanny.

"Good morning," she said as she breezed into the room. Hope gave her a big smile. Athena and Phoenix spent as much time as possible with their child, but Maria Elena coped with the little rascal for much of her waking hours.

Phoenix was about to hand Hope over to the nanny.

"Sit her up next to you," said Maria Elena, placing herself on the opposite end of the sofa.

Phoenix did as Maria Elena asked.

Hope sat upright for thirty seconds. She looked at the three faces surrounding her. What were they expecting her to do? She patted her hands on her thighs; they smiled and cooed. This was fun.

"How long has she been able to do this?" asked Athena, "we've never tried it."

Hope slid gracefully towards Maria Elena, who scooped her up and placed her on her stomach on the carpet.

"Yesterday was the first day," she said, "watch her try to scoot along the floor. She's not there yet, but she'll crawl in a few weeks."

"We'll need eyes in the back of our heads then," said Phoenix. "Sharron was into everything once she became mobile. We had to keep breakable items out of harm's way. They don't stay babies for long."

Maria Elena had no clue who Sharron was. She imagined Phoenix had a younger sister.

Athena watched as Hope moved her hips with her head raised. Maria Elena was right; crawling was just around the corner. If only they could spend more time together. The clock had moved past nine o'clock without them noticing, engrossed as they were in their daughter's antics.

"We're late for the morning meeting, Phoenix. Come on; we need to make a move."

They dashed along the corridor to the meeting room. Maria Elena and Hope watched them leave from the doorway of the apartment.

"Mama y Papa volveran pronto," she whispered in Hope's ear, "they'll be back soon."

Hope thought that was easy for her to say. It was hard enough learning to sit up unassisted without being bi-lingual at five months.

Minos and the others were deep in conversation when Athena and Phoenix arrived.

"Leaves on the line," said Phoenix by way of explanation.

Athena took her seat at the head of the table and ran through the morning's agenda.

Rusty brought the agents up to date with the retraining. Henry Case passed Athena a folder containing the psychological assessments of the twelve men in the system. Giles reported what new data they collected on The Grid over the past twenty-four hours.

Minos and Alastor confirmed that their investigations into the proposed new Olympians' backgrounds were complete. Achilles, Daedalus and Ambrosia, had been given the all-clear. There was no reason to exclude either of them from the next meeting in Manchester on the second of July.

Reservations over Jean-Paul St Clair proved unnecessary. The industrial designer and inventor had taken his wife, Simone, on holiday to the south of France for two weeks, and they returned to their home in Wales together.

"Our surveillance photos, both in Nice and at home,

portray a happily married couple," added Alastor, "in fact, several photos were a trifle indiscreet. The tabloids would pay a fortune for them."

"Well, that's one less concern," said Athena. "I'll send that information to Zeus as soon as we finish here. That and the progress on the retraining will be welcome news."

"Everything is in place for Monday and the fresh intake," said Rusty. "The stable block and the old worker's cottages will be more crowded than usual. We have solved potential accommodation issues, so male and female trainees get separate billets. We've added extra shifts for our permanent in-house personnel to bolster the canteen and the recreation areas; extra rations are due this weekend. I think we're ready."

"Well done, Rusty," said Athena. "I've no idea how you've managed this with the missions you and Phoenix have been on this month. My greatest concern isn't the logistics of getting these reinforcements geared up to move into the field after twelve weeks. It's how we explain the sudden surge in numbers to the Charity Commissioners on their next visit."

"Perhaps Alastor and I need to prepare cover documents for these men and women?" asked Minos.

"The timetable for handing over security control from International Security Assistance Force to Afghan forces was agreed at the NATO summit in Lisbon back in November 2010," added Alastor. "Task Force Helmand closed at the beginning of April this year, and they handed Camp Bastion over to Afghan security forces. We still have four to five hundred combat troops on the ground who will train, advise and assist local Afghanis. Their role will end in October, and we can bring them home."

"What will this whole campaign have cost since 2001?"

asked Artemis. "In monetary terms, not the thousands of dead and wounded."

"The best estimate is forty billion pounds," said Alastor.

"And the Taliban are still not defeated," said Rusty.

"Unless we send troops to war zones during the summer, it will be increasingly difficult to justify sizeable increases in the numbers of combatants returning to the UK suffering from PTSD," said Minos. "We shall have to tread carefully."

"I appreciate your concern," said Athena. "I know I can rely on you two to devise a method to convince the inspectors there's no anomaly to investigate."

"The last thing we need is a snap inspection," said Rusty, "what did they say when they were here last time?"

Athena smiled.

"We might never receive a surprise visit again after their last inspection. Could you explain, Minos?"

"Their last visit was mid-April while the Reverend Gough was staying here. I escorted the Commissioners around the estate and bumped into Henry and the vicar in the walled vegetable garden. They assumed she was our resident chaplain and were pleased we provided pastoral care for our patients. As a result, the frequency of checks has reduced. However, it will benefit us to take proper precautions."

"Exactly," said Phoenix, "you can't trust these organisations. A change of government, a new broom at the head of the Charity Commission. Without warning, all bets are off, and they'll add extra demands to the already long list of things with which we need to comply."

"Over to you then, Minos," said Athena, "give us a good smokescreen."

Henry Case had perked up at the mention of Sarah Gough's name.

Artemis spotted his reaction.

"How is Sarah, Henry?"

"Without a vehicle at the moment," he replied, "her camper van finally pegged out. Athena, is there any chance I can have a weekend off in early July?"

"Of course you can, Henry," said Athena. "I suppose we don't need to ask where you might visit?"

"Village fete, the padre said," Henry was embarrassed and starting to get flustered. "Wondered if I wished to pay her a visit."

"She told you she was free to officiate at Hope's christening in late August, I take it?" asked Athena.

"She did. While I'm in the village that weekend, I must ask her how she's getting to Larcombe. Now Maggie has gone to the VW dealership in the sky."

"I think it's wonderful that you two get on so well," said Artemis.

Henry thought so too, but he was wary of committing himself in case certain matters came to light.

Across the table, Phoenix and Rusty shared a glance. They, too, wondered whether the security head and the vicar indeed had a future. Since his arrival at Larcombe, Phoenix had lost count of the criminals who failed to surface after Henry had taken them to Level Three and his suite of interrogation rooms in the ice-house.

"I'll leave you to make the arrangements, Henry," said Athena. "You can drive over and collect her, or I'll send one of the transport section guys to do the honours."

"Righto, Athena," said Henry, glad that this conversation had ended.

"What's left on the agenda?" asked Phoenix.

"Are you rushing off again?" asked Giles.

"Rusty and I need to fine-tune our plans for the next

mission; debrief the last one; that's our itinerary for today. All things being equal, we'll take tomorrow and Sunday off and spend time at home for a change."

This time it was Athena and Artemis who shared a glance. Two days free from worry. Several times in the past month, there had been dangerous moments where they feared they might not see their partners again.

Athena closed the meeting and switched back on her mobile phone. There was an instant message. She read it and asked everyone to stay seated.

"This has just come in from Zeus," she said, "it concerns Dawn Prentice, the candidate rejected at last month's meeting for elevation to the senior Olympus leadership."

"She was to become Aurora," said Minos, "but there were grave concerns over her renewed contact with drug dealers. Specifically, those trading in designer drugs."

"We discovered she was financing the raw materials for a large shipment on its way to UK streets," said Alastor, "what about her?"

"She's missing," said Athena.

## Chapter Four

As soon as the agents left the room, their plans for the day, and possibly the weekend, had altered. Giles Burke and Artemis returned to the control centre in the ice-house to track Dawn Prentice's movements.

Phoenix agreed to meet Rusty in the orangery in an hour. Giles would uncover something in time. Meanwhile, the debrief of recent attacks and future mission plans had to take priority.

"Athena and I will grab lunch, relieve Maria Elena for an hour or so, and spend time with Hope. I'll see you at one o'clock."

"OK," Rusty nodded, "lunch alone again for me. Catch you later."

Henry Case contacted both training teams to tell them Rusty was unavailable until further notice. Any queries that arise should come to him.

Minos and Alastor set to work straight away on constructing feasible backgrounds for the twelve agents who returned to these shores. They decided that the recruits arriving on Monday would be far easier to handle. After completing their time, they either came directly from the armed services or had only been on civvy street for twelve to eighteen months.

As for the men and women who survived over five years working undercover in a foreign trouble hot-spot, they could present a host of problems. Athena understood that when she assigned the role to the Two Amigos. There were no better men for the task.

Back in their apartment, Athena asked Maria Elena to rustle up a light salad for lunch. Phoenix sneaked a cold beer from the fridge, flopped onto the sofa, and took a long pull at his drink. Then leant forward with his arms on his knees to watch his daughter.

"Blink, and you miss it," he said.

Athena had returned from the kitchen. She joined her husband on the sofa.

"What will I miss?" she asked.

"Do you remember the days when she needed us every waking minute?"

"How could I forget?"

"Look at her now," said Phoenix.

Hope was lying on her back. For a week or more, she had realised her hands helped pick up things. They could touch her feet too, which Hope wasn't sure her parents could do. So, she was showing off her newly acquired skill, clutching at her toes and rocking from side to side. After a minute, Hope spotted her parents watching her and gave them a huge smile. Watch this, she thought and rolled onto her tummy.

"She's learning to play on her own," said Athena. "We're not redundant yet, but she's growing up fast."

"What are our plans for her to have a brother or sister?" asked Phoenix.

"Let's enjoy things as they are for a while," Athena replied. "We still have time to have another baby, but these are dangerous times. I worry about the risks you have to take,"

Phoenix took her in his arms and kissed her. Maria Elena started to bring lunch from the kitchen, but seeing them, she thought lunch could wait.

As she pulled the door quietly towards her, she noticed Hope.

The excited squeal made Athena and Phoenix separate and look.

Maria Elena hurried into the room and pointed. Hope had climbed to her feet and was resting against the end of the sofa staring at them. As soon as they turned towards her, she sat on the carpet with a bump.

"As I was saying," said Phoenix, "blink, and you miss it. This little lady is growing up way too quick."

"Lunch is ready for the three of you," said Maria Elena. "I'll bring it in and then leave."

"Thanks," said Athena, "I'll see you in two hours. I hope I can persuade her to repeat that trick and take a picture. I'm sure Mummy and Daddy would love to see it."

"Are they even in the country now," asked Phoenix, tucking into his salad with relish. "Or did they fly off to the continent as soon as they went home after the wedding?"

"Mummy has a check-up with her physician in Harley Street coming up soon. The outcome of that will decide their travel arrangements for the summer. We'll see them over the weekend at the end of August, whatever they're up to. They won't miss Hope's christening for the world."

Phoenix polished off his food and drained the dregs from his beer bottle.

"Right, I need to get ready for my session with Rusty. I have to love you and leave you, I'm afraid.

He kissed Athena on the lips, then kissed Hope on her forehead. She was enjoying her pureed meat and vegetables. Thanks to her mother spooning it into her eager mouth. One spoonful missed as Hope realised Daddy was leaving and twisted around in her high chair to see where he'd gone. The contents of the spoon ended up on her shoulder.

"Daddy will be back later," said Athena wiping Hope's shoulder with a tissue.

I've heard that one before, thought Hope. She turned towards her mum and opened wide for more sweet potato and chicken. Yummy.

Phoenix collected the files he needed for the orangery and headed off to meet with his colleague. He arrived well before Rusty and sat in his favourite spot. He looked over the gardens and thought back over the past three weeks. The week after their trip to Solihull, where they eliminated Piotr Kowalczyk, he and Rusty had moved on to strike at the Grid's operations in the North West.

Kowalczyk had controlled the slave labour trade in the West Midlands. The demise of Kowalczyk and his criminal colleagues significantly damaged the finances of that part of the business. The Liverpool and Manchester regions were just as lucrative to the Grid. Both cities were bases for drug trafficking cartels. Phoenix had been aware the area's criminal gangs were less territorial than gangs they had tackled in the capital. They were also more active on international fronts. The northern cartels smuggled cocaine and heroin into the UK, plus the Netherlands and the Iberian Peninsula. Add in the weapons trade and the contract killings that were a speciality of the two cities; then, the North West was bandit country.

He and Rusty had carried out their accustomed detailed preparations in the early part of the week, and then on Friday afternoon, they drove north to meet their agents on the ground. Rusty completed the drive to Chester via the M5 in three and a half hours. The meeting place for the sixteen agents was a motorway service car park on the M53.

The crime gangs they were targeting trafficked drugs worth many millions of pounds. Local agents had provided data to Larcombe Manor over six weeks.

These gangs operated in the heart of both cities, not in the leafy suburbs or remote, detached properties in the countryside. They worked and flourished on dozens of housing estates, cheek to jowl with honest, hard-working citizens.

Drugs were smuggled to Scotland by car or train by couriers. The information the Lancashire and Merseyside Olympus agents provided had passed to their colleagues over the border. The noose tightened up there too. In the coming weeks, the whole network in Glasgow and Edinburgh would get identified, and direct action sanctioned to eliminate its leading lights.

Phoenix wanted to demolish these organisations brick by brick. It was a slow process, but Olympus had to choose its targets. Time was against them, and resources stretched. The Grid's all-reaching spread needed disrupting; failure was not an option.

Rusty had parked his van in the furthest corner of the car park, well away from the entrance and exit roads and the longest walk from the franchised buildings. Three more dark vans pulled alongside in a designated box formation. Fourteen agents joined Phoenix and Rusty inside the square space provided by the vans. The time was then eleven forty-five at night. Each agent wore black clothing. Black ski masks and night-vision goggles completed their outfit.

"We'll hit our target properties in Manchester at two o'clock, in teams of four," said Phoenix, "there are to be no prisoners. If any of the three strike teams lose the element of surprise and meet stiff resistance, they will call for immediate backup. Team Four, you will be on standby at the lay-by marked on your map. From there to each of the properties, the travel time is the same, six minutes, give or take a minute. Remember, no member of our teams must be left behind. Let's move into position. Contact me when you arrive. This late at night, traffic won't be an issue. Any questions? OK, let's roll."

Two ex-SAS men transferred their kit to Rusty's van and joined him and Phoenix inside. One by one, the vans headed towards Manchester into what Phoenix had termed the Bent Triangle.

They took up their positions among the sleeping residents of Beswick, Hulme, and Cheetham Hill. The occasional vehicle still occupied the roads, and several shiftless pedestrians lingered on the pavements. No big city ever truly sleeps.

Phoenix had received the check-in messages from Teams Two and Three. Team Four confirmed they had parked up, ready to respond at a moment's notice.

"Now, we wait," said Phoenix. "Drug dealers don't keep sensible hours, but at two o'clock, they'll either be tucked up in bed or relaxing after arriving home. Synchronise your watches. On my count, it's now one-fifteen. We strike at two."

They had waited. Phoenix didn't know what the others were thinking inside the four vans, but he was rechecking his plans. Planning was everything. If you imagined every step of the mission and prepared detailed methods for reacting, you would always succeed.

That was his mantra. Those thought processes had never failed him. He could still see the folders in the metal filing cabinet underground in Shaw Park Mines. He had completed those at eighteen years of age, just married, with a tiny daughter, and full of anger at the world.

"Twenty-eight years," he said.

"Sorry?" asked Rusty.

"What, did I say that out loud? I just realised how long I've been at this game, in one form or another."

The two agents in the back seats shared a look. Phoenix had as much experience taking out the bad guys as they had in total, and they thought they were battle-hardened.

Phoenix passed his final message to the other team leaders.

"Check your weapons. Put on balaclavas and night-vision goggles. Good hunting."

Rusty led the way. He had parked twenty yards from the target house in Hulme. The residential street, busy from morning to night in the daytime, was eerily quiet. The places they passed as they made their approach varied in character. Some were little more than a dumping ground for rubbish, with scrap cars elevated on bricks, discarded children's toys, dog turds, broken bottles, cans, and fast-food outlet packaging.

Here and there stood properties occupied by older residents. Their patch of garden at the front tended with loving care, the windows of their pristine homes sparkling clean and unbroken. Phoenix recognised the signs. He'd lived on an estate just like this. They were fighting a losing battle, but they kept struggling. They resembled that single daisy, desperate to survive, thrusting its way through a cow-pat for a glimpse of the sun in a cloudless sky.

The intelligence gathered over the previous weeks told them forty-seven was the Whitman family's home. Father and head of the gang Billy, forty-two years old, had been a familiar face in local law courts since he nicked the emblems from the grills of luxury cars aged fourteen.

The switch from violent crime to peddling drugs occurred in his mid-twenties. At the time, he was separated, with two sons, Ben and Ken. His wife had got lonely while he was in Strangeways prison for the third or fourth time. The grapevine informed Billy that the frequent footfall had damaged the path to his front door.

The boys followed their injured mother to Salford soon after he left prison. They lived with her and a series of blokes until they were teenagers. As soon as they reached school-leaving age, and the authorities didn't have to chase after them for not attending any longer, they moved back in with their Dad.

Ben and Ken were now twenty-one and nineteen. His two sons followed their father's career path, collecting an impressive collection of ASBOs before they were old enough to vote. The Whitmans were fully paid-up members of the organised group of criminals operating in the Bent Triangle. People associated the Whitman name with violence, fear, and misery in the communities where they plied their evil trade.

The side door to number forty-seven was the best point of entry. A black shadow emerged from the rear of the house; Rusty set to work on the lock.

Phoenix watched the second hand on his watch as it flicked its way to the top. When it read two o'clock, he nodded. The door opened. The two local agents moved through the kitchen, guns raised, ready to fire. They cleared the rooms on the ground floor. Phoenix and Rusty slipped inside the house to join in the action.

Rusty stood poised at the bottom of the stairs; each step could be a potential alarm. One creaking stair would awaken the three men sleeping in the bedrooms. It was inevitable they had weapons close to hand. The first-floor layout had been in the data passed to each of them for scrutiny. He inched his way upwards. Phoenix and the others followed.

Rusty trod on a squeaky toy.

The first three attackers forgot any element of surprise. Phoenix and Rusty charged into the bedrooms assigned to them and struck. The Whitmans struggled to wake up; a bedside light switched on in one of the front bedrooms. Phoenix heard someone scrabbling around inside the back bedroom. The sound of a window opening. The double-tap of the fatal shots had come in perfect unison.

Billy Whitman clambered out of bed naked and wielded a machete. Rusty killed him. Ben turned the light on to see what had woken him from a drunken stupor. He didn't have time to think of reaching for the handgun on the bedside cabinet. One bullet to the chest and a second to the skull left him with a permanent look of surprise to carry into whatever hell awaited him.

Phoenix crashed into the back bedroom to find Ken throwing bags out of the window and perched on the sill, preparing to launch himself onto the shed roof.

"Going somewhere?" Phoenix growled. Ken was hit twice under the armpit as he pitched forward. When Phoenix reached the window, he saw Ken's body spread-eagled on the patio.

"All accounted for," said Phoenix.

"I'll bring the van to the door," said Rusty. "Get any hoard of drugs and cash visible collected, then load it and the bodies into the back,"

Team Two reported in from Cheetham Hill. Four gang members were dead. The agents had stored the bodies in the van but abandoned the hunt for drugs and cash. The burst of activity attracted the attention of nosy neighbours.

Beswick had been a different story. Team Three encountered seven people at the bungalow they raided. Intelligence indicated five males would be present, in their mid to late twenties, and from the Indian sub-continent. The agents smashed their way in and took out two men sleeping on the floor in the lounge. The other three young men emerged from a bedroom and tried to shoot their way out. One Olympus agent died in the firefight, and another got hit in the shoulder.

Team Four were on the spot in six minutes. They discovered the three remaining agents had completed the mission but had a problem; one of the young men invited his grandparents to stay. They were in the main bedroom. The two gang members in the lounge gave up their beds for the elderly couple. Team Three team leader wanted to know what to do with them.

"We've tidied up the gear from the house, and the bodies, Phoenix," he said. "I need to get out of here fast. Do I leave these two?"

"I don't think we've got a choice," said Phoenix, "this mission was supposed to leave no one in either house. Our dead and wounded need to be removed along with the gang members. Head for the safe house as planned. Take them with you alive for now."

"Problem?" asked Rusty as they pulled away from number forty-seven.

Lights came on in several neighbouring houses, but nobody was brave enough to stick their heads outside. Hulme was not a stranger to the odd bit of gunfire. The dark clothing might deter them for a while longer. It was okay if they mistook the agents for the police. The police didn't attract an audience around here either.

"An old Indian couple staying with their drug-dealing grandson? Who could have foreseen that?"

Phoenix was annoyed. He didn't appreciate something derailing his best-laid plans.

Rusty left his friend to work through his options. The drive to the safe-house would take an hour. They made for Barnston, a village in the centre of the Wirral Peninsula and a detached property with one and a half acres of land attached. They would park the vans in the large barns at the rear of the property, a distance from the narrow lane that threaded its way across the countryside.

Phoenix considered what to do. The plan had been to store the bodies overnight, then he and Rusty would drive south to Bath in the morning, leaving the local teams to dispose of them. There was room to spare out on Thurstaston Common. He waited until morning. He would call Athena first thing for a decision. If she needed to refer the matter to Zeus, it meant delaying their return for a few hours. Phoenix knew he couldn't ask others to do the job; if that was the outcome. He must dispose of them, innocent or not.

Phoenix heard the others talking about how the mission went and their lost colleague. They patched up the guy with the injured shoulder with a field dressing; he was a tough nut. He agreed to wait until morning before one of his mates drove him to a friendly former army doctor for treatment.

"Where the heck did that squeaky toy come from?" asked Rusty, "there was no intel of the Whitmans' having a dog."

"They did own Pit Bull Terriers, but they got put down last year," said the Team Four team leader. "No excuse, though; we should have flagged it as a possibility."

"Sounds as if your action went smoothly?" Rusty asked the guys from Team Two.

"It was fine," said one agent, "they didn't grasp what was happening until I started firing. By then, it was too late."

"The trouble came from the proximity of the other houses in the cul-de-sac," added another. "We had an audience when we carried the bodies out to the van. You should have seen what we left behind us. There was a family-size suitcase crammed full of heroin. We never had time to do a proper search. I'll bet there was more upstairs, and there must have been more cash too."

"I found a plastic supermarket bag full of notes by the side of a sofa," said his Team Leader. "But it was the high-end electrical gear they owned I wanted to put in the van. It looked like a modest home outside, but the plasma TVs, laptops, and music systems told a different story. They lived in luxury."

"Not any longer," said Phoenix.

He turned to the Team Three leader and his men.

"Do you want to talk us through it?"

The Team Leader took a big breath.

"Sam led from the front, as usual. I provided cover as he dealt with the two sleeping on the floor. Lenny joined Sam inside. James and I watched them move forward to the two bedrooms. Our survey told us to expect five men. The gunshots alerted the others, and it became a shit-storm in seconds. I called Team Four straight away. Sam was on the left, and Lenny on the right, moving to the main bedroom. The door opened slowly, and instead of three young thugs running out, they met an eighty-year-old Indian bloke in a night-shirt, with his wife in her dressing-gown and slippers hanging onto his arm. Then the second bedroom door burst open, and three buggers came out firing. Sam was on that side and directly in their line of fire. He ran towards them, firing at will. Sam took one of them out but got hit half a dozen times. Sam died before he hit the carpet. Lenny got hit in the shoulder but wasn't hurt enough to be out of the game. His covering fire allowed James and me to cross the lounge to get shots off at the last two standing. It was over in the blink of an eye. Our backup arrived in minutes. The rest, you know."

"My fault," said Phoenix, ruing the loss of yet another brave agent. "I should have arranged for Giles Burke to supply drones equipped to count how many heat sources there were in each of the houses."

Nobody slept well that night.

Phoenix called Athena at dawn.

"Sorry to call so early," he said, "but we have a problem."

"Are you OK?"

"I'm fine. We lost a good man last night, though. It was a mess. There were two unexpected guests in the Beswick house, and we now have two octogenarians we don't know how to handle. They don't speak English, and their grandson's body is in a van with the others in one of the outbuildings."

"What do you suggest we do?" she asked, half asleep.

"We removed the bodies to reduce the evidence the Grid and the police had available. We cleaned up as best we could in the time available. The police will find enough blood to identify the twelve gang members. Sam, the agent who died, won't be on their radar. The British Army will have his records, but they have no reason to follow that route. When a dozen members of a major drugs gang disappear without a trace, then I imagine the police breathe a sigh of relief rather than mount a nationwide search — removing as much of the drugs and cash as we can manage points the finger at rival gangs. The Grid will seek revenge. We need to be vigilant. When they make a move on a gang up here, we'll hit hard again. If there are casualties on both their sides, so be it."

"You haven't told me what you think we should do with the old couple."

"That's because I don't bloody know," said Phoenix. "I can't pull the trigger on two innocent people. The gang members who died tonight deserved everything they got."

"Let the local agents cope with the dispersal of corpses across the Wirral countryside over the next few days as planned. Then, you and Rusty can return to Larcombe Manor with our unscheduled guests. We'll leave them in Henry's capable hands. If anyone can persuade them to forget what they witnessed, he can. If that proves impossible, perhaps we'll fly them back home."

"What, to Derby?"

"Oh, I thought they were on holiday or something," said Athena.

"We checked the old lady's handbag; Rusty found her library card. He'd never seen one."

"At least you haven't lost your sense of humour. I can't wait to get you home. Thank goodness you're both safe."

"I wasn't joking," said Phoenix, "we'll be back by ten

o'clock. Warn Henry to expect his new arrivals. Apologies for disrupting his weekend."

Phoenix was disturbed from his memories as Rusty arrived for their afternoon session.

"Penny for them, Phoenix," he said, joining him at the table in the orangery overlooking the lawns,

"I replayed the night's events in the Bent Triangle earlier in the month," Phoenix replied. "Sam's funeral has taken place, and his family received a cover story they could swallow. Lenny's on the mend. He'll be back on active duty in no time."

"It was almost the perfect mission," sighed Rusty, "losing Sam was a real blow. He was a hero. As for the old couple, I don't think we could have done much else as it turned out."

Phoenix wouldn't forget that drive back from the Wirral to Bath in a hurry. They secured their prisoners in the van to be on the safe side, and Rusty headed for the motorway.

They endured four hours of abuse in Punjabi as the older man and woman shouted and screamed at them. Phoenix had no idea what language they spoke, but Rusty recognised the occasional swear word. He said it was the first thing a squaddie picked up in any foreign tongue he came across.

Henry stood waiting for them when they got back to HQ. He and an escort took the pair to the interrogation suite in the ice-house. A thorough search made an unexpected discovery. The older man wore a body belt under his loose clothing; the pouches contained nine kilos of heroin. When they tipped the contents of his wife's handbag onto a table, something made Henry take a closer look. The bag had a false bottom. Inside was a seven-inch blade, a kirpan.

That news gave Rusty and Phoenix a jolt. They thanked

their lucky stars they had tied the couple up before driving south.

Henry interrogated them for several hours. Giles carried out background checks in Derby. Far from being innocent bystanders, the couple took four trips a year for the past three years back to Mohali. They weighed more on the return journeys than when they left, not from a surfeit of good food.

Henry reported his findings to Athena at the following day's morning meeting. She gave the order to proceed with their removal. Henry reminded her that the coppicing in the woods at the far edges of the estate had yielded a significant amount of cut wood.

"We completed our forestry management cycle at the end of March. There's ample wood to build two pyres. We can cremate their bodies to comply with their Hindu heritage, and I'll arrange for the all-male burial party to scatter their ashes in the stream that runs past the pet cemetery. It's not the Ganges and far better than they deserve."

Athena had been grim-faced when she replied. "Waste not; want not."

Phoenix and Rusty had been on the south coast that morning on another mission against the Grid. There was no rest in the fight against evil.

## Chapter Five

Phoenix and Rusty spent the rest of Friday afternoon in the orangery. There was no more talk of the Jagpals. The mission to the Bent Triangle was now a closed book. Rusty knew better than to remind his best friend despite his meticulous planning, mistakes occurred.

Details that should have been passed on to Phoenix by others in the loop got dismissed as unimportant. Checks on the Hindu couple at the safe-house had been sloppy. An error Rusty was convinced could have resulted in Phoenix having his throat cut on the homeward journey before he could have saved him.

As they went through the events of the latest action against the Grid and prepared plans for next week's, Rusty kept reminding himself Phoenix couldn't continue to carry this burden alone for long. It was too much for one man.

He helped as far as possible, but in the future, Olympus needed others to step up to share the load. He resolved to talk to Athena on the matter when he caught her alone.

Two weeks ago, the pair managed an operation in the

Portsmouth area. Agents from the Olympus cell based in Southampton were responsible for events on the ground. If they needed support from Larcombe, it was only a two-hour drive away.

Phoenix had rubbed shoulders with several of this team when the Titans were at large. He had been driving like a madman through the New Forest, trying to avoid being killed by Hermes. Athena was with him and pregnant. They had spent a Sunday afternoon in Lymington relaxing on Erebus's yacht 'Elizabeth'. The drive home was interrupted. The cell leader and a crew drove to their rescue.

Two of those same agents had been working undercover in Portsmouth for the past eight months. The nature of their work spanned a vast range, from risk-free to potentially lethal. The gang they infiltrated majored in immigrant smuggling and money counterfeiting. The head of the outfit was Albanian. Other senior roles contained fellow-countrymen, but most of the gang were British and hard-core. The agents understood from the outset. One wrong move could give them away.

Giles and his team in the control centre constructed the cover stories and alibis they used with great care. It was always a meticulous job. Giles was well-versed in the art of deception, with similar plausible backgrounds needed for hundreds of agents worldwide.

Rusty knew criminals grew increasingly aware of undercover officers infiltrating their organisations. There was no evidence to suggest the gang traced a link between the men and the Olympus cell. If they had been police officers, the gang could have watched cars going in and out of the area's police stations. That was a potential weakness for the boys in blue but not for an Olympus crew. They lived what appeared to be normal lives on residential estates. If their cars got followed, the gang bosses would have learned nothing to make them suspicious.

The head of their cell talked to the men at least once a week. He appeared anonymous to anyone watching when they met up for a round of golf. Three hours of hacking around eighteen holes and a chat in the bar afterwards were enough to pass on any news. The leader wore a wire so they could record it for posterity. The meetings provided a release valve for the agents. That constant sustained pressure of working undercover was challenging to manage. The regular debriefing and support that those rounds of golf offered were essential.

The methods used to smuggle illegals into the UK varied. Hundreds arrived from the continent in the backs of lorries on ferries. Similar numbers came in shipping containers from Africa, the Middle East, and Asia. The price these desperate migrants paid ranged from five to ten thousand pounds per head.

Portsmouth was only one of the dozens of smaller ports used since security at Dover and Folkestone had been tightened. In times of austerity, security could only operate in a limited number of places, despite the potential dangers of that policy. Rusty told Phoenix it conjured up the image of the little Dutch boy with his finger in the flood embankment.

Phoenix started to count the number of potential leaks around the coastline and gave up, "We would run out of little boys and sink under the oceans."

The Southampton agents' role within the gang had been to act as couriers. They drove the unmarried men to hand car-wash sites in towns from Bognor Regis to Bournemouth. The gangmaster in the town took control of them from there. He found accommodation, and they would work ten hours a day, seven days a week. Phoenix and Rusty knew what conditions they endured and who looked after their finances.

The undercover agents rarely dealt with families. They got moved by other gang members, delivering them across the country in lorries. The network was well-established and trouble-free. Transport the gang used on these runs was maintained to a high standard. A cheapskate operation would soon attract attention. Motorway police pulled over vehicles that looked overloaded or dangerous. With the vast sums of money raised by the smuggling trade, it was worth spending money on keeping things running smoothly.

The rest of the courier work that the agents covered involved single women. The young ones unwittingly ended up as sex workers in seaside resorts along the south coast, while the older ones found themselves little more than domestic slaves, trapped in a vicious cycle of work, sleep and no play.

Week after week, the agents passed details of the network on to their team leader. Olympus now possessed data on a comprehensive cobweb of crime that stretched from West Sussex to Devon. The plan was not to raid each property but to cut the head off the snake.

An anonymous phone call to the authorities by Giles Burke or Artemis would provide a tip-off concerning the whereabouts of illegal immigrants. In time, they could free them from the awful conditions they had fallen into, and in most cases, they would face deportation. Always assuming the authorities found the human resources available to respond.

The call for urgent help in Portsmouth arrived ten days ago at lunchtime.

Phoenix and Athena were in their apartment. Rusty and

Artemis were enjoying a rare day off. The cell team leader, Frank Bolano, arrived at the golf course for their regular ten o'clock tee-off time. He waited an hour, but the agents never made contact. He called two of his colleagues. They visited the agents' houses with ladders, squeegees, and buckets of water. There was no sign of either man, upstairs or down. There were no cars on the driveway or in the garage at the first house. A vehicle stood locked and empty in the carport of the second. They called their boss. He contacted Phoenix.

Phoenix and Rusty sped south to Portsmouth. Frank Bolano met them at Cosham, a suburb on the outskirts. The news was not good. The local radio station had reported a firearms incident near The Guildhall. As they approached the city centre, sirens filled the air.

It was impossible to get any closer. A cordon surrounded the immediate area. Traffic officers signalled for them to move on, away from the centre. Rusty saw officers with guns running up side streets. They drove to the car park for the designer outlet centre on Gunwharf Quays; the three agents then walked back towards the centre.

Rusty had run ahead and asked local shopkeepers if they knew what had happened. He heard that someone dumped the bodies of two men near the Central Police Station on Winston Churchill Avenue. Five minutes from The Guildhall. The local radio said the shootings took place in Southsea at noon. The police received anxious calls from neighbours.

Rusty put the jigsaw together piece by piece, shop by shop. He filled in a few gaps they didn't understand. The two agents had driven to meet Frank Bolano as arranged. The first agent collected his colleague and went towards the golf course with both sets of clubs in the boot. Members of the gang intercepted them.

Eye-witnesses phoned the local radio with details of a high-speed car chase. Two cars, a BMW and a VW Passat, pursued a Ford Fusion along Victoria Road North. A third vehicle, a dark blue van, pulled across the front of the speeding Fusion at a crossroads. It was unclear at first whether this was deliberate or not. Then, two men with handguns leapt from the BMW and got into the rear of the Fusion. Shots fired. Neighbours who called the police and eye-witnesses who contacted the radio station were uncertain how many shots they heard.

They agreed it was in double figures.

The driver and passenger in the Fusion got dragged from the car. Their bodies got thrown into the back of the dark van. That vehicle's role then became clear. The Passat had already left the scene, while the BMW drove off towards Portsmouth, followed by the dark van. Each of the three vehicles at this stage travelled under the speed limit.

Armed officers arrived in Southsea twenty minutes after the shootings. Within minutes there was a significant police presence, but the only thing they found was the abandoned Fusion, with all four doors open, blood spatter throughout the front compartment, and two sets of golf clubs in the boot.

In Winston Churchill Avenue, the dark van slowed at a set of lights, and the rear doors opened. Two bodies fell onto the pavement. The van then sped off. Police began hunting for the three vehicles.

Rusty found Phoenix and their colleague to relay the news.

"They must have made them," said Rusty.

"We may never know what alerted the gang," said

Phoenix. "But we're not going to let them get away with killing two of our own. We'll take our revenge."

"I want to be on that mission, Phoenix," said Frank. "I owe those lads that much."

"I don't attach any blame for this on what you've done, Frank. Rusty and I have overseen your actions every step of the way. You handled everything extremely well. Textbook. No, something ridiculous lay at the bottom of it. No doubt, Henry Case will be able to extract it from one of the gang leaders in time."

"If any of them live long enough to be transported back to Larcombe for questioning," muttered Rusty.

"There aren't many positives to take out of this mess," said Phoenix.

"I can't see any," said Frank.

"The gang believed these two were undercover police officers," said Rusty.

"Exactly," said Phoenix, "dumping the bodies fifty yards from Police HQ sends a message about who ran the show in town. That's the only positive I can see."

"Olympus security remains unscathed then," said Frank, "until the bodies start piling up around here when we get busy."

"We must be cautious, Frank, as ever," said Phoenix, "vengeance will be swift but not reckless. Our actions must not draw the attention of the police to our door. We could not prevent the bodies of those two agents from falling into the hands of the authorities. The gang may have believed they were undercover cops. The police will know they were not. The cover stories for our agents are excellent, and enquiries will hit a dead end. Our best hope is that as these two played the role of gang couriers, we can let the police find evidence they had their own scam running. Maybe I'll ask Giles to plant regular cash amounts in their cover bank accounts, or we'll hide cash in the houses they occupied. It won't be difficult to convince the police these two were just casualties of the dirty game they were involved in."

There was little more to be achieved that afternoon, so Phoenix and Rusty returned to Larcombe. Frank Bolano returned to Southampton to break the sad news to his team. Later that evening, the three vehicles had been found burnt out on a housing estate in Fareham.

In the days that followed, the misinformation appeared wherever the police would be bound to search. Giles and his team made every attempt to cover Olympus's tracks. So far, the Hampshire Police investigation had failed to uncover any cast-iron motive for the slaughter of two men on the city's streets. The overall level of crime in the region continued to frustrate them, and resources stretched even further. Two low-level gang members were dead. A dozen new cases involving the living arrived on their desks overnight. With each successive day, the case slipped further down the list of priorities.

At Larcombe Manor, when Phoenix told her the news, Athena shed a tear at the loss of two more agents. They knew taking the fight to the Grid would bring casualties. Unfortunately, it didn't make it any easier when reality hit. She considered the problem for several days as Giles and Artemis weaved their magic.

Her orders at this Wednesday morning's meeting were clear. Zeus had sanctioned the direct action against the Grid's members in Portsmouth. It would take place on Monday. Five of the gang's leaders were their targets. One was coming to Larcombe to be dealt with by Henry Case.

Now, late on Friday afternoon, the thirtieth of May, in the orangery, Rusty watched as his friend placed photos on the display boards Erebus deplored. Phoenix worked in silence as if his friend wasn't in the room.

Rusty waited as Phoenix worked on his plans with every addition to the boards. The whole layout took forty minutes. Phoenix stood back and viewed his handiwork. Headshots of the men who ran the operations, details of their roles, and criminal records. Additional photos of the homes where they lived, their families, the cars they drove — lists of potential sites where they could be on Monday. Maps of every street they used daily in the past eight months. Rusty was still working through the masses of information Frank Bolano, and his team gathered.

"You told Frank this was a textbook operation," he said, "the sheer volume of material they collected beggar's belief."

"Yet we still lost two agents," replied Phoenix without turning around. He was still running through every possible scenario. It was true they had more than enough data. But was his interpretation of it and the plan he devised going to be successful?

"Are you ready to take me through it, Phoenix?" asked Rusty.

"As ready as I'll ever be," Phoenix replied. "When I planned my crusades, the only person who stood to get hurt if something went wrong was me. Even so, when a mission didn't go as planned, I was the only one in the shit. I thought on my feet, made my decision instantly, and acted to get myself out of trouble. These days I'm responsible for others, and I'm having doubts. Little niggles creep into my head, and I question every step I've planned over and over."

"I know," said Rusty, "you can't do everything, mate,"

Rusty was even more certain he should talk with Athena about getting her husband help.

They spent the next hour running through the various stages of the planned operation. Rusty had questions. Phoenix had the answers. When it ended, Rusty could find no fault with the logic behind his boss's plans. Yet, he could see a slight frown on his friend's face. Even as they tidied up the mess they made in the orangery and walked back across the lawns to the main building, Phoenix still checked he hadn't missed a vital step.

"Sleep well tonight," said Rusty. "I'll see you in the morning."

"I hoped for a break this weekend," groaned Phoenix, "but we need to hear what Giles and Artemis have found out about this poor woman Prentice."

### Saturday, 31st May 2014

Athena awoke bright and early. Phoenix was no longer beside her. She sensed he was troubled last night when they went to bed, but he hadn't been in the mood to talk. It was clear he didn't sleep well. Hope, on the other hand, was sound asleep when Athena poked her head into the nursery.

Athena walked through to the kitchen. Her husband had already eaten; a coffee mug was missing from the shelf. He was at work in the meeting room or the orangery. Athena made her own breakfast and then collected her daughter; soon after Hope let her mother know she was awake. Maria Elena would be in this morning to look after her while they held a brief meeting. Until Maria Elena arrived, Athena could only spend time with her little princess and brood over what troubled her husband.

Athena breezed into the meeting room at nine o'clock

on the dot, ready for action. Minos and Alastor sat together, smartly dressed as ever. Not suited and booted as on weekdays, but only one degree less formal. Athena could never imagine them attending in jeans and a t-shirt. They weren't the sort of men to understand the meaning of a dress-down day.

Rusty and Artemis arrived. Watching them, clearly in love and at ease in each other's company, was terrific. They were kept apart so much by their various duties at Larcombe. Yet, Athena sensed they grabbed every second they could be together and enjoyed it to the maximum.

Athena spotted Giles Burke and Henry Case through the window, walking side by side from the stable block. They would come through the door in seconds. Where was Phoenix?

"We're still one short," said Rusty as Henry and Giles joined them, "is Phoenix having a lie-in?"

"He was up and gone before I awoke," said Athena with a rueful grin. "I'm guessing none of you has seen him?"

The sea of shaking heads greeted her.

"Phoenix will be in the orangery," said Rusty, seizing his chance to raise the subject he had been mulling over. "He'll be checking next week's agenda for the ninety-ninth time. We discussed it in detail yesterday evening, and I couldn't see any potential pitfalls. This Grid business is getting on top of him. He needs a release valve. Someone to share the load."

"We each do what we can to give him the tools for the job," said Minos, "and he's the best I've seen at what he does. His success rate is higher than any agent we've ever had."

"There have been a minimal number of occasions when the fall-out from one of his direct actions has threatened to expose Olympus as being the architect," added Alastor. "He's a genius. However, Rusty has a good point. An expert in operations planning from a combat background would be a great acquisition."

"I agree," said Henry, "we need to find someone to do the groundwork. That would allow Phoenix to fine-tune prepared skeleton plans of proposed missions. He wouldn't need to devote the extra working hours he does at present, covering every minute detail. The poor chap will burn out if we're not careful."

"I'll introduce the subject gently," said Athena, with a sigh, "but he won't like it. As the joint leader of Olympus here at Larcombe, I must ensure we protect our assets. We can't afford for him to burn out. As his wife, I'd love to have him here with Hope and me more often. With luck, I can persuade him to see sense. Henry, do you have any contacts from the old days who might fit the bill?"

"No one off the top of my head, Athena," replied Henry, "but I'll get my thinking cap on and report back as soon as possible."

"Thanks, Henry," said Athena, "perhaps we should get on with hearing what you've uncovered, Giles?"

At that moment, Phoenix entered the room.

"Sorry, I'm late," he said, "I needed to check a few things. What did I miss?"

"Not a lot," said Rusty, "we chatted about you most of the time."

Phoenix sat next to Athena and nodded to her.

That was his apology for wandering off without a word, she thought. He didn't bite at Rusty's comment either. He always made sarcastic comments when Erebus headed up the morning meetings. Athena had lost count of the times she stifled a laugh as Phoenix brightened up proceedings with his dry humour.

Least said, soonest mended, she thought and nodded to Giles to carry on.

"Before I take you through what we found yesterday, I'd like to recap on the Wirral and Portsmouth missions, if I may?"

"Keep it brief," said Athena, "carry on."

"The disposal of the bodies from the Manchester affair is complete," said Artemis, "the safe-house will now go on the market. The proceeds will be substantial. We intend to buy two smaller properties in Macclesfield and Runcorn. The laying of false trails in Portsmouth and Southampton has been successful. We believe Phoenix's suggestion to 'dirty up' the reputations of the two undercover agents was what the police wanted to hear. It saved them from having to work too hard on the case. The case has left the mainline and is now on a siding gathering dust."

"As for our disappearing drug charity worker," said Giles, "we have identified a few leads, but there are no sightings in recent days. Artemis found Dawn Prentice on CCTV on Friday the second of May."

Artemis handed copies around the table.

"This group of females were on the pavement outside the charity building. Dawn is highlighted; we believe they just finished work. CCTV captured Dawn's car on camera in Kensington High Street. That would be one route she might have taken to get home to Notting Hill Gate."

"Do we have evidence of her reaching her home?" asked Athena.

"Inconclusive proof," said Artemis, "she stopped in traffic near the cinema, as you can see in this image. The timestamp shows it shows it's six in the evening."

"Are there no cameras in her street?" asked Rusty.

"Sadly, none," said Giles.

"So, where does this leave us?" asked Henry.

"We trawled back through earlier CCTV images from the cinema area on the off chance," said Artemis, "and found this."

She handed around copies of a series of additional images. While everyone studied the photos, Giles continued:

"This man was seen on the street on five occasions, either walking alongside Dawn Prentice or following her at a short distance. The time stamp on these includes successive Saturday lunchtimes. Dawn was a regular customer at a deli on Notting Hill Gate. She doesn't appear to know him or be comfortable in his company. He is a convicted felon, mostly for aggravated assault. Dominick Nagy works as a minder for a drug dealer called Adam Kovacs."

"Did Kovacs supply her with drugs back in the day?" asked Rusty.

"He fitted the profile," said Artemis. "The neighbourhood fits. He's added the designer drug angle to his menu, too, so we checked the financials to see if he was the one blackmailing Dawn."

"I didn't trace where the actual payments went when we carried out the checks for her Olympus candidacy," said Minos. "Zeus hoped we could give her a clean bill of health. We found enough evidence to suggest she reopened links with her past. That was enough to rule her out as Aurora."

"Understood," said Giles, "we found a regular payment to an overseas account that was cancelled only days before the confirmation of her disappearance."

"The timeline we have put together indicates Nagy

approached Dawn on behalf of Kovacs at least six weeks ago," said Artemis. "Nagy was caught on CCTV stalking Dawn, as you have seen. He approached her on Saturday lunchtime. The payments began the week after. Dawn was on her way home on the second of May. She didn't arrive at the charity on the fifth. Nobody was over-concerned; she was a volunteer. By the nineteenth, her colleagues started to worry. She didn't answer her phone; she didn't appear to be in her flat, although her car was in the street. On Wednesday of that week, they contacted her solicitor. Dawn informed her workmates she was leaving her fortune to charity in her will. They discovered one of his cards on her desk. The solicitor accompanied the girls to the flat. He rang the bell and got no reply. He tried the door. It was open. They found signs of a struggle and phoned the police."

"How did you fill in the gaps?" asked Athena,

"I visited the flats myself last evening," replied Artemis. "I could get done for impersonating a police officer, but it was easy enough to slip back into the old routine. I even persuaded a young guy on the top floor to admit he'd got home on the night of the second to stumble over a pizza delivery by her door. He took it upstairs and polished it off."

"That's my girl," smiled Rusty.

"You were tied up in the orangery for the afternoon. Giles thought I could do more good on the ground. I left at half-past two and caught several occupants already at home, the others as they returned from work. I got back here at just after ten. Giles and I finished putting this together for today, and you were asleep when I reached the apartment."

"So, where's Dawn Prentice been since the second of May?" asked Henry.

"Kovacs certainly has her," said Giles. "Where he has

her is something we're pinning down. I've got people hunting for properties he's known to use. My major concern is the solicitor stopping the payment. If she's still alive, Kovacs might decide he has no further use for her."

"Then we need to find her fast," said Athena, "get back to your search. Good luck."

Phoenix had contributed nothing to the meeting since his late arrival. He finally spoke as everyone collected their things together and prepared to leave.

"Why would Kovacs kidnap her? He had already blackmailed her into setting up regular payments. So, it wasn't for money. He must have taken Dawn for another reason. What else could he want her for except to finance his designer drug supplies? Whatever it was, she's been at his mercy for over three weeks."

"I can't see this matter ending well," said Henry.

"Not for Dawn Prentice, I agree," said Phoenix, "and not for Adam Kovacs."

## Chapter Six

**Monday 2nd June 2014**

Sean Walsh dreaded Monday mornings. Tommy always phoned him from Belmarsh the first chance he had. He wanted to hear family-related things. Had Sean seen Colleen over the weekend? Did he know how his kids were? How was Sean's daughter Saoirse getting on at school?

Sean could only give an honest answer to one question. Colleen hadn't been to his place for weeks, but Tommy wouldn't want to hear. Because he hadn't seen Colleen, he didn't know what was happening in Marbella either. Except temperatures were in the mid-forties now. The only thing he knew for sure was that Saoirse spent more time out of school than in, according to the attendance officer who had become a regular visitor at Sean's house.

Tommy didn't need to know that either. So, when he called this morning, it would have to be bullshit again.

Sean looked at the clock on the mantelpiece. Half-past

eight. Saoirse was still in bed. Another duvet day. He decided to call Colleen to catch up on her news. At least he could try to have something genuine to give to his brother-in-law. Sean sighed. This could become a real chore with Tommy inside for thirty bloody years.

Colleen picked up on the second ring.

"Who's that?" she barked.

"It's me, Sean," he said, "touchy, aren't you, sis?"

"I'm busy," Colleen replied. "I'm clearing out Tommy's gear. There's stuff he'll never get to use again."

"Hold on," said Sean, "what do you mean? What sort of stuff?"

"Old clothes, for a start. Nothing to fit you. Odds and ends Tommy's had in the wardrobe for years. He never used them on the outside. He'd never need them in Belmarsh or Durham."

"Yeah, he mentioned Durham on the phone last week, but a transfer isn't confirmed yet."

"If it is, we need to try to help him escape. It may be impossible to spring him from prison, but the transfer journey offers many opportunities."

"I'll mention it to the boss when I see him later," said Sean.

"Don't tell that bastard a thing, Sean Walsh," said Colleen. "He washed his hands of Tommy as soon as his cell door slammed shut on the first night. No, we'll do it together, the Walsh family. You choose the team. I'll put up the cash."

"It will cost a fair bit, Colleen," Sean replied, "where are you going to get that amount of money?"

"You'll find out soon enough, Sean. I'm downsizing. The cars have gone. Tyrone and Rosie are looking for something more reasonable in Marbella. I'm clearing Tommy's things, so I have less to take when I move."

Sean was struck dumb. Who was this person his sister had become? Ever since she and Tommy had got together when she was fourteen, she had been under his thumb. He said jump; she asked how high. Sean had seen the evidence on her face when she had questioned Tommy O'Riordan. Suddenly, she was decisive and full of action. It unnerved him. What was she going to do next?

"Have you thought this through, sis?" he asked. "What about the appeal? Tommy reckoned last week it was going ahead."

"Listen to yourself, Sean," Colleen scoffed, "you're as naive as him. There are no grounds for appeal, nor is there a snowball's chance in hell of a reduction in his sentence. The only way he's coming out is if we get him out. He can't stay in this country, so we'll need to smuggle him overseas. It shouldn't be hard. Thousands enter this country illegally every year. All we need is to get one bloke to travel to the continent. From there, he can fly to a country without an extradition treaty with the UK."

Sean's head was spinning. Colleen had thought this through.

"This downsizing is to get the cash together for Tommy's escape, then?"

"You're catching on, Sean," said Colleen, and after promising to keep in touch, she ended the call.

Colleen smiled to herself. It was as easy to pull the wool over her brother's eyes as it was Tommy's. She had no grand plan for a life abroad if Tommy was ever set free. The attempted escape plot was what Sean would expect of her. Tommy still had long arms, no matter which prison he occupied. If it failed, Tommy would stay inside for thirty years. If he escaped....well, she would cross that bridge when she came to it.

Time to carry on with the clear-out, and then she could start packing things she wanted to take with her to her new home in the sky.

Across town, Sean still chewed over what he had learned this morning. Far from picking up hints about what to discuss with Tommy, he was deeper in it than before. He didn't have long to wait for his phone to ring.

"Hello, Sean," said Tommy, "who were you talking with for so long? I had to join the back of the queue again."

"Nobody," lied Sean, "the phone must have been off the hook, mate. How are you?"

Tommy brought him up to speed about the conditions inside and asked the usual questions. Sean made all the advisable responses on the status of the appeal. He told Tommy to stay positive. He said he had heard Tyrone and Rosie were having a busy time in Spain but didn't go into detail. As for Saoirse, she was a popular young lady. People at the school were always asking after her. Somehow, Sean winged it and got through the ordeal. There was an impatient queue behind his brother-in-law this week, so things were cut short. When he put down the phone, Sean breathed a massive sigh of relief.

That was out of the way for another week. Now all he had to worry about was Hugo Hanigan. The orders would come thick and fast when the boss reached his office at noon. He needed to be on his toes. There was no cause to mention Tommy's appeal. Or the potential transfer to Durham. Hugo didn't have any interest in Tommy O'Riordan.

For the past few weeks, the Grid leader had only two

things on his mind. He thought Sean had slipped up in appointing Seamus McConnell as his lieutenant and never missed an opportunity to rub it in. It didn't help that Seamus had an annoying habit of cocking up every job Sean let him do alone. He had to wet-nurse the guy and supervise everything he tackled. Sean had known Seamus had limited ability, but the talent pool from which he had to select a second-in-command was shallow.

Hugo's second and most pressing problem was the unexplained number of deaths of members of gangs from the Grid network. Sean tried to convince him that it was natural wastage. It was a phrase Tommy had used. Late at night in the social club, after hours, with a bottle of Jameson's in front of them, demanding to be finished.

"The game we're in, Sean," Tommy would say, "ain't one where you get a long-service medal. Villains end up in the nick or the cemetery. You and me, we're old school and have kept out of trouble so far by using our wits. Time served on the streets has provided us with a good supply of nous. The trouble with kids coming into this caper today is they haven't got time to learn the ropes. They want it all, and they want it now. Live fast, die young. So, we can expect to lose a few hotheads along the way. Raise a glass to them, and move on. That's the best you can do."

Sean thought it ironic Tommy had ended up in the nick despite his street smarts. A dollop of spit on a strip of sticky tape had done for him. A quick clock check told him he'd better grab a coffee and a sandwich. Time marched on. Hugo would be calling.

There it was — ten past twelve. Sean swallowed hard and picked up.

"Yes, boss, what can I do for you?"

"We've got a problem," said Hugo.

Sean could tell he was on speakerphone. Hugo paced up and down, wearing out the luxury carpet in his office, constantly fidgeting. Forever on the move, his boss. A bundle of screwed-up energy, ready to explode at a moment's notice. Sean didn't ask what the problem was; he waited for Hugo to speak next. Anything he said might be the trigger for an explosion.

"The month of May is finally over, thank God," Hugo continued, "thirty-one days of headaches. You know how good I am with numbers, don't you, Sean? That's what you and the others pay me to do. Before last month we had a steady line of growth in our business. The Grid grew stronger every day; we had our setbacks. Your brother-in-law getting sent down for one; the disruption of our plans to murder the High Court Judge was another. Since I returned from Dublin, that steady growth has faltered. Supplies to dealers in the Guildford area have been interrupted after the police arrested four of our West Indian friends. One of our rising stars in London, Lay-Z Gordon, was gunned down, and his sister Abigail arrested."

Hugo still paced. Sean held his breath. Would there be a question for him? Should he risk a comment?

"Are you listening to me, Sean?" yelled Hugo.

"Yes, boss," Sean replied, "but these are isolated incidents. A few people have left the game, but there's no shortage of people wanting to take their place."

"You think? No, Sean, I think you listen. Add up these numbers. Two Roma and seven Poles in Birmingham. Fourteen in Manchester. How many's that?"

"Twenty-three?" said Sean.

"Yes, give the man a cigar. Twenty-three people who relied on us for their living were either found dead at home or disappeared. Add in the people I mentioned earlier, and we've got almost one every day in May. How can that be right?"

"It's not right, boss, but it's the game we're in," said Sean, hoping for the best. "We've got people up North asking questions. The word on the street is someone took them out to absorb those districts into their business. I'm waiting to hear which outfit was responsible. We need to teach them a lesson if they're not working with us."

"What if they're part of the Grid already?" asked Hugo, who had stopped pacing.

"We congratulate them for showing initiative, boss," said Sean, crossing his fingers. "It reduces our overheads."

"There might be a future for you yet, Sean Walsh," said Hugo. "If they're a new outfit looking to horn in on our patch, they need sorting, is that understood? And it needs to be painful."

"Yes, boss," said Sean, breathing more easily.

"Keep me informed on progress. Make sure the slack these deaths caused is taken up by our people or new faces that sing the same tune. I want June to show that a steady growth trend is back on track."

Hugo ended the call. Sean walked across the lounge to the drinks cabinet and poured himself a large one. He needed it.

---

Athena and Phoenix were back in their apartment, having lunch with Hope. The morning meeting had been brief. Giles and Artemis gave a quick update on progress, then returned underground to collate the latest data they had gathered on Adam Kovacs.

Minos and Alastor had nothing further to add except

that they continued to prepare background stories for the recruits. Henry, too, was eager to show his face in the training rooms to welcome the new arrivals. Rusty left the meeting with Henry to check in with their senior trainers. The meeting may have been shorter than usual, but actions speak louder than words.

Phoenix and Rusty were to meet in the orangery at two o'clock. Artemis was to join them for a meeting for the first time. So far, she had only been invited inside once, with Athena on a guided tour soon after she arrived at Larcombe.

The plans for direct action against the Portsmouth gang were put on hold until they resolved Dawn Prentice's disappearance, one way or another.

"It seems we'll be off to London later tonight or first thing in the morning," said Phoenix.

Hope had finished her lunch and looked for something to play with; she was bored. Athena picked up one of her soft toys and handed it to her in her highchair. Phoenix and Athena carried on eating and chatting about what lay ahead over the next forty-eight hours.

Hope looked around for a place to drop the little bear. Down it went.

"Oops," said Athena, "where's Benny gone?" She leant over, picked it up, and then placed it back on Hope's tray.

Phoenix kept an eye on his daughter. Sure enough, Hope checked again to see where she could drop Benny. She watched as it fell this time, seeing how fast it fell. Hope giggled when it landed far enough away that someone had to get up to fetch it this time.

"She's got us on the run-around," said Phoenix as he walked behind Hope's chair and collected the soft toy. He threw it onto the sofa. Hope's bottom lip quivered.

"Do you want to sit with Mummy and Daddy?" asked Phoenix, and he lifted his daughter out of her highchair. Once she sat upright on the sofa between her parents, the bottom lip was back to normal.

Benny was in her mouth, and peace reigned for at least two minutes. That settled Athena's next half-hour until Maria Elena returned. Phoenix cleared the lunch things and said goodbye to his wife and daughter. Then, he set off to the orangery.

When Rusty and Artemis joined him at two, he had formulated his plan, even though he had no idea where Kovacs was holding Dawn Prentice. My programme's flexible, he shrugged. Choosing the timing will be more critical than any location.

"No wonder you two keep disappearing here as often as you can," said Artemis, dropping her folders on the desk.

"Yeah, it's very relaxing," said Rusty. "We always get more positive results from missions planned in the orangery."

"It's no big surprise," said Phoenix, "it's the influence of the vibes Erebus left behind. I tune into his spirit and let Erebus guide my hand."

Rusty and Artemis shared a look. Was he joking?

"Erebus was the god of darkness and shadow," said Phoenix, with a sly grin, "we had better get on with it. We don't want to be in here when night falls."

"You're terrible," said Artemis, "you had me going for a minute."

"Let's get cracking then," Phoenix said, "what have you found out about the building Kovacs is using to hold this woman prisoner?"

"Giles has narrowed the search to two properties. The first is a ground-floor commercial unit off Portobello Road.

The place has been vacant for three months. Kovacs bought it in 2010. I guess it's a convenient business to launder at least part of his drug money. According to the estate agents, it was a sandwich shop in its last disguise, with a decent footfall."

"This sounds interesting, Artemis," said Rusty, "why hasn't it been snapped up?"

"They've had people interested," said Artemis, "but Kovacs hasn't seemed in a hurry to sell so far. The floor-plan shows a small storage room at the back of the shop and stairs to a corridor running the width of the building. The agent said the conditions are rank in the cellar area. Neither use nor ornament."

"Show us the second option then," said Phoenix, "but it will need to be bloody good to top that."

Artemis produced the photographs and notes on the next property; they showed a warehouse in Park Royal. There were several interior rooms for offices and secure storage. Some had windows, and others didn't. There was racking on the exterior walls of two sides and tables in the open area in the middle.

"We know Kovacs is switching his focus to designer drugs," said Artemis, "this has got to be where he stores his raw materials. His people then convert those into the finished product. It's possible Dawn Prentice is being held here in one of the secure rooms."

"Unlikely," said Phoenix, "too many people coming and going. No, the shop is the odds-on favourite. She could have been in that cellar for weeks. It explains why he won't entertain a sale."

"Then she's alive?" asked Artemis.

"She was," said Rusty. "While the money still appeared in Kovacs's bank account."

"There's still a chance, though?" pleaded Artemis.

"I'll contact our nearest team. If I'm reading these drawings correctly, each unit on this side of the street has a rear entrance. Delivery vans have access via a narrow lane, opening into a semi-circular loading and unloading area. They can break in and report on what they find."

"All we can do is wait and hope," said Rusty.

"Far from it," said Phoenix. "No matter which way this goes, we're hitting Adam Kovacs and his operation. Artemis, get me his home address and that of any office he uses, and then return here in an hour."

"On it," she replied and hurried off to the ice-house.

Phoenix made the call. The closest cell team leader was now the agent who assumed control after Des Finch died at Eton Wick, Simon Garrett.

"What do you need, Phoenix," Simon said," great to hear from you again."

"Simon, congratulations on your appointment. Last July and that firefight with the Bulgarian gang seems a lifetime ago. I need you to do a spot of breaking and entering off Portobello Road today; I've emailed you the details. The place has been empty for a while; you shouldn't be disturbed. I want a two-person team fitted with body cameras to attend. Giles Burke will liaise with you from here at Larcombe. We want to see what you see as you search."

"Roger that," said Simon. "What are we expecting to find?"

"If I'm right, you'll know as soon as you reach the stairs to the cellar."

"Understood."

Phoenix ended the call and rang Giles Burke in the ice-house. Rusty sat grim-faced and listened to the conversation. Giles was left to get his side of the link-up organised and talk to Simon Garrett. They would watch the scene unfold in London if the technology played ball and worked one hundred per cent.

"What's the plan for Kovacs?" asked Rusty when Phoenix had ended the call.

"Something painful but swift," said Phoenix, "fingers crossed, Artemis will give us the perfect setting for his demise. Don't make any plans for this evening. We're off to London as soon as your good lady passes us those addresses."

"Give me a list of what to collect from the armoury," said Rusty, "it will save time. I don't need to hang around, waiting for her to get back."

Phoenix produced a list of items from his folder.

"Drop into the transport section on your way over to the armoury. I asked them to prepare a nondescript van for today, like the 'Scott & Bailey' disguise we used in Chiswick. It should be ready to collect. Come back here as soon as you've loaded the van, and we'll get on the road."

"On my way," said Rusty, glad to see action. The walk to the transport section only took a minute. He spotted the battered Transit, with ladders on the roof, outside one of the garages. The logo read 'Clearview Cleaners'. One of the mechanics threw him the keys when he saw him arrive.

"Here we are, Rusty. I need these garage windows done if you've got five minutes, mate. Can't you have a word with your boss? Everything's a rush job with him."

"That's the game we're in, mate. Sorry. Thanks, though."

He soon parked by the door to the ice-house and was due to enter when Artemis emerged from the lift.

"We meet again," she said, pulling him into the entrance hall for a hug.

"Phoenix is waiting," said Rusty, tousling her hair and kissing her neck. "As much as I'd love to take this further, I need to get below for the equipment we need tonight."

"Oh, you're off to London already? Keep safe."

They kissed and clung to one another for a while; then, Rusty opened the lift doors. Artemis walked across the grass towards the orangery. Rusty watched her go, then made his way to Level Two and the armoury.

Artemis found Phoenix sat in the same position she had left him an hour ago. He went through his mission folder, page by page, checking and re-checking his plans.

"Ah, there you are," he said, looking up with a start, "did you bump into Rusty?"

"Do I look flustered?" she asked, with a grin, "your transport looks fine, and Rusty is in the armoury already. I've got everything you'll need right here."

She laid out the photos and notes on the two properties known to be occupied by Adam Kovacs regularly.

"His home address is in McGregor Road, W11. As you can see, the property benefits from off-road parking. This image shows the double gates to the left-hand side of the building. Kovacs lives alone in the ground-floor flat he purchased for three-quarters of a million. Check the signs at the gates. CCTV covers the parking site and the entrance. Giles is working on disabling those cameras as we speak. The big red sign warns, 'No parking in front of these gates. Access required 24 hours a day.' As for his office, that's midway between his home and Notting Hill Gate. His walk to work takes five minutes."

"A further five minutes would have taken him to Dawn Prentice's front door," said Phoenix. "No wonder it was so easy for Kovacs to get his hooks into her again. They were near neighbours."

"The short distances involved explain how they kidnapped her and had her hidden in that cellar without raising any alarms. It would have been over in minutes."

Phoenix received a message on his phone.

"It's Simon Garrett," he said. "He's disabled the alarm, and they've entered the vacant shop premises. We don't have a screen here. Erebus banned them because they spoiled the ambience of the place. Let's dash over to the meeting room in the main building. We can watch things unfold from there. Leave a note for Rusty. Tell him to join us when he's ready."

They watched a grainy, intermittent image flickering on the screen two minutes later. The sound was perfect, even if the pictures weren't. Simon Garrett had led the way into the shop through the rear storeroom.

"All clear, Phoenix," he said. "I hope you're getting this. The storeroom is empty — empty racks, discarded packaging materials on the floor, nothing more. We've got a counter, display cabinet, and boarded-up windows here in the shop. There's nothing to see. So we're making for the stairway now."

Phoenix and Artemis watched as Simon reached the top of the staircase. His head turned to the wall on his right. He had found the light switch; the image flared with sudden brightness. Phoenix saw the steps leading to the corridor.

"Think yourself lucky you've only got sound and vision, Phoenix," said Simon.

Behind him, the second agent was gagging at the smell that must have been coming from the locked room.

The green-faced agent appeared from behind Simon, carrying a pair of bolt-cutters. The padlock on the door broke in seconds. The door swung open.

"We've found your missing person, Phoenix," said Simon as he stepped inside.

"How close is our nearest medic?" asked Phoenix. He could now see the grim tableau that had greeted the two agents.

"In traffic, at this time of day, possibly fifteen minutes," replied Simon.

"Contact him and get him to give you a clue as to the time of death. We can't do the autopsy ourselves. You'll need to cover your tracks. Fit a new padlock, and convince the estate agent first thing in the morning that rats have been traced back to the property. Tomorrow, Simon, you will be a rat-catcher from the council. Once the estate agent makes the awful discovery, we can let the authorities take over."

"Understood, Phoenix," said Simon. "Sorry we couldn't rescue the poor woman."

Artemis had sat quietly, watching and listening.

"How horrible. Dawn Prentice was alone in that dark cellar for weeks. She was secured hand and foot. There was a bucket close by. Did you notice? I've seen a few dead bodies in my time. I guess she's been dead several days, but not more than a week. She bore no visible wounds to suggest she was shot or stabbed. There was bruising, of course, and sores near her bindings. We could be looking at a drug overdose."

"I knew your policewoman's eye would come in useful one day," said Phoenix.

"Does what I told you help?" asked Artemis.

"Yes, without question. In due course, the official cause of death will give some explanation, but we may never know why Kovacs kept her there all that time. That troubles me. I could drag him back here for interrogation, but I don't have time to waste."

Rusty entered the room.

"What did I miss?"

"Garrett discovered Dawn Prentice dead in the cellar. They're removing every trace of ever having been inside the premises, and then tomorrow, they'll assist the estate agent in discovering her body."

"The van's ready, and the kit loaded. Shall I drive?" asked Rusty.

"Yes," said Phoenix. "I'll run along the corridor to tell Athena we're off. I'll see you outside in two minutes."

Rusty turned to Artemis.

"Was it bad?"

Artemis replayed the film of the few minutes Phoenix had taken the precaution of recording.

"I'd hazard a guess at a drug overdose," said Artemis. "Just one question? Why leave the authorities to handle the autopsy and everything that follows but rush off to deal with Kovacs? He's behind her murder, so why not let the police arrest him and any of his thugs involved?"

"If Olympus handled the body, we couldn't be sure the authorities would release the funds tied up in Dawn's will. Phoenix wants the charity she worked with to receive her fortune. We must help the work they do in the fight against drugs as much as possible. Her work in that area brought her to Zeus's attention in the first place. We would have no option but to dispose of her body, so Olympus never connected to this business. This way, the police will work out who was responsible."

"What will they make of Kovacs dying the same day Dawn's body turns up?"

"Don't worry, Phoenix has thought of that. A classic

piece of misdirection. He's struggling with the volume of work, yet he still comes up with the goods."

"Off you go then," said Artemis, "your chariot awaits. The sooner you go, the sooner you'll be back."

After he trotted off to join Phoenix, Artemis tidied the meeting room. She smiled as she listened to Rusty attempting a George Formby impression.

He was singing, 'When I'm cleaning windows.'

## Chapter Seven

Phoenix was in the van's passenger seat when Rusty walked outside the main building. He jumped into the driving seat and drove down the main driveway. It was now four o'clock.

"We should be in London by half-past six," said Rusty, switching on the radio.

"Do me a favour," said Phoenix, "reprimand whoever used this vehicle before us. One, they've left their fast-food packaging in the glove compartment, and two, the radio's tuned to Heart FM. Both are designed to clog your arteries. Find me something more relaxing."

"Kerrang it is then," groaned Rusty.

"Why can't we install CD players in Olympus vehicles?" asked Phoenix, "we could choose our music then. I'm happy to listen to one of yours for every two of mine. Fair's fair."

"Hang on, how's that fair?" said Rusty.

"Seniority," said Phoenix.

Rusty shook his head and suffered the hard rock music in silence for the next hour as they joined the M4 and travelled east.

Phoenix switched off the radio when they passed the Newbury turn-off.

"Do you agree with my logic on this one, Rusty?" he asked.

"I don't have a problem getting rid of scum like Kovacs, boss. I'm concerned about collateral damage. Is that tied in with the misdirection?"

"Of course, I do everything possible to avoid innocent casualties on an Olympus mission. You know that. Others are not so concerned."

"Which will steer the police in the direction you want them to go," said Rusty.

"They've not failed us yet, Rusty."

Phoenix called Giles Burke in the control room.

"How's progress on the CCTV situation, Giles?" he asked.

"I've located the two cameras that would cause you problems. They had a sudden failure ten minutes ago. It only lasted two minutes. I'll interrupt their feed at regular intervals over the next two hours, increasing the length of the break on each occasion. How long will you need to complete your mission once you move into position?"

"A maximum of eight minutes, Giles," said Phoenix. "I'll let you know when we finish, and you can reduce the breaks in recording over the following four hours. If we're lucky, Kovacs might not check his cameras that often. If he does, I guess he won't pay for an emergency call-out when the problem appears minor. He might leave it and call a repairer tomorrow morning. By then, it will be too late."

Rusty found his way to St Luke's Road and turned into McGregor Road at six forty. There was no option but to do a slow drive-by, as traffic was still heavy.

"I couldn't live up here," said Phoenix, "too many people going nowhere."

They passed the building and the double gates; there was no sign of Kovacs inside the ground floor room. Rusty found a nearby car park. The two friends wandered back up McGregor Road. Phoenix nudged Rusty as he saw a car slow by the entrance to their target's off-road parking spot. Rusty produced a battered copy of an A-Z street map of the city from his jacket. He and Phoenix stopped fifty yards away from the gates. Anyone on the street would have thought they'd got lost and stopped to check directions. Nobody would have offered to help. People here lived their own lives; they knew better than to talk to strangers.

Phoenix watched over the top of the booklet as Kovacs reversed his BMW into the parking space. The drug dealer could afford the top-of-the-range model he locked behind double gates. Everything went to plan. Kovacs disappeared indoors.

"Now, we wait," said Phoenix. "I'll keep on the move and watch out for when he makes a move. You get back to the van. Be ready to drive back here at a minute's notice."

"How sure are you he's coming back tonight?" asked Rusty.

"Giles provided me with a timetable of his social habits gathered over a reasonable period. He has a pattern; most people do. Kovacs is showering and changing now. Then he'll drop into that cocktail bar on the corner. He has three favourite places to eat later. A French restaurant in Notting Hill, a Chinese on Bayswater Road, and a traditional Hungarian in Cricklewood."

"So, does he walk, or will he take the motor?"

"Cricklewood is a hike. He takes the Tube. Too posh to

use the bus, which is daft because it's only two quid on the 326."

"Giles found that out for you, didn't he?" asked Rusty, turning to make his way back to the car park.

"It's good to know if you get stuck," said Phoenix. "I file these little gems away in my head. Over the past four years, I've spent a fair bit of time up here. As a result, I'm beginning to find the quickest and cheapest ways to get where I need to be."

Rusty was already out of earshot. Phoenix started his surveillance. He moved from one end of the street to the other, crossing from time to time. He couldn't stay on McGregor Road for too long. That would attract attention from a curtain-twitcher or an old dear out walking her Pekinese.

Phoenix spotted activity at the front of the building. Adam Kovacs was on the move; he was walking towards the cocktail bar. So far, so good. Phoenix was on the opposite side of the road, heading in the same direction. Luck was still on his side. He was a hundred yards behind Kovacs, and dozens of cars passed between them, preventing Kovacs from noticing someone was following him.

Phoenix waited until he saw Kovacs enter the bar and order a drink. He called Rusty. They could park in front of the double wooden gates in two minutes, no matter what the sign said. He called Giles to trigger the latest in the series of camera-feed interruptions.

"Give us two minutes to get the van into position, then shut the feeds for eight minutes,"

"Consider it done, Phoenix," said Giles.

Phoenix could see Kovacs chatting to customers at a table near the window. He was satisfied the drug dealer was comfortable for a while. They had sufficient time to do what he'd planned wherever Kovacs decided to dine afterwards.

The window-cleaning van turned onto McGregor Road and trundled along the street, coming to a halt by the gates in the gap between parked cars. Rusty fetched the ladders from the roof of the van. He opened the back doors. The buckets, sponges, and cloths he needed were ready for action.

Rusty put one set of ladders up against the ground-floor windows and got to work. Phoenix collected his tools from the van and climbed over, using the other ladders leaning against the locked double gates. Rusty watched the street from his elevated position.

"These windows needed a clean," he called out.

"Any chance I'll be disturbed?" asked Phoenix as he crouched by the BMW.

Rusty looked up and down the street. The light was fading; the sun would set in another thirty minutes. Traffic was minimal, and the pavements were almost deserted.

"All quiet on the western front," said Phoenix.

Three minutes later, Rusty had finished cleaning the windows and put his ladders onto the van's roof. He returned his cleaning materials to the van when Phoenix scrambled back over the gate and dropped to the pavement. His ladders were soon next to Rusty's, and they were good to go.

They had no sooner sat in the van when there was a tap on the driver's side door. Rusty lowered the window.

"You're new to the area, aren't you?" asked the elderly gentleman. "I could do with someone to clean my windows and hand wash my car. What do you charge?"

"Thirty quid. It's too dark to do it tonight. We haven't

got a business card with us, sorry," said Rusty. "Look us up in Yell, and give us a call."

Rusty closed the window and drove out of McGregor Road. The old bloke sauntered home.

"Only thirty?" asked Phoenix, "that seems cheap for London prices."

"We might have hit on a gimmick," said Rusty, "your windows and your car. Not too many businesses offer an all-in service."

"The BMW is no cleaner than it was when I climbed the gate. We wouldn't get much repeat business if we were that sloppy."

Phoenix called Giles, and the CCTV cameras switched on again. Intermittent delays would continue until after midnight. The drive back to Bath was uneventful. Rusty turned onto the Larcombe Manor driveway at half-past eleven. He left the van by the transport section garages; they could return the borrowed kit in the morning. He and Phoenix made their way upstairs to their apartments; for them, tomorrow was another day.

Adam Kovacs left the cocktail bar at nine o'clock. He made his way along Bayswater Road and enjoyed a sumptuous Chinese meal. It was midnight before Kovacs returned home. Inside his flat, worse for wear, he stood in the kitchen and stared at two snowy screens.

"What's the matter with this CCTV?" he shouted. He gave the top of the unit a sharp smack. The screens miraculously sprung into life. He had perfect views of his car and the front of the building.

"That's better," he said and staggered into the lounge — time for a large brandy before bed.

## *Tuesday, 3rd June 2014*

Adam Kovacs never heard the dawn chorus. He was always still fast asleep. The triple-glazed windows prevented much of the street noise from reaching his ears. It was ten o'clock when he finally stirred and made his way to the bathroom.

Despite the alcohol he had drunk last night, he remembered the strange incident with the CCTV cameras. As he reached the kitchen after his shower, he double-checked. Everything was fine. No worries. With his first mug of coffee in his hand, he walked into the lounge.

The sun hurt his eyes. He squinted at the windows. Something didn't look right, but he couldn't work out what it was. He sat, facing away from the street. That bright sunlight didn't help his headache.

He called Dominick Nagy.

"Be here at a quarter to twelve," he ordered, "we're taking a trip out to Park Royal. I need to make sure it's ready for the next delivery."

"Yes, boss," said Nagy. He was still in bed. He looked at what he had brought home last night and groaned. She seemed to be in her late twenties in the subdued lighting of the nightclub. Now, lying naked with her mouth open and her make-up smeared, he wouldn't have been surprised if she wasn't in her late forties.

The minder headed for the bathroom. With luck, the girl would have taken the hint by the time Nagy had showered, shaved, and done the other things he needed to do.

The flat was empty when he emerged from the bathroom. Nagy breathed a sigh of relief. Things were looking up. He had time for breakfast in the café up the road. Then he'd walk over to the boss's house.

McGregor Road is never empty; there are always cars there, either parked or passing through it. They get their fair share of cyclists and pedestrians. At eleven forty-five, Dominick Nagy rang the bell for Adam Kovac's flat. His boss trotted down the steps to the pavement, and they made for the double gates. Kovacs undid the padlock, and Nagy pushed open the barriers to either side of the entrance.

"You can drive," said Kovacs, "I might still be over the limit,"

Nagy didn't question his boss. He wanted to say he was taking a risk himself driving this early too, but he needed the job. It didn't pay to go against Adam Kovacs.

Dominick took the keys and opened the driver's door. His boss got in and fastened his seat belt; Nagy didn't bother. He had to get out and lock the gates as soon as they cleared the entrance.

The bomb was fixed magnetically to the car's underside beneath the passenger seat. Phoenix was grateful to Giles for adding the extra touches that helped their direct actions go so smoothly. Those hours watching the drug dealer's movements came in useful. Nagy drove forward and applied the brakes. That was the trigger.

The minder got out, and a young mother with a toddler in a pushchair nearly bumped into him. He stood back to let her pass.

"How am I supposed to get by with these gates open?" she asked, "it's very inconsiderate."

Nagy didn't want to hang around talking. He shrugged, shut the gates, secured the padlock, and shouted after her: -

"Have a nice day, yeah?"

There was no reply. Nagy got back into the BMW and belted up. Kovacs looked at his watch; Nagy took the hint. It was time to drive to the warehouse at Park Royal.

At Larcombe Manor, the morning meeting was ending. Athena had kept things moving along at a steady pace. Her main focus was to allow Phoenix to proceed with the direct action in Portsmouth later this afternoon. She knew he would be keen to have a final run-through of his plans with Rusty before they drove south.

The day's first task had been to ask Henry to update them on the new intakes' first day's training and whether they continued progressing with retraining agents recalled from overseas postings.

"I can't fault Rusty's training schedules, Athena," Henry reported. "Thomas and Longdon have a particular style which resonates with the older agents. They seem a happy bunch. I wish my old boarding school teachers had made learning such fun. I wouldn't have been in tears at the end of each holiday, dreading my parents dropping me off for another five weeks of torture."

"How are the newbies settling in?" asked Athena.

"I thought Kelly Dexter was a shock to many of the men in this set. She rules her sessions with a rod of iron and takes no prisoners. She will be the first female trainer many of them have encountered. Hayden Vincent plays the role of good cop and adds the right amount of encouragement without undermining her authority. As we know, he's not as intimidated by her in their day-to-day life, but the trainees aren't privy to that information. That couple adopts a different approach to our ex-armoury guys, but it will produce the results we seek."

"Excellent," said Athena. She turned her attention to Giles Burke and Artemis.

"Is it too soon to have learned much from yesterday's missions?"

"The visit to the shop premises off Portobello Road

helped solve the disappearance of Dawn Prentice, with the tragic outcome we feared," said Giles.

"Yes," sighed Athena. "Artemis informed me while Phoenix and Rusty were en route to London to carry out our response."

Phoenix looked at the clock on the wall.

"We should learn more on that soon," he said.

"Good," said Athena. "I contacted Zeus and broke the news to him on Aurora. He wishes to hear about today's events."

"The estate agent handling the sale of the shop premises was due to be persuaded to show the cellar to the pest control inspector from Kensington and Chelsea Borough Council this morning," continued Giles. "He's better known to us as Simon Garrett. The emergency services will have been alerted by now, and we'll follow up on the case as soon as we get back to the ice-house. However, it might be a few days before they establish a time and cause of death."

"Understood," said Athena, "can you take the rest of the team through what happened yesterday evening, Phoenix?"

Phoenix had updated his wife this morning over breakfast. Artemis had been asleep when Rusty got to bed last night and had gone to the control centre to start her shift at six o'clock. Well, before he was up and about.

"The window-cleaning cover worked a treat. It worked so well that Rusty picked up extra business for our dynamic duo. I'm not sure we'll be available to carry it out. I attached the device to the BMW, and the electrical circuit was completed when the driver used the brake pedal for the first time. That will have initiated the timer. The surveillance carried out by Giles, and his team suggested an average journey time to Park Royal in all traffic conditions is twenty-two minutes."

"How did you know Kovacs would head for the warehouse this morning?" asked Artemis. "He might have been driving anywhere."

"Not likely. This is thanks to Giles's attention to detail again," said Phoenix. "Kovacs makes only two trips in the daytime by car with his minder. Either to the warehouse or the shop. I discounted a visit to the shop. He has no reason to visit it now Dawn Prentice is dead. He wouldn't collect the body himself and dispose of it. He has thugs in his employ to do his dirty work. There's no chance of them doing that in the daytime. They would operate under cover of darkness. Either he hasn't issued the order yet, or they weren't in a hurry to get the job done. That was their loss; and our good fortune."

"We shouldn't have long to wait for news," said Giles. "Kovacs rarely went anywhere much before noon."

All eyes turned to the clock. It had just clicked past noon.


Dominick Nagy was cursing his luck. A lorry reversing from a loading bay across the road from the warehouse had brought them to a halt; seconds ticked past. He could sense Adam Kovacs losing patience. He edged forward.

Nagy tried to nudge through the gap. He was keen to get the BMW into the parking spot eagerly anticipated by his boss. The lorry driver realised he was holding someone up, took his time to manoeuvre his truck and as he straightened up, he gave Dominick the finger through his cab's windscreen.

"English bastard," cursed Nagy.

The road ahead was now clear, and the lorry drew alongside. Nagy accelerated forwards to swing in front of the warehouse building. It was eight minutes past twelve.

Time was up.


Athena and Phoenix had finished lunch. Hope played on the floor while they were chatting on the sofa.

"What time are you leaving?" asked Athena.

"In an hour," replied Phoenix. "Rusty is in the armoury collecting the things on my shopping list. We are travelling by car."

The phone rang. Athena answered; it was Minos.

"Turn on the TV," she said to Phoenix, "this is what we've been waiting for."

The scenes that greeted them were from Park Royal. The police cordon restricted the camera views for the gathering media scrum to long distance. Ahead of them was mayhem. Fire appliances, paramedics, and police officers milled around in organised chaos. The camera broke away from the centre of the blast and switched to a reporter interviewing a senior fire chief.

"A car bomb rocked this industrial estate a few minutes after noon. The blast blew apart the car, believed to be a BMW, and shattered windows in buildings a hundred yards in either direction. It's believed there were two people inside the car. They died in the explosion. The site was busy with vehicular traffic in the middle of the day. Lorries driving past or parked on the forecourts of nearby units were damaged by the force of the explosion. The pall of smoke from the car was visible five miles away. Fork-lift truck drivers working outside and dozens of warehouse staff from these units got cut by flying glass and falling equipment. At this stage, none of the injuries sustained appears to be life-threatening. Ambulances are removing the injured to local hospitals."

Athena muted the sound but left the images on the screen.

"That's a relief," said Phoenix, "there was a risk the bomb would go off in traffic. They could have hit a trouble-spot our surveillance team didn't factor into their calculations."

"Your misdirection had the potential to go wrong," said Athena, "but it was a gamble worth taking, I suppose?"

"I thought so," said Phoenix, "let's look at the possibilities. The police will soon identify the dead men. There's an established link between Kovacs, this Park Royal warehouse, and the premises off Portobello Road. It will be simple enough for Giles to make an anonymous call to suggest that the police find it useful to have a peek inside the warehouse. To check what type of business he was running."

"How will we help explain who might have killed Kovacs and his driver?" asked Athena.

"My plan relies on his actions disrupting the money supply. Kovacs kidnapped Dawn Prentice, and that led to the ending of the money supply. His partners on the continent will have been surprised by that move. Access to tens of thousands of pounds every month was a godsend to their operation. What was the first question the gang would ask? Why did Kovacs slow the transfer and conversion of their raw materials into street-ready drugs? A little nudge in the right quarter will point the investigation towards his partners-in-crime as having the best motive for killing him. We could intimate Kovacs was intent on getting more money from Dawn Prentice to allow him to cut out the middle man. To suggest that was the reason behind the kidnap.

The loss of profits for the gang across the channel would be more than enough to make them act to remove Kovacs and send a message to other UK gangs not to cross them. If the police follow the trail of clues that we leave, we could kill two birds with one stone. Avenge Dawn Prentice's murder and destroy this particular supply line of designer drugs onto our streets."

"If everything goes to plan with Simon Garrett, the discovery of Dawn's body will soon filter through to the people handling this bombing," said Athena. "Could the manner of her death change their way of thinking?"

"Difficult to say. The post-mortem will be key. We need to get hold of those results as soon as possible, to understand the nature of the misdirection we must spread to achieve the outcome we prefer."

"You had better get ready for Portsmouth, darling," Athena said, "Rusty will have finished shopping. I'll keep on top of things here and follow up on how Simon got on. You must meet up with our Southampton crew, avenge our agents, and come home safe."

Phoenix left the main building and walked across the lawns. He had passed the stable block when he spotted Rusty by the entrance to the ice-house. His pal was struggling. There were no supermarket trolleys in the armoury. He had to bundle the items into the lift and transfer them to the car's boot. Phoenix slowed his walk. No rush; Rusty was almost done.

"Are we good to go?" he asked when he reached the car.

"Would you drive while I get my breath back?" asked Rusty.

"Old age doesn't come alone, does it?" laughed Phoenix. He caught the keys Rusty threw, and they were on their way.

Two hours later, they were in Cosham. They waited in the same place as before. In minutes, Frank Bolano had joined them. He had three other agents waiting in his van.

"Run me through the background we have on our targets again, Frank," said Phoenix.

"These three played a major role in the murder of our undercover agents. Konstandin Elizi is forty-seven years old. He is the head of the gang. He arrived in the UK eighteen months ago. His criminal record should have excluded him, but he appealed because his life was in danger if he returned to Kosovo. The authorities swallowed that, and he repaid them with violence and intimidation. Dalmat Januzaj is his second-in-command; he is thirty-nine years old. He was one of the gunmen who murdered our boys. The third man and the second shooter is thirty-six years old Egzon Lumani. He works as the gang's fixer. When any of the women they've smuggled in step out of line, Lumani roughs them up or rapes them. He's a nasty piece of work."

"No great loss, then?" said Rusty.

"That goes for all three, Rusty," replied Frank. "The Albanians control prostitution in the Portsmouth area now, no matter how hard the home-bred criminals believe they are. Some of the individuals concerned, such as Lumani, are capable of extreme violence. It's the trademark of Albanian gangsters. The crime families first arrived in the UK after the Kosovo war at the end of the last century. The families are relatively small but strongly bonded by a code of honour and blood feuds. As they have made their way across Europe over the last fifteen years, they've fought for control with groups as tough as the Italian Mafia and always come out on top. These are serious guys to mess with."

"Guess what?" said Phoenix. "From this month, Albania became fully integrated into the European Union. Does it make sense to let these criminals have free movement across the whole of Western Europe?"

"Too late to moan now," said Rusty, "the beggars are here. It's up to us to thin out the worst of them."

"I intend to," said Phoenix.

## Chapter Eight

Frank Bolano returned to his van and led Phoenix onto and along the M275. The two vehicles eased their way through early evening traffic as they drew closer to the city centre.

"This paints a similar picture to the one we see in London, doesn't it?" said Rusty.

"I know what you mean," said Phoenix, "look at the streets we visited last night. Decent houses, selling for eye-watering prices, bordering on streets with national monuments, museums and beautiful parks. Half a mile away lie the council estates, full to bursting with thousands of families on the breadline. Half the boroughs in London have that contrast on their doormat, yet they crow about being part of a culturally diverse multi-national community. Talk about rose-coloured glasses."

"Every major city in the UK suffers from the same issues," said Rusty.

"They don't have to worry about the house prices as much up north," said Phoenix. "The gap between the rich and poor might be less, but it's still real."

The two agents looked out onto the streets they passed. Portsmouth was a city in decline. They may have splashed out money on things such as the Spinnaker Tower and Gunwharf, but many parts of the city were little better than a toilet. The drive from North End through Fratton was one of total misery. On either side of the street, they saw boarded-up shops and graffiti.

Money-lenders, charity shops, and ethnic supermarkets dotted liberally every few hundred yards; idle teenagers wandered pavements and gathered on every street corner. Phoenix and Rusty noted that nationality defined each corner; the unemployed poor were males, either Eastern Europeans, Kosovans or Iraqi Kurds. The Kurds were most likely refugees or convinced someone from the local council that they qualified.

"Remember that job we did in Chiswick in March?" asked Phoenix.

"What, McTierney and his mob?" asked Rusty.

"The people he had working for him, they used teenagers. Some of them were as young as fourteen. It was part of the expansion programme they were operating, spreading the misery from London to the provinces. Portsmouth was one city they targeted. These kids brought the drugs here on the train. It brings a whole new meaning to an away day, doesn't it?".

"When you look around, it's easy to see why they thought they had a marketing opportunity," said Rusty.

Frank Bolano's van was indicating left. They followed him into the car park for Tamworth Park. Once they parked alongside one another, Frank and Phoenix got out and sorted out their next moves.

"What brings us out to this side of the island?" asked Phoenix.

"Don't laugh," said Frank, "it's Elizi. He's due here for his health. He's got a penthouse suite on Gunwharf Quays, which cost him six hundred grand. That's a thirty-minute drive away from here. Over the road is the NHS Treatment Centre, where he's having a heart scan at nine in the morning. He'll have a driver bring him across and wait for him to run him home afterwards. I reckon this will be a better place to collect Elizi."

"I agree," said Phoenix, "the hospital car park will be busy, but it has plenty of cover. We'll let him go inside, neutralise the driver, and then accompany him on his onward journey. How many people are you using?"

"Two agents," said Frank.

"You and another experienced hand?" asked Phoenix.

Frank nodded. Phoenix was happy.

"Where do we find the other two?" he asked.

"It's possible that Januzaj will be the driver. Elizi has more than one lieutenant, but dropping in for a heart scan might be seen as a sign of weakness. He wouldn't want to give his senior people any ideas. If someone else is the designated driver, we'll find Januzaj in the club by the Guildhall. He'll have gang members surrounding him, so we must wait until he's outside and on the move. We know where Lumani lives on Milton Road, but if there's a problem to fix, he could drive anywhere from one end of the south coast to the other."

"So, we'll wake him up before he has a chance to choose what he's doing tomorrow," said Phoenix. "Leave that to us."

"My other two agents will be at one of our safe houses on the outskirts of Southampton," said Frank. "I'll text you the details later tonight. Let's get you a place to sleep tonight. The two houses we used for our undercover boys are still on our books. You can use the nearest one if that's okay?"

"I'm not superstitious," said Phoenix.

"Follow me then," said Frank. "It's a mile from here."

An hour later, the Southampton crew left for home. Phoenix and Rusty settled in for the night.

"Here's the folder with everything you need to know about the gaff where Lumani lives. Get an early night because we'll knock on his door at dawn."

Rusty studied the pictures, read the detailed notes, cleaned his guns, and checked his ammunition. Then, finally, he was ready; as he headed for his bed, he looked at Phoenix. Hia friend was staring into space. Rusty knew he was going through every step of tomorrow's action.

"Goodnight," he called, but his friend didn't hear him.

### *Wednesday, 4th June 2014*

The big red key's first strike was at five; the streets were empty. The noise sounded loud enough to wake the dead. Egzon Lumani was roused from a heavy sleep by his back door, crashing against the kitchen wall when it burst open. He was out of bed in seconds. The gun he kept on his bedside table was in his hand. He stood near the top of the stairs, waiting and listening. Anyone coming upstairs would be dead before they reached halfway. He was a veteran, not a wet-behind-the-ears kid to be caught napping.

The hallway sounded eerily quiet. Lumani could hear someone creeping around downstairs in the lounge. Was it only a break-in? A local druggie who didn't know who lived at this address? Lumani edged closer to the half-wall of the landing. He risked a quick peek over the top to see if his intruder was on his way up or pissing off home.

He raised his gun and looked downstairs. There was nobody there.

He could hear a voice from the lounge. The guy was talking to someone on his bloody mobile phone. Cheeky bastard. Lumani stood exposed at the top of the stairs, poised, ready to fire. He shouted: -

"What game do you think you're playing? Get out while you can. Don't you know who you're messing with?"

Phoenix climbed onto the next-door neighbour's roof and edged his way into position. Then, while Rusty distracted their target and messed with his head downstairs, he lowered himself to start work on the extractor fan in the bathroom window.

With his feet braced against the brickwork, he had secured a neat square hole. Egzon Lumani heard the sound of the unit as it struck the pathway. As he turned around, he saw a dark shape and the barrel of a gun.

The bullets that ripped into his chest from the Sig Sauer P226 ended the fixer's life before he got the answers to his questions.

Phoenix was already on his way to the ground. Rusty met him by the back door.

"A quick tidy-up, and we can be off," said Phoenix.

They had Lumani's body in the boot within a minute and were driving towards Tamworth Park.

"We've got time to wait until Elizi turns up for his appointment," said Rusty.

"It's a quiet spot. You can get your head down for an hour or two if you wish," said Phoenix.

"You're pretty cool," said Rusty. "There were several things that might have gone wrong back there."

"Such as?"

Rusty counted off the problems on his fingers.

"The neighbour could have heard you on the roof, and the extractor fan might have been impossible to remove. The bathroom door may not have been open. Lumani might have fancied his chances against one man and charged downstairs to confront me. Where was my backup? Hanging around outside."

"Oh, ye of little faith," chuckled Phoenix. "I must remember to include *all* the details in the notes I give you to read. Preparation is everything, Rusty. Frank's people checked up on the old girl who lives next door; she's stone deaf. Statistics on bathroom doors suggest they're closed ninety-nine per cent of the time someone is inside using the facilities. The same percentage applies in reverse; it's open, so everyone knows it's vacant. As for the extractor fan, it's amazing what a boon YouTube videos can be. I sat up late last night watching one a dozen times after you went to bed. Most people remove them from inside the house because it's easier, I grant you, but lateral thinking and the odd adjustment can achieve the same end. If Lumani had gone downstairs, you would have done what you always do. You would have coped. As you keep telling everyone, I can't keep doing this alone."

Rusty caught the inference of the last comment.

"What, you knew?" he asked.

"I've been aware of my tendency to overdo things and not to delegate for a while, Rusty. The fact people care is much appreciated."

Rusty decided he'd lost yet another argument with Phoenix. Nothing changed. They were soon parked close to Tamworth Park. Rusty settled into his seat with the dawn chorus in full swing and a peaceful countryside around them and nodded off to sleep.

Phoenix called Giles in the ice-house. He hoped to catch him before he got stuck into his daily tasks. The morning shift began at six am; Artemis and the others would be there, working alongside him. Their responsibility was the never-ending gathering of data for Olympus. The knowledge enabled agents to complete missions such as this morning with apparent ease.

"Giles? Good morning. Do we have any news on the autopsy report for Dawn Prentice yet?"

"I expect to get a copy by noon today, Phoenix," replied Giles.

"Good," said Phoenix. "I'll get back to you after we've completed this morning's work. One down, two to collect."

After seeing his friend fast asleep beside him, Phoenix ended the call, closed his eyes, and attempted to relax. A tap on the window of the car awoke him with a start.

"Rise and shine, Phoenix," said Frank Bolano.

"What time is it," asked Phoenix, stretching his stiff limbs. Clambering around on rooftops in your mid-forties was not recommended. Beside him, Rusty, too, stirred from his slumber.

"Twenty-five to nine," replied Frank, "Elizi is on his way. Januzaj is his driver today, so we're in luck. Everything went to plan this morning in Milton Road, I gather?"

"No worries," said Rusty. Phoenix smiled to himself.

"Any changes to how you want to play this, Frank?" asked Phoenix.

"Can you two be on hand when I need back-up? If so, my other two lads can head off towards Southampton and get things ready to receive visitors to the safe-house."

"Send them to us first. The lads can take Lumani. We'll

stay here until you give us a call. No sense in taking up valuable parking space at the hospital. Try not to shoot anyone and put extra pressure on an already stressed A&E Department."

"We'll do our best," said Frank Bolano.

A second Olympus van arrived and reversed up behind Phoenix's car. The agents switched Lumani's body to the van, and Phoenix and Rusty watched them leave. They wouldn't have long to wait.

At ten to nine, a Lexus glided into the car park. Frank and his agent Curwen watched from their van. Curwen got out and opened the rear doors. He lowered a ramp from the interior, climbed into the back and moved a wheelchair into position. Curwen and the chair were on the tarmac within a minute.

Konstandin Elizi got out of the Lexus by the entrance door. The gang boss wasn't one to walk too far. His lieutenant could waste ten minutes hunting for a vacant bay. Januzaj moved off to begin his circuit of the car park. He stopped at a pedestrian crossing to allow a guy pushing a wheelchair to cross.

Januzaj spotted a space and reversed into it. He had a good view of the entrance. All he had to do was find his boss and drive round to collect him. It wouldn't take long. The tricky bit was to estimate how long after his appointment time, Konstandin would get seen.

Curwen noted the number of the parking bay occupied by the Lexus and passed the details to Frank Bolano. He pushed the wheelchair through the entrance door and followed the signs to reception and waiting areas.

Elizi had registered that he was here and on time. The staff asked him to wait to hear his name called. Curwen parked his wheelchair on the end of the row of chairs where Elizi sat and joined the queue for the desk. He informed the girl on duty that he was waiting to return Mr Elizi to his car. Problems associated with the pre-existing condition that necessitated his heart scan meant he had difficulty walking long distances. The girl seemed happy that she didn't have another question to handle, and Curwen moved away from the counter and took a seat directly behind the gang boss.

Frank Bolano still sat in the driver's seat of the Olympus van.

"Stand by, Phoenix," he said. "Curwen is inside with Elizi. Januzaj is still with the Lexus."

"We'll drive around the car park as if we're hunting for a place to park," said Phoenix, "then stop right in front of the Lexus. Point us in the right direction when you see us arrive. We'll be with you in two minutes."

"I know this goes against your nature, but could you two have a domestic? Perhaps get out of the car and push and shove one another. While Januzaj is distracted, I'll move in."

"That will work, Frank," said Phoenix. "Rusty, can you get in touch with your feminine side?"

Rusty glared at Phoenix.

"Are you having a go at my Scottish ancestry?" he snapped.

Phoenix stood on the brakes; he leapt out of the front seat. Rusty got out of the passenger door, slamming it behind him. Dalmat Januzaj stared through his windscreen at the two middle-aged fools squaring up to one another.

"Well, you guys wear skirts," said Phoenix.

"A kilt," said Rusty, "aye, I've worn the kilt on ceremonial occasions. Never a skirt."

"They say people with red hair have a short fuse," said Phoenix, pushing Rusty back towards the Lexus.

Frank Bolano had silently slipped behind the Lexus and was poised just behind the driver's door. With his arm across his throat, Phoenix grabbed Rusty, shoved him onto the Lexus bonnet, and pinned him down.

Januzaj sounded the horn. Then he shouted at the two men. He threw his door open and got out, his face as black as thunder. Frank Bolano had him in a chokehold in seconds. Januzaj slid to the floor, unconscious. Rusty and Phoenix helped secure him with ties and bundled him into the boot of their car. Frank injected him with a dose of morphine.

"You two can certainly put on a show," said Frank.

"Who says he was acting?" said Phoenix.

"We'll meet you back at the safe-house," said Frank. "Elizi will be in there for a while yet. Curwen told me the hospital is running late."

"Let's go then," said Phoenix. "You can drive, Rusty."

"Where am I headed?" he asked as they returned to the car.

"Eastleigh, a borough to the north of Southampton. We're visiting Botley, a village on this side of the airport. Don't worry. We're not going to the west. That's where Shirley is."

Rusty didn't bite. He had heard of Shirley. All the shops and houses, and no character.

At St Mary's, Curwen still waited for Elizi to go for his scan. The gang boss was getting agitated. Just as he would jump up and complain, his name appeared on the screen above the counter. He had to go to Room 11. Curwen watched as Elizi waddled off. He had time to get a coffee from the vending machine.

Frank Bolano was in the van, ready for a signal from his agent they were on their way. If a free space closer to the entrance door became available, Frank slipped into it. Twenty minutes later, Curwen said Elizi was walking towards him. The van was now three spaces from the door.

After he had finished his coffee, Curwen dropped the cup in the waste bin and visited the toilets. The bag he carried contained a blue porter's top and a lanyard with an official-looking ID. Curwen changed. When he returned to the waiting area, he collected the wheelchair.

Elizi was five yards from the doorway. Curwen hurried to catch up and slid the chair into the back of Elizi's knees as he paused for the automatic doors to open. A firm hand on his shoulder and a polite request to take a seat did the trick. Elizi sat with a bump.

"Please allow me to take you to your car, sir," said Curwen. "A gentleman with a heart condition deserves a free ride on the NHS. That's why you pay your taxes, isn't it?"

Elizi was confused. Taxes? Who was this fool? A sharp scratch on his neck annoyed him. He tried to swipe the offending insect away, thinking it was a wasp. Frank Bolano had already moved the van to the front of the building. The ramp lowered. Curwen ran up it into the back of the van, pushing the now semi-conscious Elizi inside. Frank slammed the doors behind them, and they set off for the safe-house.

"Not a bad morning's work. Three gang members out of the game, and it's not a quarter past ten," he called out to Curwen.

"We'll be in Botley in thirty minutes," replied Curwen. "I'll call ahead and ask the lads to boil the kettle. Thirsty work this portering."

On the edge of the village of Botley, Phoenix and Rusty arrived at the safe-house.

"Picturesque," said Rusty, "a distinct improvement on many of the dumps we've used.

"It's a roof over their heads," shrugged Phoenix, "I doubt they get too attached to it. Look at what happened to the two undercover agents. Our job is to ensure our guests don't enjoy their brief stay. Let's make ourselves known to the guys indoors. Frank Bolano will arrive soon."

"That's me told," said Rusty. The double garage was on the left of the detached house. Its doors faced the property. Rusty parked their car by the side of the garage, screening its presence from the main road.

Phoenix had walked across to the side door. He knocked; a face appeared at an upstairs window.

"Okay, it's them," called the agent, and his colleague opened the door.

"I'm Gary, and Vince is upstairs," he said. Rusty followed Phoenix inside.

"Where's Lumani?" asked Phoenix.

"Still in the van, in the garage. Frank didn't want to make the place untidy," said Gary.

"Frank should be along in a few minutes," said Phoenix.

"They're on their way. No problems. Frank called to say get the kettle on."

"Good thinking," said Rusty. "It's been a long time since breakfast."

"What's your plan once Frank arrives with the two gangsters?" asked Vince.

"How close are your nearest neighbours, and how much passing traffic is there?" asked Phoenix.

"On this side of the road, a hundred and forty yards back the way you came in, there's a farm and a row of terraced houses sixty yards further up the road. On the opposite side, houses and bungalows stretch into the village.

The nearest three-bedroomed bungalow is opposite, behind that high hedge. Traffic is brisk in both directions, with two cars every minute, at least during daylight hours. It tails off in the early evening."

"Thanks," said Phoenix. "Rusty and I don't want to have to spend the night if we can help it. No offence. We need to get back to Larcombe Manor. There will be fallout from this mission and the ones we've completed in London to handle."

A door slammed outside. The sound of the garage door opening announced the arrival of Frank and the second van.

Curwen appeared at the side door. He walked into the kitchen.

"Where's the coffee mugs, Gary? And the choccy biscuits?"

Frank came in from the garage, and the six Olympus agents gathered in the large country-style kitchen. Gary and Curwen fixed the coffees; Vince unearthed the chocolate digestives.

The two gangsters could wait; elevenses was an important ritual.

"Who's going to do the honours, Phoenix?" asked Frank Bolano, blowing on his hot coffee.

"They were your agents, Frank," Phoenix replied. "Lumani was lucky. His death was quick. We won't stand in your way if you want payback with these two."

"Thanks," said Frank, "we'll set up something."

When they finished the packet of biscuits and piled the coffee mugs in the dishwasher, Frank took his guys out to the garage.

"How long before we head back?" asked Rusty.

Phoenix led him through to the lounge.

"We may as well have a comfortable seat for an hour or two," he said, "as soon as they're ready to finish the job, we'll drive home."

Outside, there was a burst of activity. Gary drove one of the vans out of the garage and parked it near the gateway. That stopped a vehicle from getting onto the property and gave passers-by something to see. Then he closed the garage doors behind him with Frank and the others still inside.

From the back of the van, Gary removed a power tool. He ran an extension lead from the kitchen to the drive and plugged it in. Both the rear doors of the van were opened wide. He looked the business with his ear defenders, hard hat, and safety goggles. If anyone saw him from the road, it would look to all the world like he was using the angle grinder to carry out repairs to the van's bodywork.

Phoenix and Rusty heard the angle grinder when it screamed into action.

"That tool has the second-highest noise level going, only bettered by a jet engine at take-off," said Phoenix.

"I know, and just below the threshold of pain. Nice touch," said Rusty.

Outside, Gary had finished playing with the angle grinder for a while. He walked to the gateway and looked in both directions. He saw the odd car on the road but nobody on foot within a hundred yards. Gary banged on the garage door and got back to work.

Frank Bolano emerged from the garage two minutes later with his fingers in his ears. Gary caught a glimpse of his team leader and turned off his kit. The safety equipment and the grinder went back into the store cupboard in the garage.

"All done?" he asked Frank.

Frank Bolano nodded.

"I'll go inside and see Phoenix, bring him up to speed, and then we'll get ready to drive into Portsmouth."

Frank found the two agents in the lounge watching daytime TV.

"If you want to get back to HQ, then everything's tidied up here," said Frank. "I left it to Curwen and Vince to decide how they wanted to avenge their friends' deaths. Elizi and Januzaj got the triple capping. Knees, elbows and ankles; low-velocity gunshots to the bone joints to maximise the pain."

"Did you tell them why they needed to suffer?" asked Phoenix.

"I did," said Frank, "I told them the two lads they killed were working for me, not the cops. That came as a shock. Then we showed them Lumani's body and told them the gang would never operate in the same way again. Elizi yelled a bunch of threats, but he knew the game was up. I gave them time to think about the error of their ways before I finished the job. The three bodies are in the back of my van. It's twenty minutes from here to the police station on Winston Churchill Avenue. We'll drop them off right next to where they dumped our two lads. The police can make of it what they will."

"They'll be at a loss as to what's going on, won't they?" said Rusty. "Two bodies out of nowhere, now three that should at least be familiar. They must know the gang structure in the city, even if they've never had the evidence to arrest them."

"Giles will be busy," said Phoenix. "I asked him to boost your lads' fake bank accounts and plant cash in their houses only the other day. My first thought was we might convince the police they were running a scam and got caught. Then, when three prominent gang members turn up dead soon after, the police will automatically think of a gang war. Then, maybe, one piece of good can come out of this mess."

"What are you thinking?" asked Frank.

"When we get back, I'll get Giles to nudge the police towards the addresses in towns where your undercover lads delivered those immigrants. If that can help them expose the racket involving slave labour and sex trafficking, they will latch on to a 'win-win' situation. Taking on two gangs involved in a gang war will be beyond their capabilities, and there would be no guarantee they'd solve it."

"Cheeky," said Rusty.

"Pragmatic," said Phoenix, "there was only one gang, after all."

Frank Bolano smiled.

"Safe trip home, lads," he said, "I've got a delivery to make. Shut the place up nice and secure when you leave."

"We'll be right behind you, Frank," said Phoenix, "but I want to see the end of this programme first."

"It's only a repeat," said Rusty.

"Oh, you've spoiled the ending now. We might as well go," said Phoenix.

Frank shook his head and left.

# Chapter Nine

***Thursday, 5th June 2014***

Hugo Hanigan stood in his penthouse suite looking out of his window on the world. His world, the City of London, was that square mile famous for the United Kingdom's trading and financial services industries. That was where he made his fortune, and the Grid continued to thrive. The beating heart of the network of criminal organisations of which he was the leader.

A month ago, he visited his mother's grave in Dublin. In the weeks before his annual pilgrimage, he had issued orders to his various gang leaders that they must send a message. Those in authority in the government, and the police, should hear and understand that message. Those in opposition to him, who operated gangs too stupid to see the benefits of joining the Grid, should fear his reaction to their ignorance.

People died the length and breadth of the country. The

stranglehold the Grid held over the nation was demonstrated. The message was crystal clear.

Yet, Hugo was a troubled man. The financial voice on his shoulder told him that the overall business was up and profits were higher than ever. Someone thwarted an attempt to pervert the course of justice by murdering a High Court Judge, it was right, and Tommy O'Riordan would be in Belmarsh for the rest of his life. Hugo hadn't prevented that. Yet things hadn't been disrupted in his gang's manor to any great extent, nor across the country.

Sean Walsh had slipped into Tommy's seat while it was still warm. He was doing a grand job, even if his lieutenant Seamus McConnell was useless. No, they didn't miss Tommy. His appeal was a joke and bound to fail. Colleen, his wife, ran around like a headless chicken, flogging off Tommy's cars and sorting her kids out. Not before time for those two spongers. It was plain she had cashed in whatever she could to give herself a chance of seeing out her time without ever needing to work for a living. She'd never had to graft while Tommy was a free man. He'd looked after her ever since she was fourteen. It was time she found out what happened in the real world.

Hugo continued to tick off the list of things that didn't worry him. Even those that had annoyed him at the time. All the while, a tiny voice on his other shoulder asked him why there were deaths and disappearances of Grid employees around the country he couldn't explain.

It was fast approaching eleven o'clock. Sean Walsh would arrive soon. They met at least twice a week, and Hugo kept the meetings as brief as possible. Sean was never comfortable up here in these surroundings. Hugo couldn't imagine why. The view was to die for; he laughed aloud at his unintentional joke. Hundreds had perished over the years; they needed to so that he could afford this place.

The meetings were necessary for him to keep in touch with his roots. Sean helped him do that. He told him what was happening on the ground in Kilburn and the boroughs that bordered it. Hugo understood the big picture. The way the Grid operated across the UK. Sean could never grasp that degree of complexity, but they had grown up together on the seven streets in Dublin.

Those ties ran deep. It was where the street gang mentality became ingrained in all of them. Hugo possessed the brains. Tommy O'Riordan and Sean provided the brawn. That mentality had been transferred to London, and Hugo ruled the roost. He looked up to see the clouds scudding above the building. Today they were so close he could almost touch them. What was it Cagney had said?

"Top of the world, Ma! Top of the world!"

The lift pinged to announce the arrival of Sean Walsh.

Hugo turned from his glimpse of heaven and greeted his second-in-command.

"Sean, how are you this morning?"

"Which would you want to hear, the good or the bad news?"

Hugo sunk into his chair and groaned.

"Now, what has Seamus McConnell done? That man is an eejit."

"No, it's not Seamus. He's been harmless this week so far. I heard from Tommy this morning. He queues up to ring me first thing every Wednesday. It's never the best start to my day. The rumour they might transfer Category A prisoners to Durham became a reality. They start moving them in batches of four from next Monday."

"Does that count as good news or bad? Why do we even worry about Tommy O'Riordan? He's yesterday's news."

Sean looked at his boss. He had better tread warily.

"He's still my brother-in-law, boss. Colleen has said since the day he went to prison. We should try to help him escape."

"Ah, the faithful Colleen. Sean, I know she's your sister, but come on. You know full well she's turning everything into hard cash. The cars have gone, the Marbella place has gone, and Tyrone and Rosie have been scratching around, looking for a new place to live. Do you think I've taken my finger off the pulse of everything around here, whether it's important or not, Sean?"

"She's financing the appeal, boss. I've tried to convince her it's money down the drain. You try telling her, but she insists Tommy expects it of her. As for the breakout, I told her nobody had ever escaped from Belmarsh. The last time I talked to her, the transfer rumour got her fired up. She's ready to pay for the boys and me to whisk him away from his security guards on the trip north. I can't refuse her; she's family. Tommy will be on the phone again before next week, asking me if I have a plan."

"Do you, Sean? Have you been scheming behind my back? I laughed when I heard she still believed the appeal had a prayer, it was doomed from the start. Fine, go ahead if she wants to spring Tommy with his own money. You'll get no help from me. Good luck getting him out of the country. He'll never be safe on these shores, nor back in Ireland. Either the police will catch up with him or the enemies he made in the past. I won't protect him; the Grid is bigger than one man. Tommy O'Riordan used to have our protection. That no longer applies."

Sean knew where he stood. He expected nothing less

from Hugo. He would turn a blind eye to Colleen's plans to help Tommy get abroad to a place of safety. Tommy and Colleen were irrelevant now, as far as Hugo Hanigan was concerned. Sean resolved to talk to his sister tonight. She was due to visit Tommy this afternoon. She might know more about the move by then, and they could try to develop a workable plan.

"Let's forget the good news, bad news stories for a while," said Hugo. "I need you to help me with something else."

"Anything you need, boss, you know me," said Sean. He hoped it wouldn't take long. The sooner he was in that lift, the better. It wasn't a fear of heights or the expensive artwork on the wall. It was from Hugo. He was coiled so tight; Sean didn't want to be within a mile of him when he snapped.

"Every unit inside the Grid is doing well, Sean. Every aspect of the businesses we are involved in is growing. There are gangs in parts of the country determined to go it alone, but I remain confident we can persuade them to join us in time. None of them is strong enough to take us on in a fight to control their patch, and yet here and there, we have suffered casualties."

Sean had a puzzled look on his face. They had been over this already.

"I'm not sure where this is going, boss," he said.

"Take the Midlands," said Hugo, "in Solihull, where that Polish guy and half a dozen party guests were gunned down. The police have no leads. Our men locally pointed the finger at a dozen rival gangs within a fifty-mile radius without proving it was any of them. We could find nothing to link anyone to the killings. Then those fifteen low-level criminals disappeared from the Manchester area. Nobody knows where they've gone. No bodies have surfaced, and the police aren't searching for them. We replaced the gaps these deaths and disappearances leave behind. It's a nuisance, not a crisis. I wish I understood what happened."

"The thing is, boss," said Sean, "what you've got to remember is this, gangs are essentially local. Remember where we began? Our gang was formed from members of families who lived on those seven streets. Our parents and grandparents were at the heart of it. Other families, newcomers, and foreigners formed separate gangs. We bumped heads with each of them to see who was the strongest. Over here in London, it was no different. Hundreds of small street gangs existed when we arrived, and those who survived were the toughest. Members of the ones that fell by the wayside have joined gangs like ours. You have spread the net so that almost all the major gangs are now united."

Hugo sat open-mouthed. Sean Walsh had more of a grasp of things than he believed.

"Go on, Sean," he said, "I'm listening."

"The way I see it, the Grid is a jigsaw of interlocking pieces. You haven't got the pieces to complete the picture. In an ideal world, once you get the last piece and insert it, that will lock the Grid together into one cohesive unit."

"That's my dream, Sean," said Hugo.

"There's a problem, boss," said Sean, hesitating in case Hugo snapped, "each piece is interlocked by activity, not by culture. Some nationalities major in human trafficking, others in drug dealing, some favour contract killing, and others make money ripping ATMs out of walls: different nationalities, different religions, and different skills. A few of the gangs try to cover every one of the bases. Others only have one line of business and do anything to protect it. The common denominator is money. So you've got everyone with the Grid feeding the money through the Glencairn Bank to cleanse it."

"So, what you're saying is, the money is the glue that holds it together. There will be ties between businesses with a common interest, but rivalries too."

"Exactly," said Sean, "you need to ask these questions. Did these guys get killed or taken by members of a rival gang outside the Grid? If so, they wanted that slice of the action. It may only affect a tiny percentage of what that area's gang covers. Did our people kill them? Was it part of an internal power struggle?"

"We should make an example of those who try to steal a share of our business, Sean," said Hugo, "no matter how small. The internal slimming of our operations doesn't concern me as much. Thanks, Sean; I feel happier now. I need to get to the bank. I'll see you on Friday morning."

Sean was happy to leave. As he walked to the lift, he called back to Hugo.

"There is another possibility if it's not inter-gang rivalry or in-fighting. Again, it's far-fetched, but what if it's an outside agency?"

"What? MI5, or the United Network Command for Law Enforcement? You were doing so well, Sean. That's the sort of daft idea I'd expect from Seamus. I'll see you on Friday."

While Hugo Hanigan and Sean Walsh met in London, the Olympus agents were hard at work in the West. Phoenix and Rusty arrived home to Larcombe at five o'clock yesterday afternoon. Phoenix searched for Athena and brought her up to date on a successful mission.

Rusty had found Artemis asleep in a chair in their apartment. Her shift ended at four. Ten hours of fine-tuning items of misdirection aimed at Portobello and Portsmouth and gathering valuable data for future missions.

This morning's meeting started at nine o'clock sharp.

"I'm sure we're pleased to see Phoenix and Rusty home, safe and sound," Athena began.

"Yesterday's mission avenged the deaths of those two poor undercover agents," said Artemis. "Our losses have been small compared to the casualties we've inflicted on the Grid."

"Long may that continue," said Minos.

"Can you bring us up to date, Giles," asked Athena. "What's the situation in London?"

"The autopsy report on Dawn Prentice will be available from noon today. The minute I see what it says, we'll prepare our response. Our misdirection relating to the Portobello Road affair has had a positive impact. Simon Garrett and his team are in the clear."

"Thanks, Giles," said Athena, "and Park Royal?"

"We had a slice of luck there," said Giles, "or the police did. It appears the visit planned by Adam Kovacs was to prepare for a delivery. The emergency crews were clearing glass and debris in parts outside the police cordon in the early evening. A Dutch-registered truck pulled up, and the driver asked for directions. One of the firefighters alerted a police officer, and they blocked him in with a patrol car. The officer wasn't happy with the driver's answers to his questions. He appeared agitated and anxious to phone his employers. The officer relieved him of his mobile phone; he suspected he had something to hide and made sure he couldn't warn his bosses back in Holland."

"When questioned later, we've learned the driver

admitted he was carrying raw materials that could be used in manufacturing legal highs," Artemis continued. "Officers entered the warehouse from the rear, in those natty paper suits, even before they received our anonymous tip-off. The equipment they discovered inside and the traces of chemicals on the floors and tables sealed the deal. They arrested the driver and seized his vehicle's tachograph. They hope to trace the journey's origins and close that supply route for good."

"That could be an even better result than we hoped. It was a bigger bang than I would have liked," said Phoenix, "and we were lucky nobody else died."

"The collateral damage was superficial," said Rusty, "the businesses would be insured. Kovacs and Nagy are dead. Our job now is to persuade the police that a rival drug gang was responsible. We'll leave that to Giles and Artemis."

"Zeus is pleased with our progress," said Athena. "He wanted Kovacs to pay for Dawn Prentice's death. I must call him after the meeting to pass on the good news from the Portsmouth mission."

They completed the morning's agenda, and Athena closed the meeting at ten-fifty. She asked everyone to reconvene at twelve-thirty, and they would discuss what the autopsy report held.

As they were back earlier than usual, Maria Elena was outside in the garden with Hope.

"We should plan for an early lunch," said Athena. "I'll chase up Maria Elena, and we can eat at twelve. Do you have anything to do between now and then?"

"I've got plenty of catching up to do," said Phoenix, "the past weeks have teemed with meetings, planning, and direct actions. I need to browse through those reports Giles produces about current events. I'll drop in on Minos and Alastor if I can spare five minutes. It's been a while since I spoke with them. I'd like to see how they're tackling the background identities for the agents on the retraining course."

"You didn't call them the Two Stooges for once," said Athena, "do I detect a newly found respect?"

"It was always in jest," replied Phoenix, "these days, I think of them as the Two Amigos because they are true friends of Olympus. No matter how much work you pile on them, they get their heads down and get on with it without complaint. We couldn't do this without them."

"Everyone works hard at Larcombe," sighed Athena. "While people like Kovacs and Elizi and his gang are out there, that situation is unlikely to change. I'll see you as soon as I can round up our nanny and daughter."

Athena and Phoenix left the apartment together. She went downstairs, past the kitchens on the ground floor, and out into the gardens. Phoenix carried on along the corridor on the first floor to the administration offices. He looked at the growing pile of reports on his desk in the corner. The slight sheen of dust on the desk's surface told him how long it had been since he'd been here.

He flicked through folder after folder. The subject matter in the reports near the bottom was history. That could go into File B for Bin. Phoenix chose two more recent reports at random. They concerned the Government and the Prison Service; he could always use a laugh.

"I wonder what fool ideas they've dreamt up now?" he said.

He opted for a quick read through these two reports and a more extended session with the Amigos in the next-door office. Giles had highlighted a report in April on twenty-five schools in the Midlands. It was alleged that teachers and governors in secular state schools were being ousted to be taken over and run on strict Islamist principles.

Phoenix cast his mind back to the days he spent with his wife, Sue, in The Gambia. He kept in touch with events in the UK via his laptop. He gathered data that would later be used in Operation Streetcleaner when he returned home four years ago. Phoenix recalled a head teacher in Yorkshire who complained of being pressured to quit by a few influential, hard-line Muslim governors. If his memory didn't fail him, a decade had passed since then. In the following months, the press reported anonymous assertions claiming boys and girls were segregated in classrooms and assemblies, sex education banned, and non-Muslim staff bullied.

Giles had updated this file in the past twenty-four hours. Something must have hit the fan, thought Phoenix. The Prime Minister had given two cabinet ministers a hefty slap on the wrist; they couldn't agree on tackling extremism in schools. Phoenix put the file to one side. Maybe he would return to it later. It seemed ironic that a decade had already passed without a clear policy being agreed upon and implemented.

His education had been cut short by his mother, and he left school in 1984. In thirty years, our kids had fallen further down the league tables. Even Oxford and Cambridge University play outside the Premiership these days. Phoenix chided himself. I must be getting soft, he thought, using a football analogy. Then, he turned to the following report.

All thoughts of seeing Minos and Alastor in the next few minutes went on hold. Category A prisoners were being moved around the country yet again. Phoenix smiled at the memory of those terrorists and extremists they transferred to HMP Wakefield. They got lost in transit; someone could have made a film about that. They must be mad to try it again. He read the report from cover to cover.

Phoenix made a note to ask Giles to investigate further. Who was going from HMP Belmarsh to HMP Durham? How many did they expect to transfer, and when was this due to start? He hadn't been back to Durham since he dealt with Neil Cartwright. In two weeks, it would be the fourth anniversary of avenging his daughter Sharron's death. He wondered who might be among the faces selected for transfer. He set the folder aside. Depending on what Giles dug up, that might be worth a second look.

He looked at his watch; noon. It was time to head back for lunch. As he passed their door, he popped in to say hello to Minos and Alastor. They were taking a break.

"We grabbed the chance of a sandwich before we went back into the meeting room, Phoenix," said Alastor. "What can we do for you?"

"Keep chasing me to spend time with you," he said. "I'd love you to take me through the background stories you're preparing. It's valuable work. I'm sorry I haven't been available much this past month."

"No problem," said Minos. "our door is always open. We'll catch up with you after this next meeting."

Phoenix made his way back to the apartment. Noises from the kitchen told him lunch was almost ready, and Hope banged her high chair table with her tiny fist when she saw Daddy enter.

"Warning the ladies of my arrival, are we?" he asked, tickling Hope under her chin.

Athena and Maria Elena emerged from the kitchen carrying plates of snacks. All four of them tucked into the food.

"This is fun," said Athena.

"Far too brief, I'm afraid," said Phoenix, looking at the clock, "our meeting awaits."

Hope got plenty of kisses and cuddles before they left, and at half-past twelve, the agents gathered in the meeting room to learn the news from Giles.

"Dawn Prentice died from a drug overdose," he began. "There were a series of marks on the right-hand side of her neck that suggested she received injections over an extended period."

"Any chance they were self-administered," asked Henry, "given her history?"

"Not a chance," said Artemis. "The injuries to her wrists and ankles showed they held her in that room against her will for weeks. The final injection was to end her life. Either Kovacs, Nagy or one of the gang members killed her. That is clear."

"What is also clear from the main body of the autopsy report is that Dawn Prentice had traces of different chemicals in her system," said Giles.

"What type of chemicals?" asked Athena.

"Benzodiazepines and cannabis, for a start," said Giles, "they stay in the system for a month. So, it wasn't possible to establish which chemical combinations got injected and when because of the time lag. So, I can't detect which legal highs they used. But, I can deduce from the list of drugs manufactured by Kovacs and her needle scars that Dawn Prentice was receiving injections daily."

"They used her as a guinea pig," said Rusty.

"Testing different combinations on her to see which gave the best result," said Phoenix. "Cynical bastards. Well, that car bomb put a stop to that."

"That still doesn't answer the other question," said Athena.

"Which one," asked Rusty.

"Why did Kovacs kidnap her? He blackmailed her into financing his drug operation. He risked losing that regular income if she disappeared or died because of the treatment they subjected her to. It doesn't make sense."

"I may have an idea, Athena," said Artemis. "Remember what Kovacs used as a lever to get her to pay him the original fifty thousand? It was hush money. Dawn worked as a prostitute in the months before she resolved to clean up her act. Where did she work? Adam Kovacs? He continued to hold parties at his place, with drugs and girls on offer to the friends he invited. We found evidence of that. Maybe he wanted to renew their acquaintance in that area too? Dawn knocked him back, and he made her work for him another way."

"That makes sense," said Phoenix. "He probably didn't set out to kill her, but he lost his rag when the money flow stopped."

"OK, Giles," said Athena, "we'll let you two get back to the ice-house. I'm sure you've got loads of ammunition for your next gems of misdirection."

"We'll be fine with the Portobello case, Athena," said Giles, "and Portsmouth won't pose too many problems. I'm still fabricating links between potential foreign gangs and the bomb attack at Park Royal."

"Can we identify any additional men from the gang who may have dealt with Dawn in the cellar?"

"The CCTV detail is sparse, Athena," said Artemis, "but we found images of Nagy in Notting Hill Gate, so it may be possible to find others. We would need to plant evidence suggesting these thugs planned to get rid of

Kovacs and Nagy. Their motive would be simple greed. If that works, we would have gotten rid of everyone involved in Dawn's death."

"Brilliant," said Athena, "you've got your work cut out. Off you go."

"Hang on, Giles. Is that everything for today, Athena?" asked Phoenix.

"I think so," said Athena.

"In that case, Rusty and I need Giles to do more work for us too. Sorry to add to the workload, mate, but can you look at this, please?"

Phoenix handed him the notes he had made on the prison transfer saga.

"Delegate as much of the misdirection as you can, Giles," said Phoenix, "this has to be a top priority."

"Is this something new?" asked Athena. "I wasn't aware of any fresh developments."

"It was something I stumbled on before lunch. The lunatics have opened the doors to the asylum."

## Chapter Ten

Colleen O'Riordan had been a busy woman. There were black bin bags lined up by the kitchen door, ready to go to the recycling unit. The last few pieces that belonged to her husband, Tommy, stood alongside much of her wardrobe. Finally, she could afford to start anew.

Yesterday, she made the trip to Belmarsh to visit Tommy. She had gone through the now-familiar rigmarole of spending an hour in the company of the man she now despised.

Tommy didn't change the record; it was the same every week. He rambled on about the appeal. Colleen decided it was time to be blunt. She told him to forget it.

"The lawyer says he's wasting time and effort. You won't get time off your sentence, and the guilty verdict stays."

Tommy let that pass; he switched tack and asked after Tyrone and Rosie. Colleen was on a roll; she told him they were old enough to stand on their own two feet. They wanted independence. Tyrone had told her his friends joked behind his back about his family being a load of criminals.

"Give me their names," Tommy said, "I'll send some of the boys to sort them out."

"You don't have any boys anymore, Tommy," Colleen told him. "If we get you abroad next week, you'll have to keep your head down. Not draw attention to yourself by dishing out beatings to anyone who speaks out of turn."

She watched the stuffing being knocked out of her husband as he took on board what she was saying. Then, after he had no luck mentioning the appeal and his children, he moaned about her brother, Sean.

"I spoke to Sean this morning and told him about the transfer. He didn't seem convinced it was possible in such a short space of time,"

That made Colleen jump.

"What do you mean? Last week it was a maybe, now it's a definite, is that what you're telling me? What do you mean by a short space of time?"

"Oh, yeah, sorry, I thought I told you. Twenty of us are moving north to Durham. I'm transferring there on Tuesday."

"That doesn't give us enough time," Colleen complained. "Can't you appeal? It would help if you told them it's a long-distance for me to have to travel. I won't be able to do it nearly every week, Tommy."

"They'll tell you to move to Durham," he shrugged, "it'll be on your doorstep then."

"No, I mean appeal so that Sean has more time to put a team together to help get you away."

"I can't change the date, sweetheart. They've got twenty names on the list. Four go each day, Monday to Friday. I'm on the list for Tuesday. End of story."

Colleen had to think fast.

"There must be someone here who can make you ill,

Tommy. Fix you up with dodgy food, and get you moved to the hospital wing. It could buy us a few days."

It was time for visiting to end. That was three weeks in a row; they had to take a break next week no matter what. Colleen got ready to leave.

"I'll see you when I see you, then," said Tommy.

Colleen nodded. Her husband looked to have aged ten years since he came to Belmarsh.

Tommy watched his wife as she walked away. He had to get out of this place. A twenty-four-hour bug might be a tricky one to sort. It would be far easier to convince the screws he was depressed and get him placed on suicide watch. The breakout plan had to work. This prison lark was driving him nuts.

Colleen called Sean from the taxi. As she waited for her brother to answer, she wondered where the guy was who had driven her last week. Colleen gave the new driver a cold stare when she thought he was earwigging. Sean agreed to drop round to see her first thing after lunch. He was visiting Hugo Hanigan at eleven.

The doorbell rang at two fifteen.

"I'm guessing you had a late lunch then, Sean," said Colleen as her brother wandered indoors.

Sean looked around him. The hallway lay bare of the family photographs that hung there for years. Instead, he could see the minimalist look spread through the open door into the lounge.

"Blimey, sis, I don't recognise the place. Where's everything gone?"

"What did you drive over in, Sean?" asked Colleen.

"Just the car. Why?"

"Can you borrow a van? I need to get these bags to the tip."

Sean followed his sister to the kitchen. He gave a low whistle when he saw the number of black bags she had accumulated.

"I don't know what Tommy would say if he saw this," he muttered.

"We're getting him out of prison so he can have an extended foreign holiday," said Colleen. "He'll never be able to come back here whatever happens."

"Now you mention that," Sean hesitated, "when did you say it was on the phone?"

"They've got him on the sheet for Tuesday. I told him to go sick and do something to give us more time. He'll call you if there's a change."

Sean shook his head.

"What?" asked Colleen.

"It doesn't give us much time. Next Tuesday, or the Tuesday after, it will still be a devil of a job."

"Grow a pair, Sean," said Colleen. "Ever since the day Tommy got sent to prison, I told you we must try to get him out. When I saw him yesterday, he was like a little old man. He's shrinking in there. He's looking more and more like Tommy Senior used to look, and you know what a tosser he was."

"Let's start on these bags," said Sean, "we can chat on the way to the tip. Are any of these likely to leak? Only I don't want to ruin the leather on the back seats of my car. Put the dodgy stuff in the boot; I've got a liner in there."

"Yeah," said Colleen, "like these bags are our top priority, Sean. Let's load up your car. You drive, I chat, and you listen, okay?"

Colleen knew her brother meant well, but he had never been a leader. She could tell she would have to come up with ideas for this job. Sean would nod in the right places and find the muscle to carry it out, as always.

Sean made three trips to the recycling site that afternoon. Colleen hadn't shown him the scrapped furniture and picture frames she'd stored in the back bedrooms. At least it gave her plenty of time to expand on her ideas for interrupting Tommy's drive north.

Whenever it finally took place.

Sean dropped his sister at home after the last few pieces went to the dump.

"When do you think you'll be moving?" he asked. "Have you found a place?"

"I'm moving out at the end of the month. I found a lovely little flat with views over the river."

"You'll have to give us your new address. We can come over sometime. I know the missus and the kids will be keen to visit."

"Plenty of time for that, Sean; concentrate on what we discussed this afternoon. Make the calls, and hire the vehicles. Get the right men for the job. I'll front up the cash for everything we need. Can I trust you to do your bit?"

"Course you can, sis," he said, "it's what I'm good at."

"Have you ever sprung someone from prison before?"

"No," admitted Sean.

"Well then, do as I tell you, and there's half a chance you might add this to your CV."

Colleen closed the door behind him.

Sean drove home; he was going to be busy over the weekend. He prayed Tommy was feeling rough damn quick. The list of things they needed was as long as his arm.

## *Monday, 9th June 2014*

Tommy O'Riordan had asked around. There were dozens of acquaintances of his in Belmarsh but no real friends. Many prisoners knew him by reputation as a hard man, but equally, some couldn't give a toss. He got caught, just like them, so he wasn't that smart. The prison population was full of guys just trying to do their time. They didn't bother other people and didn't want people bothering them.

By Sunday evening, Tommy had been desperate. He heard there was a doctor on the next block who had been struck off for hypnotising his female patients and assaulting them. He tried to get a message through to him. Maybe the bloke could fix him up with something. He realised he needed to get a message to Sean or Colleen. They had to be ready for Tuesday, and time was running out.

Tommy arranged to make a call first thing in the morning; he chose to ring Sean. He would be arranging things; Sean had the contacts. Colleen was probably having her hair done. His problem was men's work; it stood to reason. After another sleepless night, Tommy joined the queue for the phone. There were five men in front of him. He knew the drill. Wait your turn. Give everyone space to have a few minutes of contact with the outside world. Then get in, get on with it, and get off the phone.

The line of men behind him was growing. Tommy sensed trouble brewing. He heard raised voices, and the screws were doing nothing, as usual.

He felt a shove in the back. "Get a move on,"

Tommy half turned, "Leave it out, pal. You need to learn patience."

He was staring at a chest. Shit, this bloke must be enormous.

"Patience? You need to learn respect."

The next thing Tommy knew, he was bent double in pain. The man-mountain had punched him hard in the kidney. The follow-up was swift and brutal. At least three prisoners joined in the attack. Blows rained down on his head and back. He tried to retaliate, but he was soon on the floor. His instinct was to curl into a ball, but the kicks still hurt as they struck home. The assault lasted less than a minute, but it seemed an hour before the guards dragged his attackers away and restored order.

Tommy O'Riordan went to the hospital wing. He suffered severe bruising to his arms, chest and stomach; and two fractured ribs. His face was a bloody mess. He was drifting in and out of consciousness. Tommy tried to hold on to the memory of the guy's face that threw that first punch. He would be in a bed like this very soon.

Every time he tried to move, to make himself more comfortable in his cot, he winced. Tommy knew he had been lucky. Not because he hadn't died but because it meant he was now off the Tuesday transfer list. Every cloud has a silver lining.

Colleen received a call from the prison late on Monday morning. They were very sorry to inform her that her husband suffered injuries in an unprovoked attack. His assailants would receive the appropriate punishment. The prison chaplain called to tell Colleen she had dispensation to visit Tommy tomorrow or Wednesday.

"Oh, wonderful," she thought, "another half-day traipsing backwards and forwards."

She rang Sean as soon as she thanked the chaplain for taking the time to ring.

"Tommy's transfer is off, Sean. Somebody did us a favour and gave him a beating. He's on the hospital wing.

They said I could have a compassionate visit tomorrow or Wednesday if I want."

"Of course you want to go, sis," said Sean, "tell them you'll be there Wednesday. Tommy's been in a few fights over the years. He'll be up and back to his old self in no time. Leave it until Wednesday. I reckon they'll have him passed as fit to travel by then. Ask the doctor if he's going on Thursday or Friday. You won't get a thing out of the officers, but if you flash your eyes at a medical man, he won't be able to resist."

"What do I say to Tommy when I see him, Sean?" asked Colleen.

"Tell him he's done us a favour," said Sean, "we'll be ready for the back end of the week. No problem. A beating isn't how I would have chosen to delay the move. I'd rather have the shits for twenty-four hours."

"Are you saying he asked someone to knock seven bells out of him?" asked Colleen. "From what they said, it sounded as if this bloke didn't like how Tommy spoke to him."

"I guess it doesn't matter what sparked it off as long as he's delayed his move," said Sean.

"Are you going to tell me what you've planned, Sean?"

"Not over the phone, Colleen. I tell you what, why don't I drive you to Belmarsh on Wednesday? We can see him together, see what's what, and talk it through on the way home."

"Okay, Sean," said Colleen. "I want to know everything. We can't afford for this to be cocked up."

At Larcombe, the morning meeting had ended, and Athena and Phoenix were eating lunch.

"We couldn't have hoped for much more today," said Phoenix.

"I agree," said Athena, "our misdirection tactics and tip-offs have paid off handsomely. The Hampshire Police have carried out dawn raids on car hand-wash sites, brothels, hotels, and restaurants along the coast. They've found more illegal immigrants than they've got rooms available to keep them. It's causing a furore in the media."

"Even if a smart lawyer keeps these men and women hanging around in the UK for far too long," said Phoenix, "they won't be working for Elizi's old gang. The thugs who took control of that must be bricking it."

"The truck tachograph from Park Royal opened a bag of worms, too," Athena continued. "The Met police are liaising with their European colleagues over a sophisticated smuggling route that starts from Northern Spain and travels through France, Belgium and the Netherlands before coming across the Channel. There are hundreds of leads to follow. It could mean the dismantling of a major supply and distribution network."

"Our input on these matters must always stay under wraps," said Phoenix, "but you can't help feeling chuffed when things go well. It's a shame we can't shout our successes from the rooftops."

"We must operate under the radar as we always have, darling. Despite the successes, our work is far from finished. The Grid will ride out this storm and come again."

"The report on the prisoner transfer exercise from Giles was fascinating. If only he could get confirmation of the names of the prisoners involved. The first of those transfers is already underway. We have agents following the route the van takes. When we receive feedback on that, I want to talk with Rusty."

"What did you have in mind?" asked Athena. She had finished her lunch and was helping Hope finish the last of hers. Hope had been listening intently to Mummy and Daddy rather than getting on with her lunch.

"If they're moving Category A prisoners, then these will, by definition, be dangerous men," said Phoenix. "It wouldn't do for them to find a way to escape. Rusty and I would have to ensure that it couldn't happen. Think back to the end of April and that chap O'Riordan who went down for murder. The Grid did everything to disrupt that process. We lost two good men, and those jurors and the helicopter pilot died."

"If O'Riordan is among the list of prisoners on the move," Athena agreed, "it's not hard to imagine his friends wanting to help him escape. You're right. We need to discover who travelled today, then who's on the list for the rest of the week."

"I'll drop into the ice-house and set the ball rolling," said Phoenix. "Then, on my way back, I'll catch up with Rusty and the training teams to brief him on our plans."

"Let me know how you get on," said Athena. "I'll wait for Maria Elena, and then I'll be in the administration offices."

When he arrived in the control section, Phoenix looked around for Giles and Artemis.

"Over here, Phoenix," Artemis called. "I'm watching a live broadcast from a drone of the prison van on its journey up the M11."

"Interesting," said Phoenix, "so they're taking the shortest route despite the tolls."

"That's because it's the taxpayer who's paying," laughed Giles, who appeared from the next room. He joined Artemis and Phoenix by the monitor.

"The total journey time should be under five hours," said Artemis, "via Girton and Blyth."

"I came over to ask if you could redouble your efforts and discover who is in that van. So far, I guess there's been nothing suspicious with any traffic in and around them?"

"Nothing obvious, Phoenix," said Artemis.

"Good. Let me know if you spot something. I wouldn't put it past the Grid's people to have a go at releasing a prisoner or two."

"Depending on how important they are to them, I presume?" said Artemis.

"Which explains the urgency of finding the documentation sent to Durham," said Giles. "I've got you. We'll get onto that straight away. It's not the first time, is it, Phoenix? I know where to look for the booking forms. Hard to believe it was eighteen months ago that we intercepted those extremists bound for HMP Wakefield."

"Send me the details when you have them, Giles. It will make for interesting reading."

He left Giles and Artemis to their work and took the lift to the floor below. Bazza and Thommo were assessing their trainees on the shooting range. They were engrossed in their work and had nothing witty to offer for a change. Rusty was nowhere around. Everything seemed to be going well, so he headed to the surface. He crossed the lawns from the ice-house to the stable block. Kelly Dexter emerged from the door to her quarters, towelling her hair dry.

"Hi, Phoenix," she said, "looking for me?"

"Not this time, Kelly. Have you seen Rusty?"

"He's with Hayden and the rest of the group in the pool. I was there until fifteen minutes ago. I couldn't continue. Rusty is on one of his marathon swims. First to one hundred lengths. Hayden is watching from the poolside already. Rusty has serious opposition, though, from lads younger than him."

"The mad bugger won't give up, though," said Phoenix, who had swum with Rusty on many occasions. "He can't bear to lose."

"That's what we must teach everyone in this intake and the ones to follow. Be the best."

"I'll walk over to see him," said Phoenix. "I hope he'll recover from this swim in time for our next mission."

"Next week?" laughed Kelly.

"Could be tomorrow," said Phoenix.

Kelly ran her fingers through her hair and continued to rub it with the towel.

"Perhaps I should get this cut off," she sighed, "it would be easier to manage,"

"I'll ask Hayden while I'm waiting for Rusty to finish,"

"Don't you dare," said Kelly, "he'd have a fit."

Phoenix smiled, said cheerio, and walked to the old workers' cottages, where the recreation facilities were situated. Rusty was still in the pool with three other squaddies.

"How many lengths so far?" Phoenix asked Hayden Vincent.

"Either ninety-four or ninety-six. I may have nodded off. I don't think anyone's counting. Rusty will stay in the pool until the last man quits."

Phoenix sat beside him.

"I haven't heard anything from Orion recently, Hayden. Is he working on a case for us at present?"

"He's taken his kids out of school and is on holiday in Tenerife for two weeks. It's worth risking a fine with the money he saves compared to flying during the school holidays."

"Naughty, and with him being an ex-copper too," said Phoenix.

Five minutes later, two more men quit the race. The final agent showed signs of flagging. Rusty was several lengths in front. When he reached the wall, he paused, looked up at Hayden and Phoenix, smiled, and started the return leg doing the backstroke.

"Oh-oh, he's doing a four by one hundred metres medley now. That's just showing off. When Rusty passed on a breast-stroke leg two minutes later, it was too much for his final opponent. If his front crawl couldn't keep pace with that any longer, it was time to admit defeat.

As both swimmers got out of the pool, they received a warm round of applause from the other trainees. Rusty shook his opponent's hand.

"Great workout. Well done. You're the right stuff."

Phoenix joined his pal as he sat on the poolside, recovering.

"Next time, he'll beat you," he said.

"Nah," said Rusty, "I'll suggest he swims against you next time. I'm getting too old for this. Did you need to see me?"

Phoenix filled him in on the prisoner transfers and suggested meeting later to plan for a mission.

"You think it's a real possibility?" asked Rusty.

"I do, and if O'Riordan was the target, then foiling an escape bid would be another blow against the Grid."

"Your plans had better be good then," said Rusty. "Who would want to foil an escape bid? Apart from the police and the prison authorities, of course? Unless you're very clever, you risk drawing attention to Olympus. At the very least, the Grid would know a third party was involved."

Phoenix smiled.

"One advantage of having time to sit and think is they often allow ideas to creep into my head. I was watching you swimming, and considering the exact problem you described. I've got the building bricks of a plan; we'll get together later to see whether we can make a solid structure out of them."

"Glad to help," said Rusty, grabbing Phoenix's shoulder to push himself up from the floor. "Thanks. I need to shower and get changed."

"I'll wait for you," said Phoenix, "we can walk back together and discuss the mission on the way."

Rusty headed for the showers. Phoenix wandered to the exit whistling 'Lean On Me' by Bill Withers.

"Not on your life," Rusty called after him, "there's life in the old dog yet."

While the two Olympus agents were walking across the lawns towards the old Manor house, two yards apart, Sean Walsh was home in Kilburn. He was thinking through what he had achieved towards the escape bid for his brother-in-law.

He had arranged to hire four transit vans from different garages, none within thirty miles of where he lived. The men he contacted were connections he and Tommy had developed over the past two decades. Hard men, who were familiar with guns, and fond of committing various robberies with violence. Tommy couldn't have found a better crew if he'd selected the men himself.

The team was ready. Sean knew what each man had to do for their audacious plan to succeed. So far, everything was happening at arm's length. No meetings had taken place. The police couldn't suspect a thing; there was nothing to question. He had been ultra-careful. As he ran through each step once more, Sean Walsh started to believe Tommy had a realistic chance of being a free man in the next few days. This plan really could work.

Sean poured himself a glass of Jameson's. He didn't often drink this early in the evening but needed the confidence a drink brought him. Sean knew two people would take convincing that he could manage something on this scale alone.

His sister, Colleen, would find fault. She always did of late. But he didn't need to face her until Wednesday afternoon. Hugo Hanigan, too, would sneer at the simplicity of his planned methods. Tommy always favoured brute force over finesse, and he had taught Sean everything he knew.

Sometimes, it was best to stick to what you knew. Sean thought Tommy would approve, and if that happened, Sean would be a happy man.

## Chapter Eleven

### Tuesday, 10th June 2014

Giles Burke brought news of the prison transfers to the morning meeting. Phoenix had told Athena of the plans he and Rusty had discussed yesterday. She recognised the item's importance and placed it at the top of the list.

"What have you got for us, Giles," she asked.

"We established the route the prison van will follow. It's unlikely it will alter throughout the week. Our drones followed the prisoners throughout their journey yesterday. Agents on the ground shadowed the van, either in front or behind, in unmarked vehicles. There are plenty of junctions to allow for changeovers. None of our drivers reported any problems. The prison van was unaware we were watching."

"Did they have an escort?" asked Henry Case.

"There were no escorting vehicles, Henry," said Artemis. "Belmarsh used a cellular vehicle, like the one used in 2012. I've read up on Olympus's role in what my police station termed 'The Case of the Disappearing Terrorists'. It was a great piece of theatre, rather like a David Copperfield magic trick."

"As you will recall," said Giles, "the vans are designed to hold handcuffed prisoners securely in individual cells. The driver and his mate occupy the front compartment. Two escorting officers sat in the rear compartment on this trip. They observe the prisoners, maintain security, and handle any emergency. If the need arises, they will assist with evacuating the vehicle."

"Which roads did they take?" asked Athena.

"They leave Belmarsh at ten o'clock, join the M25, and then take the M11 ramp towards Cambridge and Stansted Airport. Around Huntingdon, it's the A14, which they follow until they merge with the A1(M). Yesterday they stopped at Blyth Services around three hours into their journey. They travelled north again at two in the afternoon, and it was a quarter to four when they left the A1 at the exit for Sunderland and Durham. They arrived at the prison shortly after four o'clock."

"We have people tracking today's transfer; I take it?" asked Henry.

"What if something happens on today's journey?" asked Alastor.

"Phoenix asked me to trace the transfer documentation between the two sites. We now know who travelled yesterday and the names of the prisoners moving today. I expect to uncover the details for the rest of the week after we return to the ice-house."

"Was our man on today's list?" asked Rusty.

"He was not," replied Artemis, "but I noticed a difference between today's document and yesterday's. I think they made a substitution; for what reason, I can only hazard a guess, but someone who took a seat today was possibly originally scheduled for later in the week."

"As soon as we confirm who is moving when we need to move in," said Rusty.

"We're ready to move tonight if our target is on tomorrow's list," said Phoenix. "Who knows, maybe he won't be among the chosen few, anyway?"

"What's the scale of these transfers? I'm not sure why they feel the need to shuttle prisoners around the country,"

"You'd be surprised, Henry," replied Artemis, "around fifteen hundred people transfer every week. Sometimes, people move because of overcrowding. The moves can have a damaging impact on transferred prisoners. Sometimes people are moved from a prison they know to a busy prison where they feel less safe. The most common reasons for transfer are because someone's security category has changed. Prisoners must stay in the lowest possible security category. A further reason is sentence progression. They might move closer to home or to a prison where they can take a course that will prepare them for life on the outside and reduce the likelihood they will re-offend. Like most things in life, it's complicated."

"It seems to me transfers are inherently risky," said Minos. "To move that volume of people throughout the year increases the risk to the public. Especially when you move convicted murderers and terrorists."

Athena had heard enough; this was old ground. Olympus couldn't influence the way the authorities dealt with such issues. Their role was to clean up the mess caused by the confusion their policies left behind and reduce the volume of criminals contributing to the overcrowded prisons in the first place. A thankless task, but someone had to do it.

"Thank you, Giles. We'll let you and Artemis get back to work. Let Phoenix know as soon as you have the prisoners' identities in the vehicles for Wednesday onwards. If today's journey throws up an incident, let me know. It may be too late to prevent it, but I can alert our local agents to help in the aftermath if possible. Please ensure the cars shadowing the Belmarsh vehicle aren't spotted if an incident occurs. They must break off the operation and leave matters to the official authorities. Our local teams can stand by to act if an escaped prisoner needs to be intercepted or to ensure public safety."


### *Wednesday, 11th June 2014*

Sean Walsh had made an early start. His first visit to the drinks cabinet had been straight after breakfast. He told himself it would be fine if he weren't drinking on an empty stomach.

Today was going to be a nightmare. Sean met Hugo at eleven, then collected Colleen for the trip across to Belmarsh and a visit with Tommy. That was a triple whammy.

He had lain awake half the night thinking through his plans. Was he overconfident? Were there flaws Colleen and Hugo would spot immediately and tear to shreds? He swallowed a large mouthful of Jameson's and went over things again.

On the other side of the estate, Colleen stood by her

front door. At long last, Sean had remembered to ask 'a man with a van' to put in an appearance. Colleen watched as the young driver and his mate shoved the last few sticks of furniture onto the low loader. Then, with everything done, Colleen handed the driver an envelope.

"You don't mind cash, do you?" she asked.

"I prefer it, madam," said the driver. "I get to keep more of it this way. Give me a shout if you need anything else done. Have you got my number?"

Colleen looked at his tanned body, shown off to good effect with a sleeveless t-shirt and shorts.

"I believe I do," she said, smiling at him, "but I'm busy today."

She closed the door and gazed around the house. If things went to plan later in the week, Tommy would be out of her hair. Next week, she could visit an upmarket furniture shop and look for new stuff for her penthouse. Colleen could set aside another week for clothes and shoes for her new wardrobe. That gave her something to occupy her time until the day she moved.

Colleen was feeling in a celebratory mood. She poured herself a white wine and made a toast, "Out with the old, in with the new."


Sean slipped the hip flask back into his inside pocket. He was in the lift heading up to Hugo Hanigan's apartment. It was a minute before eleven. Despite the liquid fortification he had armed himself with, he was still nervous. The doors opened, and he was inside the penthouse.

Hugo faced the doors with his arms crossed over his chest. Not a great start, thought Sean.

"Good morning, boss," said Sean.

"Is it, Sean? Really? News received from Portsmouth and Amsterdam would tend to disagree with that view. The police are significantly disrupting our operations on both sides of the English Channel."

Sean decided not to pass a comment. He would let Hugo make the running. His head was fuzzy with the drinks he had on board. It would be too easy to say something which antagonised the boss. He waited.

"Nothing to say, Sean?"

Sean looked towards the windows. They splattered with raindrops.

"A passing shower," he said, "not a storm."

"I hope you're right, Sean," said Hugo, "and have you masterminded the release of your brother-in-law yet?"

"We're seeing him this afternoon," said Sean, "me and Colleen. Tommy got beaten up on Monday morning. He's in the hospital."

Hugo gave a bitter laugh. Sean bit his tongue.

"How the mighty are fallen, eh, Sean?"

"It helped give us more time to prepare,"

"Where will he be living next week, Sean? If your plans come to fruition."

"With a following wind, he'll be near La Romana in the Dominican Republic."

"My word, you're ambitious, Sean. So when will the delightful Colleen be joining him in paradise? Have you planned that far ahead?"

Sean hesitated. The way things had been with his sister since Tommy had been inside, he wasn't sure what to say. He wanted to get off this subject.

"As soon as it's safe, I suppose," said Sean.

"From what you told me earlier, he's not even safe inside Belmarsh. He's a marked man, Sean. It's often the way. A hardened criminal gets caught, he's in prison, and a young thug seizes an opportunity to make a name for himself. Have you vetted every single man on your crew, Sean? Can you trust them? What if one of them sees Tommy as a shortcut to the top? I might view that man in a favourable light. More favourable than a bloody numbskull like Seamus McConnell, for example. You had better watch your back during this escape bid, Sean."

Hugo enjoyed ribbing Sean. He knew the poor chap hadn't the brains to see he was joking. In truth, he couldn't care less about Tommy or Colleen.

"Well, if you think our problems will fade over the coming weeks and you've got a busy afternoon, I had better let you get going. I'll see you on Friday, Sean."

"I'll have to send Seamus, boss," said Sean. "Friday could be awkward if you get my drift."

"Ah, you might be helping someone move to a new home? I follow you. Let's leave it until Monday. You can tell me everything then. I couldn't face an hour with the other eejit; it would spoil my weekend."

Hugo shook with laughter. Sean was relieved to get away without Hugo questioning him on further details of his plan. As he travelled in the lift, he wondered whether Hugo had been behind Tommy's beating. The boss had long arms. Was Tommy's life in danger, as Hugo suggested? When he reached the ground floor, he had already started through the names of the men he had hired. Was Hugo right; had he unwittingly hired a gunman capable of killing his brother-in-law?

In his penthouse, Hugo Hanigan still pondered the news affecting the Grid. Despite Sean's insights, he wasn't prepared to allow these deaths and disappearances to continue. He resolved to call a meeting of the heads of the gangs that formed the network. It was a bold move.

Hugo had talked to each of them individually but never together. He had always contacted those furthest afield by phone or video call. He wanted their agreement to create a nationwide crime syndicate. The gangs wanted the Glencairn Bank to launder their ill-gotten gains. Hugo wasn't interested in forming friendships or spending his evenings socialising with these people. They were the scum of the earth. Their only saving grace was they could help him control every illegal transaction from Land's End to John O'Groats.

Hugo knew there were risks in choosing this course of action. How could he be sure these villains behaved when they gathered in the same room, certainly for the first time? There would be rivalries and old scores to settle. It might end up like the 'Gunfight at the OK Corral'.

Hugo spent the rest of the morning searching for ways to keep them on a tight rein. The current situation cannot be allowed to continue. He convinced himself they would see sense. Either the gangs combined to eliminate any outside threat, or they cut out cancer eating at them from the inside.

As Hugo dealt with the significant issues in his criminal world in South Kilburn, Sean Walsh had his problems. As soon as he arrived home, he needed another drink. Sean knew he ought to get food inside him. Otherwise, he'd never be in a condition to drive to Belmarsh later. His wife watched him walk from his chair to the drinks cabinet.

"Are you pissed, Sean," she shouted. "You must be stupid to risk your licence this afternoon. Think what a danger to other road users you'll be if you get drunk behind the wheel."

"Shut up, woman," Sean said, "and get my lunch. I'm going for a shower, and then I'm off to collect Colleen. We're visiting Tommy this afternoon."

As the water hit his head and body, Sean shivered. Not from cold but from fear. So many things could go wrong over the next few days. He had faced problems in the past, but Tommy had been there to support him. These days the responsibility fell on his shoulders; he couldn't get through the day without a drink. His head cleared a little. Just one swig from his hip flask when he was in his car on the way to collect Colleen would fix him. He could get through the day, then treat himself to a bottle tonight.

Sean drove to Colleen's to collect her. He had taken a swig from the hip flask earlier than he had promised himself, but his wife wouldn't stop moaning. He had to remind her who brought the money into the house so she could enjoy a taste of the good life. The kids or her neighbours couldn't see the bruises on her body. He would treat her to a holiday when this week was over. He hadn't meant to lose his temper. He was stressed.

Colleen was standing on her doorstep, waiting for him.

"You're cutting it fine, Sean," she said as she sat beside him. "Do you want a mint or something? It might take away the smell of booze on your breath."

"I'm fit to drive, sis. So don't you start," he snapped.

Sean drove them to Belmarsh. Neither of them spoke.

They passed through reception and went to where Tommy sat up in bed. He looked like crap.

"Tommy," said Colleen. "What did they do to you?"

Her concern was genuine, despite everything. Tommy nodded at Sean.

"Good to see you could spare the time to come and see me, Sean. First time since I've been in here. I should get beaten up more often. Tyrone and Rosie might come over then."

"Maybe they can come and see you without any hassle soon, Tommy," said Sean.

"What does the doctor think, Tommy?" asked Colleen.

Tommy shifted position in the cot, and they could both tell he was in pain.

"I'm on the happy pills," he said, "another twenty-four hours, and he reckoned I'll be good to go."

"Is that definite?" asked Sean. "Only we're good to go too."

"The bloke who took my seat yesterday was due to go on Friday. They won't muck around anyone else. Unless I have a relapse, I'll be in that van on Friday morning. The chaplain dropped by this morning to say my kit would be taken to the van by the escorts. I won't return to my cell. I'll go straight from here to the transport."

"Keep your head down, and be ready," muttered Sean.

"How long?" asked Tommy.

"Thirty-five minutes into the journey," said Sean.

"You're a pal, Sean," said Tommy.

"I'll talk to the doctor," said Colleen, "to make sure he still thinks you'll be okay."

"Give my love to the kids," said Tommy, "and I'll see you on the other side."

Colleen smiled and walked out of the cubicle, looking for someone who resembled a doctor. Tommy was still in dreamland. It must be the happy pills. If Sean's plan worked, Tommy would be miles away by the end of the weekend, with no chance of returning to the UK. The conversations she'd had with Tyrone and Rosie suggested Tommy had no chance of them popping over to see him anytime soon.

As for her, she was making a life for herself in London. A single life with Tommy's millions to ease the pain. The money she had put up for Sean to get Tommy out was substantial, but it didn't make much of a dent in the sums the lawyer told her she had available.

Colleen had filled a holdall full of cash to give Sean when they returned. That was Tommy's pay-off. He could live well enough on an island with two hundred thousand to get settled. In time, she would tell him she wasn't joining him, and the money he had was all there was, and he needed to make it last. It wasn't as if he could fly back and do anything about it, was it?

She saw a bloke in a white coat with a stethoscope around his neck.

"Excuse me, doctor," she said, "have you been treating my husband, Thomas O'Riordan?"

"I have, Mrs O'Riordan, it's slow, but he's coming along. He's a tough nut. I expect him to be on his feet tomorrow."

"He'll be able to transfer to Durham then?"

"I see no reason he shouldn't be made comfortable enough to manage a five-hour journey. Therefore, I have asked that they make two comfort breaks instead of the usual one."

"Thank you," said Colleen. She was satisfied Tommy was moving. The next stage was up to Sean and his crew. Now she wanted to get in his car and get off home; it was time to learn how Sean planned to pull off the escape.

Phoenix and Athena were playing with Hope when the phone rang; it was Giles Burke. He had traced the missing transfer documentation. Phoenix kissed his two girls and ran across to the ice-house.

"Anyone we know?" he asked.

"Tommy O'Riordan is moving on Friday," said Giles. "The other three are lifers too."

"If my memory hasn't failed me, the twenty they will have moved this week represents half of the Category A prisoners at Belmarsh. Is there any sign the other half is going north to the same place?"

"Not yet," said Giles. "Although the Young Offenders Institution set up four years ago may be primed to occupy the whole site in the future. There's been criticism over the way we hold maximum-security prisoners. They're in their cells most of the day, and conditions on the wing are dark, gloomy, and depressing."

"My heart bleeds," said Phoenix. "Instead of showing these critics around the prison so they can write this garbage, they should hand them a list of the victims these bastards are responsible for at the prison gate, and then tell them to piss off."

"If they didn't let them in, the press would only make up rubbish. Don't shoot the messenger. I'm on your side."

"Sorry, Giles, I know you are, mate. Thanks for the information."

Now you know who will be in the van on Friday. What will you need from us?"

"Rusty and I will drive over tomorrow," said Phoenix. "I'd like to be part of your shadowing team. I need to get a feel for the lie of the land. We'll see if we can identify spots where they might ambush the van and try to break O'Riordan out. You should continue to fly your drones, and we'll be in constant radio contact with you, so you can give us the big picture rather than the limited amount we can see on the ground."

"Rusty will drive, I presume?" asked Giles.

"He trained me to a reasonable standard when I arrived here, but he's the expert. So, he'll drive while I take notes."

"I'll send Rusty the details of the formations and the rolling change points as soon as you've left. You two need to be in Belmarsh by nine forty-five in the morning. Your contact will be Andy Walters. I don't believe you've met him?"

"The name doesn't ring a bell. What's his background?"

"Andy was a driver for senior military personnel in Iraq and Afghanistan. He left the Army in 2011 and has freelanced as an armed chauffeur for any number of Arab Royals visiting London. He wrote the book on these techniques. But, even Rusty could learn a trick or two."

"You can tell him. I'll pass," said Phoenix and headed for the lift.

He checked his watch. Hope would be off to bed soon; he and Athena could discuss his plans for tomorrow and Friday. Artemis had finished her shift at four, so she and Rusty would be getting a meal now. He ran up the stairs to their apartment and knocked on the door.

"Phoenix," said Rusty, "what can I do for you, mate?"

"Did you get tomorrow's details from Giles yet?"

"We've been chilling out. I haven't checked my emails for a while."

"The truth is he's knackered," called Artemis. "He was half-asleep in the chair when you knocked."

"I need to borrow him for an hour later," said Phoenix. "I'll grab a bite with Athena, then pick you up at eight, alright, Rusty? We can run through the driving you'll be doing tomorrow."

"Oh good, he'll be sitting," said Artemis, "probably for the best."

Rusty grinned at his friend.

"See what I have to suffer? No problem. See you at eight. I guess we're off to the orangery?"

"Where else?" said Phoenix.

### Thursday, 12th June 2014

The alarm rang at six. Phoenix was showered and dressed in fifteen minutes. Then, Athena came into the kitchen as he was drinking his first coffee of the day and munching on a slice of toast.

"I wanted to see you before you left," she said.

"Today's just a recce," he shrugged, "boring stuff, for the most part. I was trying to think last night how I would organise a breakout if I were one of Tommy O'Riordan's former colleagues."

"Who took over after he went to prison? Do we have pictures of his gang members?"

"Giles has information on the Irish gang O'Riordan ran, which controlled large areas in and around South Kilburn. Hanigan knew O'Riordan well before the Grid formed. We've established that fact. Yes, the crew they put together may be local, but with the resources that Hanigan can make available to him, whoever is heading up this operation would pick the best men in the country. We would need Giles and Artemis to sift through thousands of images to identify a driver or passenger in a suspect vehicle. It would take far too long,"

"I'll get Minos and Alastor to work on the data Giles has available while you're away today. We may be able to narrow the field for you. You concentrate on identifying the weak spots on the route the transport follows and how we would counteract any attempt made."

"Fair enough," said Phoenix, "I'd better get moving. Rusty will be sitting in the car, drumming his fingers on the steering wheel. Kiss Hope for me. Tell her I'll see her tonight."

"Don't I get a kiss," said Athena.

"Why not? He'll be playing a full-blown drum solo by the time I get there, but who cares?"

Phoenix joined Rusty by the transport garage at six forty-five.

"Take me to Belmarsh prison, driver, and don't spare the horses," he said.

"The radio's tuned to your favourite station. I had time to fiddle around while I was waiting,"

Rusty set off on the A36 towards the A303. For a change, they were driving to Hampshire to join the M3. That was half their three-hour journey time sorted.

"You can't beat Motorhead first thing in the morning, can you?" said Phoenix.

"If you say so," moaned Rusty.

Thursday morning traffic into London isn't much different from every other day of the week, whichever road you're travelling. It takes as long as it takes. The occasional roadworks, the odd truck shedding its load, a lane closed off for no apparent reason, and knobhead drivers who popped up from nowhere. Rusty had seen it all. So they left the M3 at Junction 2 and joined the M25. It was nine forty-four when they met up with Andy Walters four hundred yards from Belmarsh.

"Good to meet you, Phoenix," said Andy, "and you must be Rusty?"

"It was the creaking joints that gave it away, wasn't it?" said Phoenix.

"No, the red hair," said Andy, "plus the fact you two are Batman and Robin. You always arrive together, according to Olympus legend."

Andy introduced the rest of the shadow team, whose vehicles were scattered around the Iceland car park selected as their meeting point. He checked that each group of drivers had their instructions and led the way. Other crews would relieve the initial vehicles en route. Andy Walters and Rusty would stick with the transport vehicle the whole trip.

"I pride myself on being able to do this without them ever cottoning on to the fact I'm there. I know you've done this work before, Rusty. Are you confident you can do the same?"

"I shall do my best not to mess up," said Rusty. "If I think we've raised suspicions, I'll drop back, maybe half a mile behind them, and we'll rely on the live feed from Giles Burke to monitor their progress."

Andy seemed satisfied with that answer. It was now ten o'clock. The prison vehicle drove through the prison gates, and the shadow team eased into traffic in front and behind the van, as detailed in Andy's instructions.

"Hard taskmaster, isn't he?" said Rusty. "Anyone would think I was a novice."

"I'll leave you to concentrate on the driving," said Phoenix, "we can't afford to mess up. I need eyes on every junction to gauge the point I would strike if I were them. If that means driving to Durham, so be it. I don't want to miss anything."

"We should have brought Artemis along for the day out," said Rusty. "We could have popped in to see her parents."

"To ask permission to marry their daughter?"

"I thought you wanted to concentrate on the junctions?"

Phoenix smiled to himself. Maybe one day, Rusty would take the plunge. He began taking notes. The first leg of the journey was stops and starts. They spent more time stationary than moving.

"Pull off at the next turnoff, Rusty," said Phoenix. "I've seen enough."

The time had reached ten thirty-five.

## Chapter Twelve

"Andy Walters will think I was spotted," groaned Rusty as he parked the car.

"I'll explain it to him when we meet tomorrow," said Phoenix, "don't beat yourself up; you were perfect."

"I wish you would explain it to me," said Rusty.

"Do you fancy a decent breakfast? Let's walk into town and find a place to eat. We can talk it through over a Full English and a mug of coffee. I only had time for a slice of toast earlier."

"You'll get no argument from me," said Rusty.

"We'll play catch-up with Giles when we get back to the car to check on Andy and the team's progress. I have no doubt everything will pass off without incident today. The longer we have time to prepare for tomorrow, the better."

"Do you think you've found the best interception point so soon into the journey?" asked Rusty.

"You seem surprised? Think about it, the further north they travel, the less familiar the territory. If I assembled a team for a job like this, I would pick men who knew the region well. Where will they take him if they manage to get O'Riordan out of the vehicle?"

"A safe-house, I guess, or to the coast for a boat across the Channel."

"The second option, rather than the first, I believe. What would you do with the other three prisoners if it was you? Would you leave them handcuffed inside the van?"

"I don't need them, so I'd leave them behind," said Rusty. "What about the escorts?"

"Robbery with violence will be the stock-in-trade of the guys they pick for this job. So, the escorts are expendable as a last resort. I don't think they will kill anyone except by accident. That is if they happen to die as the result of a crash. They may take a hostage along with them as a bargaining tool, though, and we need to factor that into our plans."

The roadside café was perfect for what they needed. The all-day breakfast went down a treat, and an hour later, the agents returned to their car, ready to face the rest of the day.

"Let's call Giles for an update," said Phoenix.

Giles had little to tell them about the prison transport vehicle except that traffic was nose to tail on the M11 due to an accident, and progress was slow.

"Sounds like abandoning the shadow team was a sensible move," said Rusty.

"It's also something to bear in mind for the morning. Timings may be affected by the traffic for the criminals and ourselves.

"Are we heading back to Larcombe now?" asked Rusty.

"Let's go back via Chiswick. It'll be slow going through

the city, but once we hit the M4, we'll be home by three o'clock. We can have two hours in the orangery and spend time with our other half. It will be another early start in the morning."

They had reached Swindon when Giles called back.

"Minos and Alastor have been working on the possible makeup of tomorrow's crews. A maximum of thirty faces are right for the job and available. That's the best we can do. I've got Artemis checking back over the past four or five days to see if we can recognise any men in vehicles on the roads in question. They wouldn't go into this cold. Someone must have reconnoitred the area. Also, Alastor suggested they might use an isolated spot or an abandoned airfield, for instance, to practice the manoeuvres they plan to use to box in the transport van, so it can't escape."

"Brilliant," said Phoenix, "this will be a great help. I can reduce the workload for Artemis too. She can discount any roads further north than Ockenden."

"That's a massive help, Phoenix," said Giles. "She overheard that, and it brought the widest smile I've seen from her in a while."

"We're an hour away from Larcombe," said Phoenix, "we'll see you both later."

"Safe journey," said Giles and ended the call.

Rusty parked the car next to the transport section garage a few minutes after three. He and Phoenix made for the ice-house to get the latest news from Giles and Artemis.

"What have you discovered, Artemis?" Phoenix asked.

"I've confirmed the identities of two criminals I believe will be there tomorrow so far," she replied. "I'll keep searching. Giles is hunting for possible practice sites in the other room."

"Keep going with identifying the gang members, Artemis, and give me the details of the vehicles they're driving."

"I anticipated that and included make, colour and registration," she said, "but it's unlikely they will use those vehicles on the job, surely?"

"The two you have identified, what were they driving?"

"One drove a beat-up old van, the other a VW Golf."

"They could be what they would drive tomorrow, I suppose. So you're looking for at least eight men and a minimum of four vehicles. One of which will be big and heavy."

"I'm due to finish at four, but I'll keep going. You and Rusty will be tied up preparing for tomorrow anyway, I presume?"

"Sorry," said Rusty, "we'll only be two hours tops. Phoenix wants to spend time with Athena and Hope too. Tomorrow will be a long and tiring day."

The two friends left the ice-house and made for the orangery. It was time to run through the plans Phoenix had formulated. They relied on Artemis and Giles to provide more information before morning. When Andy Walters assembled his shadow team in the Waitrose car park in Belmarsh, they needed every scrap of knowledge at their disposal so that they could foil the breakout.

"That's as far as we can get today," said Phoenix at six o'clock, "let's quit. We'll leave at the same time in the morning. I'll visit the control centre to collect anything new they identify overnight. Can you please pick up our guns and ammunition from the armoury?"

"No problem," said Rusty. "I guess I'll catch you in the ice-house just after six, then?"

"No rest for Batman and Robin," laughed Phoenix.

### *Friday, 13th June 2014*

Despite the early start, everything went smoothly. The two agents left at six forty-five on the dot and had most of the extra details they needed. The identity of the gang members wasn't one hundred per cent complete, but Phoenix was confident his plans would work.

"Do you want me to take the same route today, Phoenix?" asked Rusty.

"No, we'll take the M4 and go north on the M25 towards Purfleet. That's where the action will be. I called Andy Walters late last night. I told him we wouldn't be travelling alongside them today. He's aware now that the gang will join the party south of the Thames."

"Are those guys carrying weapons, too?" asked Rusty.

"As a precaution, yes, but if things go well, we can avoid bloodshed."

Rusty drove to the motorway and started on the two-hour drive east. The M25 trip could vary in length depending on the usual variables; they would be in the right location by ten, with luck. They *had* to be there by ten thirty-five.

Sean Walsh hadn't slept well for days. He had been drinking more than was good for him, but he still didn't sleep. His stomach played him up, and he thought the stress had given him ulcers.

His team was ready. They had a VW Golf, a white Transit Van, a 7.5-tonne flatbed truck, and a Peugeot people carrier. In addition, he hired a woman driving a small foreign hatchback for the motorway accident. Other cars with grunt under the bonnet were on standby.

They had practised for ages on an industrial site near Barking. The place was brand new, and apart from construction vehicles parked on the sides of the roads, they had the place to themselves in the late evening.

Reports were coming in that one of those construction vehicles disappeared last night.

Sean wasn't going on the operation. Hugo Hanigan called last night to order him to stay away.

"If it goes pear-shaped, Sean, the fact that you were in the vicinity of my building could bring unwanted attention to me. I can't risk that. Can the team handle things without you, Sean?"

Sean knew they were better off without him; he was that nervous. He talked to the driver of the lead vehicle, Tony Simms. He hadn't liked the idea, but as Sean had only been riding in the people carrier, at the back of the crew as extra muscle, Simms could find a replacement.

His sister Colleen had called twice this morning to check everything was ready and if he was sure nothing could go wrong. He reassured her as best he could. Not because he was super-confident but because he wanted to get her off the phone so he could fix himself a drink.

At ten o'clock, the transport vehicle left Belmarsh. Tommy O'Riordan and his three fellow travellers were securely handcuffed in their cell.

The driver and the escort party were the same as had travelled on Monday and Wednesday. The only change to their schedule was an extra stop at a service station ninety minutes into the journey.

That allowed O'Riordan to stretch his legs and get checked out. His injuries were on the mend, but the authorities didn't want him dying on the way north. The paperwork that would cause would be astronomical. His escorts in the rear compartment had been told in no uncertain terms to handle O'Riordan with care.

The van driver noticed the gradual traffic build-up as they got closer to the Dartford Crossing. However, he didn't see anything familiar about the VW Golf that eased in front of him. Instead, his wing mirrors showed he was being followed by a white Transit van that looked like it had seen better days.

As they entered the tunnel, a flatbed truck edged alongside. The line of traffic slowed and stopped for a moment. The driver glanced across at the cab. The driver and passenger looked straight ahead; traffic began to move again.

"Dark hooded jackets in June," the driver said to his passenger.

"If they're working outside, it's sensible," his colleague replied. "We can get four seasons in a day in England, and labourers are at high risk for malignant melanomas if the sun stays out."

"A mine of information, as always, Heather," said the driver.

"This makes a change for me," Heather said. "I understand you've done this run twice this week. The doctor persuaded the bosses to have a female escort with a nursing background on this trip, just in case O'Riordan is taken ill."

The lines of traffic crawled through the tunnel, and the minutes ticked by to ten thirty-five. Up ahead lay the Mar

Dyke Interchange. Not as complicated as Spaghetti Junction, but busy enough on a Friday morning. The driver puffed out his cheeks as the traffic remained solid around him. They were behind schedule already, and this traffic jam wouldn't help. He wanted to change lanes. He searched for a gap. He thought he had one there, but no, a bloody people carrier closed the gap as soon as it appeared.

Heather looked out of her window as the traffic on the approach road suddenly braked hard. She could see nothing but red lights.

"Blimey, did you see that, Ivan?" she said. "A Corsa changed lanes in a hurry, veered into the inside lane and got shunted by a van. Loads of cars have piled into the back of one another."

Ivan Newbury wasn't watching the approach road. His eyes were on the way ahead; he slammed on his brakes. He heard swearing from the cells and the rear compartment.

"Sorry, lads," he shouted, "it's an accident fifty yards in front of me."

The female driver of a foreign hatchback had seemed to slow deliberately, so the car behind hit her bumper. She punched the accelerator and shot forward, clipping the vehicle's rear in front and spinning her car around. The inside lanes had to come to a standstill.

"Terrific," said Ivor, "I should have known everything would have gone pear-shaped today."

"Why," asked Heather.

"Friday, the bleeding thirteenth, isn't it?"

Heather had turned her head to view the chaos in front of the van. There wasn't much to see out of her window now. Any vehicle that wasn't in the accident was being held up by a JCB joining the M25. It headed the rush to merge with their lane.

The prison van was stationary and likely to be for some time. Its left-hand side was exposed. Ivan glanced out of his window. The flatbed had dropped back ten yards. The lane next to him stood empty. Typical. As much as he wanted to, he couldn't move out. They were stuck.

Heather James was thirty-two. Her thirty-third birthday was on Tuesday. When it dawned on Heather, the JCB was rushing to merge with their lane; she turned to see where it was. The grill on the articulated dump truck was the last thing Heather saw. She never had time to scream.

Ivan Newbury knew something was wrong. His van had switched lanes, and there was a roaring noise in his ears. Before he lost consciousness, he thought he saw dark shadowy figures. He was right. Tony Simms and the rest of the crew assembled by Sean Walsh had already set to work.

Inside the van, the other prisoners had been thrown around in their cells. They suffered cuts and bruises; the handcuffs chafed their wrists. Tommy O'Riordan knew it was coming. It took longer than Sean said, but the van kept slowing. Traffic must have been heavy. He had braced for the impact. Now, he sat and waited. Tommy relaxed; they were coming for him. Sean and Colleen pulled it off for him. Freedom was only minutes away.

Outside the cells, the escorts fared far worse. They weren't wearing seatbelts, so the impact sent them flying. They were stunned, shakily getting to their feet and trying to get hold of Ivan or Heather in the cab. The communications system was working, but nobody answered.

"What the hell is going on?" one shouted.

There was a noise from outside the van.

The back door flew open. On the roadway stood six men. They wore black balaclavas and dark clothing. Five carried sawn-off shotguns. One took the oxyacetylene torch that had just made mincemeat of the door lock.

Neither of the escorts could offer any resistance. They were still too stunned. The men clambered into the rear compartment, clubbed the guards around the head and relieved them of their keys. Within two minutes, four prisoners were hustled along the shoulder of the highway to cars fifty yards ahead.

The fast cars Sean had acquired sat in splendid isolation at the front of the queue of traffic in the lanes affected by the second so-called 'accident'. One prisoner and two gangsters got into each car. The JCB driver was already in the first car.

The cars then sped off, reaching Junction 29 in four minutes. As they exited the motorway, they reduced their speed and joined the morning traffic on the A127. It was now ten forty-four.

At Larcombe Manor, Giles Burke had monitored the coverage being transmitted by the drones from ten o'clock. Everything had progressed in the smooth manner of the previous four days. There was little change in weather conditions or traffic flow. Each day this week, the runs had been accident-free. If there were incidents between London and Durham, they occurred far enough on either side of the prison transport to be irrelevant.

Artemis sat in the next room following CCTV images, keeping Andy Walters updated on what was happening around him. Both agents were in constant contact with Andy and with Phoenix.

Phoenix had gambled; he drove to a spot near Rayleigh. He and Rusty were lying in wait.

At ten thirty-five, Giles had spotted the first hint of trouble. The accident on the slip-road had happened quickly, but it felt wrong, so he reviewed it.

"Andy, Phoenix, just a heads up. There's been a pile-up on the approach road. It looks dodgy, but I can't see how it will affect us at this stage."

"Define 'dodgy', please," asked Andy Walters.

"The way the car dived for a space that wasn't there, it could have been deliberate. The accident has cut the number of cars moving on the slip-road by ninety per cent. What do you see out there?"

"My shadow team are in similar positions to those we've occupied all week. Two in front and two behind. We should be well-placed to respond if anything happens. I've noted a few familiar cars and trucks; I'll pass the details to Artemis. Perhaps she can tell us whether any of them carry our suspects?"

Giles watched as the second fake accident appeared on the screen in front of him.

"Andy, watch out! There's another prang up ahead. That looked deliberate too, mate."

"My God, a JCB is hammering up the slip-road," shouted Artemis, "it's aiming straight for the cab of the prison van. The JCB hit the van and shunted it into lane two. Everything's stopped. There are men on the motorway. I repeat, men on the motorway attacking the prison van."

Andy Walters ordered his shadow team to abandon their cars. They briefed them on how to handle this type of assault. Every man or woman was armed, and they wore bullet-proof Kevlar vests. With dozens of vehicles stopped on the motorway, it was imperative to avoid a fire-fight, if possible.

As Andy made his way forward and his colleagues

joined him, they spread out across the inside lanes and used the stationary vehicles for cover. Andy received a message in his earpiece from a driver who had been in front of the prison van.

They could not help; they had become aware something happened two hundred yards behind them, and although traffic slowed, they were committed to staying on the M25 until the next junction. The two cars had left the motorway and parked by Gallows Corner on the A127, awaiting instructions.

"I'm twenty-five yards behind the prison van," Andy said. "I can see drivers and passengers on the side of the road, right in front of me, chatting and smoking. I can see a man in dark clothing by the rear of the van. He's holding a shotgun by his side. Hang on; the prisoners are out of the van now; there are at least five armed men, and they're leading them forwards. I can't get close enough without endangering the public. Can you tell where they're going, Giles?"

"They ran past the car that spun across the inside lanes and climbed into waiting cars. They've just sped away, and I'm now tracking them. Stand by."

"Got it," said Andy, "I can hear sirens behind us, moving up fast in the outside lane. Help is on its way."

"Andy," said Phoenix, "you and your people get back to your vehicles. As soon as you can get moving, make for the next junction and get to Gallows Cross. Giles and Artemis use drones to track the cars carrying the gang and the prisoners. Can you pick them out?"

"Yes, Phoenix," said Artemis. "I've got them. They've left the motorway at twenty-nine, the same junction as those two cars from the shadow team."

"Send the details to the cars at Gallows Cross. Tell them

to follow, but do not attempt to intercept. Keep us informed."

"Why aren't we heading over there?" Rusty asked Phoenix.

"Because they won't all be going the same way. It would make things too easy for the police. They'll split up at some point."

"It will take at least twenty minutes before we can get to the turnoff, Phoenix," said Andy. "The emergency services are here now, but they didn't appreciate the scale of what they were facing. The place will be crawling with police in the next few minutes after they send for back-up, but the prisoners will be long gone before we can join the chase."

"Don't give up yet, Andy," said Phoenix. "Get on the A127 as soon as possible, and be ready to drive in whatever direction Artemis or Giles tells you. The eye in the sky is our best hope from here on in."

"Andy, it's Artemis again. You were right. Tony Simms drove the flatbed you had on your list, a nasty piece of work. He's got an unhealthy CV - guilty of robbery with violence, grievous bodily harm, and assault with a deadly weapon. His passenger was Jeff Melvin, another career criminal. The drivers of the VW Golf and the Peugeot people carrier are also well-known to the police. Interestingly, they come from all over the southeast of England. They have no connection to O'Riordan's former gang. His second-in-command, Sean Walsh, is reputed to have assumed command since his brother-in-law went to prison. There's no sign of him taking part in the breakout."

"Could he be driving one of the getaway cars?" asked Phoenix.

"It's not known to be one of his talents," said Giles, "he's more likely to be used for muscle."

"OK, I've got an update," said Artemis. "It's ten fifty, and three cars have turned left off the A127. That road will take them through Hacton. Andy, your guys at Gallows Cross, need to get after them."

"Will do," replied Andy. "What happened to the fourth car?"

"I saw four cars as they let the motorway, then with the intermittent feed from the CCTV and the drones, there are gaps. I missed one car that must have turned off. Giles, can you help me find it? I don't want to stop tracking the other three."

"Could they be heading my way?" asked Phoenix.

"Give me a minute," said Giles.

"Where does the Hacton road take them?" asked Phoenix.

"Rainham, Hornchurch, Dagenham, any one of several places, why?" asked Giles.

"Railway stations," replied Phoenix, "which is closest?"

"Hornchurch, I'm diverting a drone there immediately,"

"Any news on the fourth car?" asked Phoenix.

"It's doubled back to the other side of the motorway, heading for Basildon."

"Thanks, Giles. That will be O'Riordan," said Phoenix, thumping the dashboard. "The stations are a smokescreen. They'll drop the others off to make the police think they've used a train to escape. O'Riordan needs to get abroad tonight. He's not safe anywhere in Europe in the long term, but as a stop-off for several hours before a much longer journey, Holland is convenient."

"They intend to get him on a boat from Harwich then?" asked Rusty. "Now I know why we're sitting here. I should have known."

Phoenix allowed himself a smile.

"It's an eight-hour crossing, and from here, it's a ninety-minute drive at the most."

"Phoenix, the first prisoner, has been dropped at Hornchurch station. He's wearing a light grey hoodie, blue jeans, and white trainers. They've given him a change of clothes in the car."

"Are the others still on the move?" asked Phoenix.

"Yes," said Artemis, "if you're right, they might be in Rainham and Dagenham in ten minutes."

"That will be the same time you'll meet the fourth car, with O'Riordan on board coming into Rayleigh," said Giles. "If you're right."

"We're ready," said Phoenix, "and I'm right. They can forget about catching a boat."


Tommy O'Riordan was in a car with Tony Simms, Jeff Melvin, and a driver who could give Lewis Hamilton a run for his money. He felt good. Even in this clobber, they made him wear.

"What's all this about?" he asked Simms.

"Sean insisted the four of you wore the same kit. With your hoods up, the cops couldn't be sure who they were following. The other three went in the opposite direction. It didn't matter if they got caught as long as you got clear."

"Far too clever for Sean to have dreamt it up himself," said Tommy, "where are the other lads headed?"

"That's up to them. The station they're being dropped at can get them to London, Tilbury, or even up north with a few changes. We gave them five hundred quid each in cash to help."

"Did Sean give you anything for me?" asked Tommy.

"There are more clothes, a wash kit, a passport, a plane ticket, and a few grand cash in that bag under your seat."

"I need a gun," said Tommy.

Simms shook his head.

"Sean never suggested that," he said.

"Look, I'm begging you, mate, I need a gun. Things have gone great so far, but there's no way I'm going back inside. If I have to shoot my way out of this bloody country, then I will. I'll get rid of it once I'm in the clear."

Simms shrugged and handed Tommy a handgun wrapped in a towel.

"There you go; it can't trace back to me. It's got a full magazine."

The car had now reached the outskirts of Rayleigh.

At Larcombe, Artemis and Giles continued to track the getaway cars' movements and check what was happening to Andy Walters and his team. The two lead cars were hot on the heels of the two remaining prisoners. The first car that dropped a passenger at Hornchurch headed north. Its work was over for the day.

Giles contacted Andy Walters.

"Where exactly are you, Andy?"

"We've made it onto the A127, and we're three minutes from the Hacton turning."

"I'm forwarding details of a car that's making for Stevenage. Three bandits inside; you should assume they're armed. Could you cancel their lunch appointment, please?"

"Glad to have a part to play in this, Giles," said Andy. "You can count on us."

Almost simultaneously, the other two prisoners arrived at the stations in Rainham and Dagenham.

"Light grey hoodies and jeans again," said Artemis. "It's dress-down Friday, I guess."

"It matches what O'Riordan will be wearing, I bet," said Phoenix.

"You'll be able to see for yourself soon," said Rusty. "This is them coming towards us now."

Giles Burke's timings had been near perfect. It was two minutes past eleven.

## Chapter Thirteen

In three locations across London, those interested in what was unfolding in Essex waited anxiously for news.

Colleen had got fed up with calling her brother; he must have turned off his phone. He was useless. What if the team needed to ask him for help? What if something had gone wrong? She sat in her sparsely furnished lounge and bit her nails; the radio tuned to the local station. News reports came on the hour. As the DJ linked the same mindless music with light-hearted banter, she imagined what might have gone wrong.

Colleen thought of pouring herself a drink. No, she told herself, wait. You've got champagne on ice, ready to celebrate. If everything went to plan, it was the last she would see of Tommy. He'd be on the other side of the world, with no way of getting back.

The DJ said it was ten forty-five. Colleen looked at her watch. When did time ever move this slow? She consoled herself with the thought that Sean would have called if there had been a problem. What if the police knew he was involved? Maybe Sean had been arrested?

After what seemed an hour, the DJ announced it was eleven o'clock. It was time for a news update. 'Police say long tailbacks are causing delays on the M25 Northbound after an earlier accident. One person died, and several suffered serious injuries. More on this at noon.'

The phone rang. Colleen answered.

"Sean, is that you?"

"No, Colleen, it's Hugo Hanigan. I must commend your brother on his escape plan for Tommy. That was ingenious. Sean's not answering his phone. Is he with you?"

Colleen couldn't stand the smarmy Hanigan. She wanted to talk to her brother to find news about Tommy. Had he been injured in the accident or even killed? Where was the team now if they fled the scene of the accident?

"I couldn't trust Sean to plan this on his own. I added a few of the finer touches. Tommy should be on his way to the coast by now. The others will be on trains heading into whichever part of the country takes their fancy."

"I wish him well, Colleen," said Hugo. "The police have sealed off the spot on the motorway where the accidents occurred. I doubt they realised until ten minutes ago that the prison transport was the target, and the prisoners were released. The search will begin in earnest within the hour. Every station, port and airport will be alerted. I hope your husband is quick enough to get away before they close the net."

"You couldn't care less whether he escapes or not," Colleen snarled. "You washed your hands of him weeks ago. As for Sean, you made sure he didn't taint your precious reputation. No matter what happened today, you planned to come up smelling of roses."

"My, how bitter you are, Colleen," said Hugo. "I called to congratulate you, and this is the thanks I get. If you speak with Tommy before he leaves the country, be sure to tell him to take care. There's much that can go wrong between here and his final destination."

Hugo ended the call, avoiding the abuse. Colleen screamed down the phone at him.

Colleen tried Sean again. He picked up at last.

"Sean, where have you been? Have you heard from Tommy? Is he alright?"

Sean Walsh was drunk. He sat slumped in a chair, staring out of his lounge window.

"Tony Simms texted me before eleven to say they had reached Rayleigh. They'll be in Harwich at half-past twelve. Tommy's on his way, sis."

"Sean, are you pissed again?"

"It's been a stressful morning. I needed a drink. Another couple of hours, and we can celebrate."

"The news said someone died. What happened?"

"The JCB hit the cab, not the main body of the van as was intended. The front-seat passenger died. The driver was seriously hurt. Michelle, the woman I hired for the accident, has been hurt too. She's a stunt driver, so she'll heal; you'll probably see her at work in the next Bond movie. It couldn't have gone better, Colleen. Tony said the lads got in and out of the van with Tommy and the others within two minutes."

"Bleeding Hanigan called to say, 'well done', but he couldn't resist a dig. He warned me Tommy had a long way to go before he was safe."

Drink befuddled Sean's brain, but the memory of what Hugo said drifted to the surface.

"I wouldn't put it past him to stop Tommy himself," he muttered.

"What do you mean, Sean?" said Colleen.

"When I saw him last week, he said Tommy was a marked man and might be in danger from someone I picked for the team. He said the beating Tommy received in Belmarsh could have been arranged by someone on the outside. I had my suspicions; it was him. Hugo might have been behind everything. Hugo may want Tommy dead, sis."

"Tommy's with Tony Simms then?" asked Colleen. "Can you trust him, Sean?"

"A hundred per cent. Tony's a diamond geezer. A rough diamond, but he's not Hugo Hanigan's man."

"Let me know when you hear more, Sean," said Colleen. "When he's on that boat, I can open my bottle of champagne. I wish noon would hurry up, and I can listen to the next update."

"Turn on the telly, Colleen. They'll have a helicopter over the motorway by now. I'm not sure how the police will play it. They might keep a lid on the breakout and try to intercept the prisoners without informing people dangerous men are on the loose. The shit will hit the fan in time, but the longer they have to put things right before that happens, the less fall-out they'll need to handle."

"OK, Sean, we'll talk later," said Colleen. "Oh, and Sean, stay off the booze for crying out loud."

Sean looked at the bottle in his hand. When had he stopped pouring it into a glass? He couldn't remember.

At two minutes past eleven in the ice-house, Giles and Artemis coordinated the teams homing in on Rainham and Dagenham stations. The grey-topped prisoners stood on the platforms, waiting for the next train. The getaway cars that delivered them were turning around to head home. Olympus shadow team cars tracked them.

Artemis was in touch with Olympus cells across London. She issued the same orders as Phoenix. Wherever the cars went, they should never arrive. The drivers and gang members must disappear. Andy Walters and his crew would then disperse, ready to be called into action on Olympus missions whenever the need arose.

Giles made another of his regular anonymous phone calls. He rang the Metropolitan Police and asked whether it was true three Category A prisoners were at large after this morning's crash on the M25. They declined to comment or to confirm that fact.

Giles suggested checking for passengers wearing light grey hooded jackets, blue jeans and white trainers travelling from Essex railway stations. The seeds had been sown. Olympus could only hope the police worked the rest out for themselves.


Outside Rayleigh, Rusty had waited until the car drew alongside. It had to slow for the ninety-degree bend in the road. Phoenix had convinced him to park on the apron of the side road. He guessed the getaway car had plenty of horsepower under the bonnet. Rusty knew the vehicle he drove could never hope to match it on a straight run, but in a short sprint, they had a chance. For their plan to work, he had to get this right first time.

As the gangsters' car made the slow turn, Rusty accelerated hard, wheels spinning, and shot from his hiding place. He drew alongside, and before the driver could react, Rusty edged by and narrowed the gap between his bonnet and the dry-stone wall.

There was no way through. The car collided with the wall, and the nearside scraped along it until it came to rest. The driver tried to reverse away from trouble.

Phoenix appeared above the wall and opened fire with his MP5K. The driver and front-seat passenger, Jeff Melvin, died instantly. Inside the back of the car, Tony Simms tried desperately to get out. But his door was too close to the wall to kick open.

Tommy O'Riordan struggled to get out of the car, fighting the pain from his injuries. It was no contest. Rusty waited for him, already braced in his firing position. He had aimed his Browning HP before Tommy cleared his gun from the wrappings of the towel. Rusty fired twice. Tommy sprawled back against the car door and slid to the ground. Tony Simms was stuck inside the car and in no position to find a target. He fired wildly, expecting death at any moment.

Rusty ducked back behind his steering wheel and eased away from the stricken vehicle. Phoenix vaulted over the wall and jumped into the moving car.

"Three out of four," he said, "and O'Riordan was on the run for Harwich, just as I predicted."

"I only caught a glimpse of the guy in the back, but it must have been Simms," said Rusty. "Why didn't we finish him?"

"We can pop back if you want?" said Phoenix, "but he can't identify us. From where he sat, he wouldn't know if we were the police or a rival mob. The car isn't driveable, so he has a long walk. They must have fixed O'Riordan up with hand luggage, papers, and cash for the next leg of his journey. The locals will have phoned in to report gunfire in the area. Simms runs the risk of being picked up on the grass verge somewhere with a heavy bag and plenty of explaining to do."

"Where to now, Phoenix?"

"I'm hungry. Shall we find a country pub and take time out for lunch?"

"It's not even ten past eleven. There won't be anywhere serving food yet."

"I'll find out how Giles and the others are doing," said Phoenix. "You choose the road home, but we're stopping somewhere, even if it's only for a bacon roll."

Rusty checked their exact position and continued towards Chelmsford.

"If we stay on the motorways from here, and there are no accidents, we can be home by two," he said.

"Happy days," said Phoenix.

He called Giles at Larcombe.

"Progress report please, Giles?"

"All being taken care of, Phoenix," replied Giles. "Did you stop O'Riordan from boarding his boat?"

"Rusty did. I played a supporting role. Simms is still alive, but it might pay us to have someone tell the Grid's senior bosses they're facing a formidable enemy."

"Even if they don't have a clue who they are or where they come from," added Rusty.

"Are you on your way back?" asked Giles.

"Yes," said Phoenix, crossing his fingers. "Traffic's heavier on Friday afternoons. We could be late."

"Don't kid me, Phoenix," said Giles. "I'm looking at data from the CCTV feeds around the south of the country. There's nothing out of the ordinary today."

"Ah, but it's Friday, the thirteenth, so you never know what might happen."

Colleen had another agonising wait for news. The local radio didn't break into their music schedule to update the eleven o'clock bulletin; TV news channels concentrated on the M25 incidents and how they may be related. So far, they haven't released information on the breakout. She hoped that noon brought her the good news she craved.

Sean Walsh stirred. He must have nodded off for five minutes. The clock on the mantelpiece told him it was closer to fifty minutes. It was nearly noon. He levered himself up from his chair and lurched into the kitchen — time for a black coffee.

Hugo Hanigan didn't do agonising, anxious, or drunk. He wanted to get Tommy O'Riordan out of the way, metaphorically speaking, but that was it.

He was keener on the bigger picture. If a fellow countryman and his team had pulled off one of the most audacious prison escapes in history, he would use that to his advantage. Hugo intended to stress it had been a man from the seven streets in Dublin where he had grown up who organised the breakout. A man Hugo had known all his life. It showed members of the Grid that they had joined a winning team and that resistance was futile for those who still opposed them.

Hugo, Sean, and Colleen watched the news channel at noon. After a summary of what was coming up, the newsreader handed over to a reporter outside New Scotland Yard. He stood beside a high-ranking police officer.

"Assistant Commissioner, what can you tell us about this morning's incident on the M25 and surrounding areas?"

"At around ten forty this morning, a prison van containing four prisoners and their escorts was involved in a serious incident. The van was en route from HMP Belmarsh to HMP Durham. It was the last of five trips planned for this week. We believe fake accidents slowed or stopped traffic at a specific point. A stolen truck then rammed the prison van, killing an escort. Armed men stormed the van and released the prisoners; they escaped in fast cars. The driver and escorts are receiving treatment in the hospital. None of their injuries appears to be life-threatening."

"This was a well-organised attack, then? Who do you think was responsible? Are the public in any danger from the men on the run?"

"It's too early to speculate. We are still gathering evidence at the scene."

"We're getting reports from nearby towns of high-speed chases and gunfire. Are you closing in on the men who did this?

"We are hopeful of early arrests. We can assure your viewers we take the public's safety very seriously. Every available officer has been committed to the hunt for the criminals who carried out this attack. We aim to recapture the prisoners involved as soon as possible."

"Can you tell us who travelled in the van, Assistant Commissioner? Am I right in thinking these men were Category A prisoners and included murderers and rapists?"

"No comment. I repeat, the investigation is at an early stage. We will release a statement when we have more information."

High-speed chases, gunfire, thought Colleen. Where had these reports come from; was Tommy involved? Did Sean have news? She called him.

"What have you heard, Sean?" she asked.

"Nothing, sis," he replied, "I've just this minute texted Tony Simms. They should be thirty minutes from Harwich.

The boat is waiting for them in the harbour. Tommy will be in Holland by nine tonight, at the latest."

The news channel had moved on to other matters in the background.

"Give me a shout when you hear from Simms," said Colleen.

"I will," said Sean.

The weather girl predicted a weekend of sunshine and showers. Then it was time for the rolling news feed to start again from the top.

"The time is now twelve-thirty pm, on Friday, the thirteenth of June. Breaking news…

Sean's phone pinged. It was from Tony Simms.

"Sean? I'm sorry, mate. Tommy and the others have been shot dead. We got ambushed by two blokes outside Rayleigh. Christ knows who. I'm on foot, trying to get back to civilisation. I've phoned the other lads for a lift, but I can't raise anybody. Can you get someone to give me a lift?"

Sean wasn't listening. The only thing he had heard was his brother-in-law had been shot dead. Sean had to tell Colleen. Hugo had gotten rid of him, just as he feared.

"Do you need picking up?" asked Sean.

"Yeah, you better sort it out, and quick. I never signed up for this crap."

"Tell me exactly where you are, and I'll send a driver to fetch you."

Simms looked for landmarks or road signs, but he was in the middle of nowhere, as far as he was concerned.

"Not a clue. I'm walking back the way we came. The nearest town is Rayleigh."

"I'll send out a search party," said Sean and ended the call.

He paused before ringing Colleen. There was a new report on the breakout.

On TV, he saw pictures of a wall running along the side of a road. Whatever lay behind the police screen erected ten yards away must have been too horrific to show. A crashed car, perhaps? He listened to the commentary.

"Police say the three men got shot at close range. They refused to comment on whether this incident is related to the prison van ambush this morning."

His phone rang. It was Colleen. "He's dead? My Tommy's dead?"

"Yes, sis, I'm sorry. Simms just called. Two gunmen killed Tommy and another two men I hired for this job."

"It was Hanigan, wasn't it?"

"It looks that way," said Sean, "but let me make sure first."

"He's a dead man walking," muttered Colleen.


Phoenix and Rusty arrived back at Larcombe Manor a few minutes after three. Rusty returned the damaged car to the transport section. He had some explaining to do.

"Sorry, chief," he said to the senior mechanic, "it was him or me."

"I'm sure the other guy's car is in a worse state, don't worry. We'll fix it and get it back into the pool in time. Was the mission a success?"

"There were a few sticky moments, but it went well in the end."

"Then that's all that matters, isn't it?"

Rusty headed for the ice-house to see Artemis. She finished at four, and it would be good to hear what had happened to the other getaway cars.

Phoenix dropped in to see Athena in the administration office to tell her they had arrived home safe and sound.

"I've been kept up to date by Giles," she told him. "Earlier this morning, I wondered whether you had made a massive miscalculation. The shadow team separated in the accident and was ineffective until they joined the chase after the gang had made their escape. You and Rusty were miles away from the action."

"The scale of the accidents caught us unawares, I admit," said Phoenix, "but everything panned out in the way I predicted after that. Andy Walters wasn't at fault; he did the right thing at the time. The gang focussed on their target of releasing the prisoners. Andy and his team were well-placed to protect innocent motorists if the gang had turned on them. We both believed the vehicles we had identified were to box in the prison van and bring it to a standstill on the motorway. The JCB wasn't something we anticipated."

"That poor young woman in the van," said Athena.

"Why was she there?" asked Phoenix, "they had a male escort crew every other day. That's a mystery, but when we stopped for a bite to eat, Rusty said something strange."

"What?"

"When O'Riordan got out of the rear off-side door, he moved like a seventy-year-old. Rusty had all the time in the world to get his shots off."

"That is odd. It doesn't match O'Riordan's reputation."

"Once the gang had left the motorway, we were playing catch-up. We believed the vehicles they used to stop the van would have been part of their escape plan. We didn't factor in them abandoning four or five vehicles altogether. That was clever. It made the task of emergency services even harder. The motorway has two lanes out of action now for the rest of the day. Crime scene officers will have so much evidence to collect from the road they'll drown in it."

"You anticipated the split correctly, I grant you that," said Athena, "but you couldn't possibly have known they planned to drop these three prisoners at railway stations."

"I knew O'Riordan would go in the opposite direction to the others. That felt obvious. He was heading for either the east or south coast. Once Artemis told us the others had left the A127 and which towns lay ahead, it became clear. They were using a different form of transport. The rail network had to be the best option. The police would assume O'Riordan had gone the same route. Their whole ruse centred on getting him away to safety. If the other three got recaptured, it didn't matter."

"I'm hoping to hear from Giles in the next hour," said Athena, "he's been following the movements of the three prisoners. He notified the police and gave a full description of what they wore."

"We could walk over together if you wish?" said Phoenix. "I'll tell you what happened at Rayleigh on the way. It will be better than sitting here waiting for him to call."

They took the back stairs to the kitchen door. The afternoon sun was warm on their backs as they crossed the lawn. Phoenix told Athena how O'Riordan and the others had died.

"Are you sure it wise to let this man Simms live?" she asked.

"It's a calculated risk, the same as Rusty and I waiting outside Rayleigh. That paid off, and I believe this will too. Simms will report to his handler in the O'Riordan gang, who set up this escape bid. In turn, that handler will inform Hanigan. We have wounded the Grid on several occasions in the past month. Often the wounds that fester and cause the deepest harm are those carried in mind, not body."

They reached the entrance to the ice-house and descended in the lift to the operations room. Giles Burke talked with Artemis and Rusty.

"Thanks for your help today," Phoenix said to Giles and Artemis. "You had to do a lot of quick thinking to get the result we sought. What's the current state of play?"

Giles looked at his watch.

"It's five hours since they extracted the prisoners from the van. Andy Walters and his team dealt with the occupants of the first getaway car. I contacted a backup crew in the area to reinforce the other members of his team hunting the getaway cars from Rainham and Dagenham. We received news from them ten minutes ago. I can confirm that none one of the gang members who left the scene is still breathing."

"Excellent," said Athena.

"That's another strong message delivered to the Grid," said Phoenix.

"What news on the prisoners?" asked Athena.

"Transport police are on the alert," said Giles, "they know how our men dressed. They know the identity of the four prisoners. Even on a warm, sunny day, they'll stop dozens of men wearing a similar outfit who are innocent, but the noose is tightening."

"We're monitoring the situation closely, Athena," said Artemis, "I reckon the police will find them soon enough to save face. How they explain away what happened to O'Riordan and the others near Rayleigh is a different matter."

"The actions of Andy Walters and his team will be easy enough to conceal, I presume?" asked Phoenix.

"The police won't worry too much about losing a dozen active criminals from their future caseload," said Artemis.

"Family members are prepared for the worst when loved ones choose a violent profession," said Rusty. "Tears will fall when they disappear without a trace, but they don't have many avenues they can pursue to uncover the truth."

"We'll deploy the usual misdirection tactics," said Giles, "as you did earlier, Phoenix."

"Sorry, did I miss something?" asked Athena.

"Rusty called me when they were halfway back to Larcombe," said Artemis. "They were due here at two, but he told me Phoenix needed a comfort break at Membury services."

"Not unusual on a long day's mission, is it?" asked Athena.

"The ketchup stains on Rusty's shirt suggest they took more than a comfort break," said Artemis with a grin.

"Not bacon rolls again," laughed Athena, "you two are incorrigible. Erebus was staggered by how many you managed to put away in those meetings in the orangery."

"All that action makes a man hungry. What can I say?" said Phoenix.

"Time to call it a day," said Athena, "let's take a break. Giles, you too. Delegate the monitoring to your staff overnight. We'll get together for an hour in the morning to hear the latest. Well done, everybody."

The two couples left the ice-house and returned to the manor house.

"Enjoy the rest of the day," said Athena as Rusty and Artemis went to their apartment.

As she and Phoenix reached their door, they could hear Hope's laughter as Maria Elena played with her.

"That has to be the best sound in the world," said Athena.

Phoenix thought the sound of bacon frying in the pan ran it a close second but thought it safer not to mention it.

## Chapter Fourteen

***Saturday, 14th June 2014***

Another sun-blessed morning greeted the agents as they faced a new day. The unscheduled morning meeting occurred at ten o'clock, and everyone gathered to hear what had emerged overnight.

"Over to you, Giles," said Athena.

"The three prisoners have been recaptured. The Assistant Commissioner gave the news at nine o'clock this morning. They are interviewing them as we speak. The police want to find out who helped them to escape yesterday."

"How far did they get?" asked Rusty.

"The guy who left from Hornchurch travelled to Victoria and was at Gatwick Airport when police stopped him. It appears the gang supplied each man with a wad of cash plus a change of outfit."

"Our Rainham prisoner lacked imagination," Artemis

continued. "He went to Fenchurch Street station and started looking for a woman."

"Any particular woman?" asked Henry.

"Don't think so," said Artemis. "He'd been locked up for a long time."

"How did the police find him?" asked Minos.

"He visited a bar where he thought he might get lucky and start drinking. The landlord threw him out later when he started singing and touching up any female who got within a few feet of him. The guy started a fight with the landlord and a customer. I bet the police couldn't believe their luck when they arrived expecting to be dealing with a spot of drunk and disorderly."

"And the Dagenham prisoner?" asked Alastor.

"He went to Tilbury Dock," said Giles, "and tried to board a cargo boat sailing under a Singapore flag. There was an argument over the money required to get him to their next port of call. The gang possibly gave each man four to five hundred pounds, but the captain wanted more than the prisoner had to offer — a machete featured in the argument and a lot of shouting. The dock police intervened and held both men for questioning. The penny dropped late last night that the hopeful traveller might be one of the escaped prisoners. That gave the Met's morale a lift. They could report that they recaptured all three remaining prisoners within twelve hours."

"How did they handle the rest of the story?" asked Henry.

"The AC said they had confirmed the identity of the three men killed near Rayleigh. One was the fourth prisoner, Tommy O'Riordan, former leader of an Irish gang from South Kilburn. Giles filled in the details, the aftermath of the murdered jurists, and the judge's life attempt. The others were Jeff Melvin and Dave Lumsden, both career criminals."

"Did they mention Simms?" asked Phoenix.

"The police seem unaware of a fourth person in the car," replied Giles, "or they aren't releasing that information. Difficult to tell."

"Who do they think was responsible for the breakout?" asked Alastor.

"More important for us, who do the police reckon killed O'Riordan and the others?" asked Phoenix.

"They would be searching for the gang members using the same source information we used," said Artemis. "That is still available to them until the prisoners arrive at the stations. Sadly, a fault developed overnight, and much of what followed got erased. The feed resumed after the Olympus cars had left the scene. There were no cameras in the countryside where O'Riordan died."

Giles picked up on Alastor's question.

"The police are saying they continue searching for the people responsible for the breakout. Good luck with that, and Tony Simms won't help them, even if they discover he was in the car. When the AC answered that question, he pointed the finger at the gang O'Riordan led for many years. As to why he got shot, O'Riordan received a severe beating in Belmarsh earlier in the week. It was touch and go whether he would travel yesterday. Heather James, the nurse who died in the crash, travelled on board to tend to him if he became ill on the journey. The police think the breakout aimed solely to set him free. Someone who wanted him dead used that to finish the job they'd started inside Belmarsh. Melvin and Lumsden were collateral damage or in the wrong place at the wrong time, as the AC said this morning."

"That explains why O'Riordan struggled to get out of the car," said Rusty.

"Anything further?" asked Athena.

"We're still monitoring things, Athena," said Giles. "If we need more smoke to confuse the authorities, it will be organised."

"It looks as if you've pulled it off again, Phoenix," said Athena.

"We must remain vigilant," he replied. "We haven't had a response from the Grid yet. Simms will fill in a few gaps for whoever masterminded the plan. The missing men from the breakout crew will throw up various possibilities for who got rid of them and why. It won't be long before they lash out at someone. When that happens, it will be a swift and deadly attack."


Last evening, Colleen called their children, Tyrone and Rosie, to tell them the news. They would fly home for the funeral. She didn't know how long it would be before the police released Tommy's body.

The champagne had tasted less satisfying than she had imagined. Twenty-four hours ago, Tommy was alive, a few hours from a life in the sun. He would have been stranded over four thousand miles away, out of her life forever. She could be her own woman at last.

Now he was dead. That hadn't been in Colleen's plans. Why did things never turn out how you wanted them? Tommy's death couldn't have come at a more inconvenient time. She moved into her new place in just over two weeks. How could she explain that to the kids? They thought they would come to stay here in the family home.

It was odds that the funeral wouldn't take place before

the middle of July. Then there was the hassle of the will and settling Tommy's estate. Her lawyer had tidied things up to her satisfaction while he was in prison. Nothing would have changed while he still lived in the Dominican, but now every member of the O'Riordan clan would have their nose in the trough. She might need to let the solicitor have more than a glimpse of her tits if she wanted to get away with every penny Tommy had.

Sean hadn't called back. He was probably sleeping it off. If he had ever stopped drinking, the police would knock on his door before long. It didn't take a genius to work out that Tommy's old outfit was favourite for springing him from Belmarsh. Colleen had a brainwave. She rang Sean.

"How are you, Sean?" she asked.

"Hanging, what do you think?"

"Give your head a shake and listen. Take a taxi, and get over here, now. You need a holiday."

Thirty minutes later, a dishevelled Sean Walsh stood on her doorstep.

"The police will ask questions, Sean," she said, "and you're in no state to give them sensible answers on your own. We need to get our statements lined up first. We both visited Tommy in the hospital wing in Belmarsh on Tuesday. That can be confirmed easy enough. He told us he felt in danger for his life and couldn't wait to get to Durham. They'll swallow that after the beating he took. You stayed home all day yesterday. Your phone records and mine will confirm we talked to one another, and the GPS will place us in northwest London, not out on the M25 in Essex."

"What about the calls I had with Tony Simms?" asked Sean.

"They know you're both criminals, Sean. Say it was business. You don't need to incriminate yourself. Tony will sing from the same hymn sheet if they find out he was involved. There's no way they can connect you to the breakout if Tony and the others keep their mouths shut. They haven't caught any of them, have they?"

"No, it's only the prisoners they've caught up with so far. They were expendable anyway. Tommy was the important one."

"Yeah, and we know who topped him. We'll let the police try to work it out on their own. That will take the wooden tops six months minimum. What we know, we keep to ourselves. If anyone's taking revenge for my Tommy's murder, it's me."

"So, we tell the cops the same story to keep them off my back. What do we do then?"

Colleen had been waiting for the chance to reveal her great idea.

"With Tommy not needing it, the place near La Romana is vacant, and there's loads of money in the bank. We'll get you on a plane tonight or tomorrow. Stay there until the heat dies down."

"I can't leave the wife and kids without a word," said Sean.

"No, you prat, take them with you. The kids will only miss a week of schooling, and then you'll be okay for another six weeks. After that, we can sort you out somewhere fresh to start back. We'll sell your place while you're away. The money's there, Sean, trust me. I need you around when I tackle Hanigan. I can't afford for you to go to prison."

"I'll miss the funeral?"

"I'll give him a proper send-off, Sean. Tyrone will walk behind his coffin with me."

"What about Hanigan?"

"You leave him to me. He'll need to look for a new person to front up the gang while you're out of the country. Seamus McConnell is a fool and will be history. I'll convince him it's best to keep it in the family."

"He won't work with a woman, sis, don't be daft."

"He worked with Tommy, didn't he? Then he worked with you. How hard could it be? Anyway, it will only be a temporary arrangement."

Sean thought things over with a black coffee. His head had hurt when he shook it earlier. It made more sense the longer he thought about it. Sean had been to enough funerals. It would be tough to miss Tommy's funeral, but it got him out of Hanigan's way. His family wouldn't complain at two months in the Caribbean, and a new home to return to in a different part of town could be made to work too. He needed to get back in his wife's good books after the slap he had given her when he was drinking yesterday.

"Okay, sis," he said, "let's get our brief to sort out these statements. Then we're covered if the police come calling. If things get difficult while I'm away, the family can come home in September, and I'll hide out in La Romana until it's safe."

"Well done, Sean. I knew you'd see sense. I'll make sure the money's there for you."

Hugo Hanigan had watched the same news report as Sean Walsh and Colleen O'Riordan. He was as stunned as they were. Hugo had been ribbing Sean on Wednesday when they met. Hugo never imagined someone would kill him as soon as he escaped prison. Who could have done it? Everything went smoothly; they were an hour away from the coast, and Tommy was close to freedom. It made no sense.

On Saturday morning, Hugo read the newspapers. As lunchtime approached, he listened to the latest news bulletins of the recapture of the prisoners. He kept waiting for Sean and his crew to get a mention. The police were hunting for the gang but making no inroads whatsoever. That felt wrong. Sean had done well with Colleen's help, but the police should have tracked at least one person involved. His idea of gathering the gang leaders together seemed an even better idea today — questions were needed. Answers had to be given. Who killed Tommy O'Riordan, and why?

The Walsh family flew out to the Dominican Republic with British Airways on Monday, the sixteenth of June. The coroner released Tommy's body on Monday, the thirtieth, when Colleen took possession of the keys to her penthouse overlooking Hugo Hanigan's apartment.

Colleen could now inform the O'Riordan family, the Walsh's, and those from the Kelly and O'Regan clans Tommy's sisters had married into that the funeral would be at two o'clock on Friday, the fourth of July.

Tyrone and Rosie flew into Heathrow on Thursday afternoon; a driver met them as they came through Arrivals. They were surprised to go to a hotel rather than their old home; the manager told them they had a suite for three nights.

A note from Colleen was waiting for them in their room, giving details of the funeral at St Mary's in Kensal Green. The driver would collect them at one fifteen tomorrow to take them to the social club. Their mother promised to be there to meet them. The clothes she expected them to wear would arrive in the morning.

On Friday morning, Colleen stood and watched as the

odds and ends she was taking with her went into the removal truck. Her new clothes and furniture would be waiting outside her apartment block when the taxi dropped her off at ten. As soon as the funeral was over, she would return to ensure everything was to her satisfaction. She had no intention of attending the wake at the club. Tyrone and Rosie could represent her.

With the keys in her hand and workers busying themselves behind her, she stood by her penthouse window and looked across the city skyline. There was Hanigan's nest. There sat her prey. This afternoon's ceremony allowed her to consign the past to the past. When she returned here alone, it marked the beginning of her bright future.

The limousine collected her at half-past twelve and took her to the funeral home. She sat beside Tommy's coffin and waited for Tyrone and Rosie to arrive. As she waited, her thoughts drifted back to the first day she and Tommy had met. As soon as she got home, her mother met her at the gate.

"Did I see you talking with that O'Riordan boy, Colleen? He's trouble, that one. You'd do well to steer clear of him. No good will come of it."

Her mother's words had only attracted her more to him, and although she had been proved right in time, some good did come out of their relationship. Colleen O'Riordan now had more money than she ever imagined.

Tyrone and Rosie walked in to join her, and although they had many questions, the sight of their father's coffin caused them to break down in tears. Staff from the funeral home escorted the three of them into the courtyard. The horse-drawn carriage was ready and waiting. The bearers loaded Tommy's coffin into the hearse. The procession set off to walk the two hundred yards to the social club.

The male mourners in the borough's Irish social club, tough-looking men in black suits and black ties, drained pint glasses of Guinness, then walked outside for a puff on their last cigarette. Wives and partners in their black dresses were waiting and chatting.

The funeral director ushered his flock towards the eight black limousines in his grey pinstriped trousers and black topper. It was quite a turnout. Colleen knew they were there because they needed to be seen, not out of respect, just as at Tommy's father's and mother's funerals before him, but gangland traditions still run deep.

The tall, elegant funeral director set off on foot, planting his black cane in the middle of the street. The hearse followed behind, drawn by its six jet-black horses. Tommy's hearse bore wreaths inside and out. Colleen, Tyrone and Rosie followed, arm in arm, each grieving for the fifty-six-year-old gangster in their way.

They reached St Mary's church's gates at one minute to two. Everything that followed was a blur to Colleen. The church service, and the burial in the family plot, were surreal. Family members came and offered their condolences and said what they knew they should say. All she wanted to do was to get away.

She told Tyrone to take Rosie to the social club. Everything was paid for, no matter how much the free bar cost her.

"The hotel is fantastic, Mum," said Tyrone, "but why aren't we staying home with you? Where's Uncle Sean? Why aren't you coming to the wake, even for an hour? Everyone wants to see you."

"Not now, Tyrone," said Colleen. "I need to be alone."

Tyrone watched as his mother disappeared into the

limousine. Where she was going, he didn't have a clue. She was a stranger to him.

Colleen was eager to get back to enjoy her new surroundings. She wanted to get out of these black clothes and into one of her new outfits. The champagne was ready to celebrate her fresh start. Tomorrow morning, she would start her plans to take revenge on the man responsible for Tommy's death.

## Next in The Phoenix series

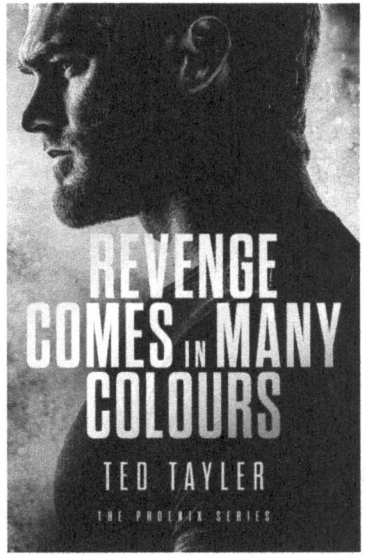

vinci-books.com/revenge-in-colours

**When an assassin strikes, The Phoenix must soar above the darkness.**

In a deadly showdown, Colleen O'Riordan consolidates power with a secret assassin, while Hugo Hanigan faces disaster. As Olympus battles organized crime, The Phoenix navigates a treacherous world where justice and vengeance blur, and the price of victory is paid in blood. Can he turn the tables on the criminals in control?

Turn the page for a free preview…

# Revenge Comes in Many Colours: Chapter One

### *Sunday, 29th June 2014*

"Good to see you again, Phoenix,"

"You too, Biggles," replied Phoenix.

"So, we're off to Bonnie Scotland this evening then, I gather?" asked Les Biggar, the pilot Olympus had on speed dial for urgent flights around the United Kingdom.

"Yes, and Rusty is coming along for the ride. He's parking the van. I've left him to carry the equipment over to the chopper on his own. Rusty will let you know how he feels in a few minutes."

"There's never a dull moment with you two," said Les.

The rear door of the helicopter flew open, and a bag got shoved into the luggage compartment. The helicopter rocked as the door slammed. Rusty Scott, the rugged, red-headed agent who was Phoenix's best friend, clambered on board.

"Travelling light?" asked Biggles.

"His lordship needed a few essentials for this job. He

forgets, sometimes, just how heavy they are. It's his age," muttered Rusty.

"Neither of us is getting any younger," said Biggles, "okay, gents, if you're ready, we'll be on our way."

"How long do you think it will take, Biggles?" asked Phoenix.

"Two hours in these conditions. It's a pleasant enough evening."

Rusty checked his watch. It read six forty-five.

"Relax," said Phoenix, "our pick-up is for nine o'clock. If we're early, we can get coffee. If the weather closes in, the Glasgow team will sit and wait until we land."

"What's the mission, lads? Can you tell me?" asked Biggles.

"A lot less dangerous than the last one we used you on in Ireland," said Rusty.

"Good, I still get the odd twinge and a few flashbacks, but it goes with the territory."

"I guess you won't be in a rush to return?" asked Phoenix.

"Been there already. I've ferried a few racegoers to meetings at Cheltenham and Newbury and then home again. Apart from a few drunks, there's been no problem. Afterwards, either get back in the game straight away or check out. I chose to keep flying. I'll go wherever the money is, Phoenix."

"Well, this Glasgow trip will be easy enough. It was a direct result of our Manchester mission a few weeks ago," said Phoenix. "We cleared out a fair number of the Grid's gang members based in the Bent Triangle."

"Where's that when it's at home?" asked Biggles.

"The area containing Beswick, Hulme, and Cheetham Hill," replied Phoenix. "The whole place is rife with people for whom law and order is only the name of a TV programme."

"Drugs were being smuggled to Scotland by car or train, using couriers from the region," continued Rusty. "We passed the information gathered by the Lancashire and Merseyside Olympus agents to our colleagues over the border. They had to follow up on our leads."

"The fact you're travelling north suggests progress has stalled somewhat then, am I right?"

"Yes, and no. Our agents acted on the leads we provided, and the noose has tightened," said Phoenix. "The whole network in Glasgow and Edinburgh has now been identified. Zeus sanctioned direct action to eliminate the leading faces in the organisation, but resources are stretched to the limit by other demands around the country."

"Sometimes, Olympus should avoid getting caught in the media headlights," added Rusty, "and let the authorities take the credit."

"This mission aimed to expose enough of the network that even the police can uncover and clean it up," said Phoenix.

Biggles laughed.

"Am I right in thinking an anonymous phone call will be your last act before I fly you home?"

"We're so predictable," groaned Rusty.

The rest of the trip proved uneventful. Les Biggar landed at Glasgow Airport at eight forty.

"Leave your gear in the storage compartment, Rusty," said Biggles. "Follow me, we can get checked in, and then I'll start scheduling our flight plans for the return flight. Do you have any suggestions on timing, Phoenix?"

"First light in the morning, Les," he replied, "I don't intend hanging around up here any longer than necessary."

"Fair enough."

"Will we have time for that coffee?" asked Rusty.

"We'll make time," said Biggles.

They were checked in and drinking a mug of coffee by nine o'clock. Phoenix kept a weather eye open for movement on the tarmac outside the window. The single-storey building stood on the airfield perimeter, and pilots of helicopters and small private planes used it. They were the only people in the place tonight.

"Here they come, right on time," said Phoenix.

A black van motored towards Les Biggar's helicopter. It stopped, facing the building, and the driver turned his headlights off and then on again. Ten seconds later, he switched off the engine, killing the lights. The area around the parking bays was bathed in a dim amber glow from lamps high overhead. It felt eerily quiet.

"Not a bad night for it, Sunday," said Rusty, "it's peaceful."

"We still need to be off this airfield as quick as we can," cautioned Phoenix.

The three men emptied their coffee mugs, carried them to the sink, and swilled them under the hot tap.

"Can you tell we've been house-trained recently?" laughed Rusty.

"Leave them to drain," said Biggles. "I'll pop back and tidy up once you've left. Then get to sleep for a few hours, so I'm ready to fly you south at around a quarter to five."

"I'll call you if there's a delay," said Phoenix. "Although, there's not much room for anything to go wrong on this trip."

"Famous last words," muttered Rusty.

The night was warm outside the building, and the breeze was no more than a whisper. The driver's door opened as they approached the van, and a short, stocky man stepped out.

"Jimmy McLean, as I live and breathe," exclaimed Rusty, "how are you, my friend? It's been a long time."

"I volunteered for this gig when I heard who was coming," the man replied, "our team leader Greg is in the passenger seat. Apologies, but he's on the phone with our lads on the other side of the city."

Phoenix walked around to introduce himself.

"You two have met before then?" asked Biggles.

"We trained at Hereford together on both occasions," replied Jimmy. "When we applied to join the SAS, then again in 2005 when we formed part of the first intake for the Special Reconnaissance Regiment. I left in 2008, the year before Rusty had a difference of opinion with a superior officer."

"He thought he was proficient," said Rusty, "I told him he was a bleeding liability,"

"OK," said Phoenix, returning with Greg, the Glasgow team leader.

"If you two have caught up on the old days, we'll get moving."

"We're off to Barrhead first," barked Laidlaw, "get your kit stowed, and climb in."

Greg Laidlaw was a tall, angular man in his mid-thirties accent pure Glaswegian. Rusty reckoned he had been born and raised no further than five miles from Govanhill. He knew how rough that district was and had a degree of respect for a man who dragged himself up from there to a senior post in Olympus.

Biggles smiled as he watched Phoenix offer to help Rusty carry the heavy bag. Rusty patted his arm away and slung the equipment over his shoulder. The pilot knew the score. No way would he let his old SAS comrade McLean think the years had caught up with him.

"I'll see you guys in the morning," said Les Biggar, "good hunting."

Phoenix and Rusty raised a hand in acknowledgement as the pilot trudged towards the building. They got into the van, and Jimmy McLean drove away from the airfield. They were soon leaving the motorway and heading along the A76.

"Another fifteen minutes, and we'll be there," said Jimmy.

"What's at Barrhead?" asked Rusty.

"A town that has seen better days, with a population of twenty thousand," said Phoenix. "The gang leaders selected this place for its variety of industrial estates. Plus, it's accessible by road and rail from Manchester, with none of the risks associated with being spotted in the heart of Glasgow. So they rented several units across the town, and most of the face-to-face meetings needed were in a bar in Cross Arthurlie Street, just up from the railway station."

"Thanks for the history lesson, Phoenix," said Rusty.

"My pleasure," Phoenix replied.

"We're coming up to our first warehouse just now," said Laidlaw, "so let's park, and I can go through the layout with you."

"Who's running this outfit?" asked Rusty.

"Gregor McGrath," replied Greg Laidlaw. "He's quietened a touch as he's grown older, but he was a wild one in his teens. His reputation with a blade has left him untouched for forty years. Nobody has threatened his position as the head of the organisation covering Glasgow and Renfrewshire and lived. Yet there's nothing to suggest McGrath's laid a finger on anyone in the past three decades.

On the contrary, he has a loyal crew of enforcers who carry out his orders without question."

The four men sat in the van one hundred yards from the warehouse that was their target. The building was in darkness, just what you might expect, late on a Sunday night. There was no sign anyone was on the premises, let alone that it was a potential hive of illegal activity.

"Do we have a backup team in place?" asked Phoenix.

Laidlaw nodded and unfolded a drawing that showed the ground surrounding the building, plus the layout of all three floors.

"We have a van here and on the far side. Each vehicle holds six agents. It doesn't take a genius to work out why we can't see signs of activity because we're looking through the windscreen at a two-floor warehouse building. The drawing shows the layout of the basement. That's where the workers are grafting away, converting the product transported from Manchester into a street-ready product. It's a slick operation, and quality control is variable by design. They put every kind of rubbish into the gear to sell to junkies and cut the crap content the further they move up the social scale; they've got the process off to a fine art. Stocks of every grade match demand to the ounce. They never hold excess stock. Just in time and continuous improvement were management tools in the Nineties; now these buggers have taken it to a new level."

"Kanban, and Kaizen," said Phoenix.

"Those names sound more like sumo wrestlers," said Jimmy McLean to Rusty Scott.

"Watched that every week, didn't we?" replied Rusty, "did they ever fight that Hawaiian giant, The Dump Truck? Davy Glass was a big fan, I remember. What happened to him?"

"He came out of the mob and returned to Edinburgh. That was three years ago. His wife and kids had moved south within six months. He found it difficult to adjust. She couldn't handle his moods. The last I heard, he was living on the streets. I keep meaning to look him up, to see if I can help,"

"Damn shame, he was a good lad," said Rusty.

They sat silently for a few minutes, reflecting on the times the three had lived, fought, and socialised together. Along with the rest of the regiment they had served in, how things had changed. The spell broke when Laidlaw issued an order.

"Time to move in," he said into his mouthpiece.

The action against the Grid's gang members was underway on the far side of the warehouse. Eight heavily armed Olympus agents burst into the ground floor and descended into the basement. Laidlaw ordered Jimmy McLean to drive to the right-hand end of the building.

Phoenix and Rusty could hear flashbangs, smoke bombs, and brief bursts of gunfire.

"The best point of entry for the teams was at the opposite end," said Laidlaw. "We should see activity here in a tick."

Phoenix and Rusty were out of the van and grabbing their gear from the bag. McLean and Laidlaw had already moved to within ten yards of the building.

"Cover the far door and subdue anyone who tries to escape," shouted Laidlaw. "Once we finish that part of the exercise, we'll head inside. You're aware of the layout now. The stairs on the left take you to the basement and bring you into the rows of storage racks. Not every gang member carries a weapon, but you must be careful as you progress. The other team will inform me of how much resistance these guys offer. We can adapt our tactics from 'subdue' to 'eliminate' as required."

The metal door was suddenly flung open, and two men ran out onto the ground. McLean and Laidlaw overpowered them in seconds. The bright light from the doorway showed Phoenix that the men were only teenagers from Southeast Asia.

"McGrath seems to be an equal opportunities employer," said Rusty.

"I doubt they were born and bred in Barrhead," said Phoenix. "I guess they were trafficked in and set to work long hours for little or no pay."

"Well, it keeps the profit margins high, which will please the Grid's hierarchy," muttered Rusty.

"We need to get inside," shouted Laidlaw. "Our lads have dealt with another half dozen kids like these. As many again remain with handguns keeping them occupied. We've suffered no casualties so far, thank goodness. Let's give these gunmen something to think about."

The four agents edged towards the open door; McLean led the way inside. The hallway was empty. He signalled to the others to follow as he descended the stairs one at a time. Rusty moved ahead of Phoenix and Laidlaw to join his former colleague.

"Just like old times, Jimmy," he whispered.

They crept past the first rows of roof-high racking. There were cartons dotted here and there but plenty of gaps, which gave them a chance to look across the whole width of the building. There were no gunmen near the back wall yet.

Jimmy indicated to Phoenix and Laidlaw to replace them.

"We'll make our way across to the far wall," he whispered.

"Take care," said Laidlaw.

As he and Rusty moved from one stack to the next, they checked the gangways for any sign of opposition. Halfway over, the sound of automatic weapons caused them to stop and hit the floor.

"That was our lot, opening fire again," said McLean, "but I've no idea where."

"The low ceiling in this basement and the metal racking are causing every sound to echo," said Rusty, "but we're no help lying here. So let's head for the far wall, as planned, and make our way forward. Keep Greg and Phoenix well behind us. I don't want us to engage with the enemy simultaneously if they move past us towards the exit. It might get hairy."

"Agreed," said McLean, and they set off at a run, crouching low. Finally, they reached the relative security of the far wall. McLean contacted Laidlaw and said they were moving forward.

"We've had two agents hit in the past few minutes," Greg told McLean, "only flesh wounds, nothing terminal. They've eliminated two shooters. There are three to sort out, and they're in the centre of the room, just beyond the final row of racking."

"All received," said McLean, and he and Rusty inched forwards.

"There," said Rusty, grabbing his friend's left arm and bringing them to a temporary halt.

He could see the three gunmen through the gaps in the racking. They were shielded from the other teams by a forklift truck and steel cabinets that housed electrical equipment. The two agents could see the rest of the layout as

Greg's plan had shown. In the distance was the racking for the Inward Goods. There were tables for the preparatory work and then the final assembly. Nothing was left to chance. It was a lean, mean production plant.

The gunmen were still concentrating their attention forwards where the initial attack had started. They weren't expecting an attack from the rear.

"Let's finish this," said Rusty.

"Permission to eliminate the threat, boss," McLean asked Laidlaw.

"Affirmative," replied his team leader.

"Here goes nothing," cried Jimmy.

He and Rusty stood up from their crouching position and burst into the open. They skirted the rows of racking, firing as they ran. The gunmen half-turned, aware of the danger at last; it was far too late. They fell in a hail of bullets.

"Clear," Jimmy McLean called to his team leader.

Phoenix and Laidlaw emerged from the other side of the racking, and four other agents joined them. A final sweep by two colleagues soon confirmed that each of the three warehouse floors was under Olympus' control.

"How are your wounded?" asked Phoenix.

"Embarrassed," came the reply.

"They live to fight another day, unlike the Grid's casualties," said Rusty.

"We've got a group of Vietnamese teenagers to hand over to the authorities," said Laidlaw. "I'll start the ball rolling on that later. But, for now, we need to clean up in here. Then, my crew will dispose of the bodies."

The agents looked around them. A clean-up crew would soon dispose of the bodies. But the explosions and the gunfight had disturbed much of the product the warehouse was handling. The air was full of white particles, and the floor looked like a carpet of snow.

"What's the plan?" Rusty asked Phoenix.

"Any scrap of information within these walls to help the police track the source of the drugs backwards to Manchester and the distribution network onwards will be accessible to them. The young lads will be next to the tables they were working at, awaiting their arrival. Trussed up like chickens, perhaps, but alive and well. Greg's men will leave as few clues as possible that we were here. The anonymous phone call will hint at a turf war. The workers don't know any different and pose no threat to Olympus. Our best bet is for McGrath to believe this was a police operation driven by a tip-off of the illegal immigrants. The uncovering of a drug network was a happy coincidence."

"Let's hope he swallows that," said Laidlaw. "If we can dispose of the bodies and spread misinformation on the whereabouts of the gang members within the police system, then we buy ourselves valuable time."

"It's a ploy that's worked well for Olympus over the years," agreed Phoenix.

"We had better make a move," said Jimmy McLean, "you guys need to transfer to your next target site. Greg will look after the wounded here and make the call when the place is shipshape."

With a quick nod of gratitude to Greg Laidlaw, Phoenix and Rusty followed Jimmy McLean outside. They crossed the open ground to the van quickly and quietly. Once they had stowed the gear, Jimmy started the engine, made for Glasgow on the M77, and then took the M74 towards Edinburgh.

"Sit back and enjoy the ride, lads," said Jimmy. "We'll be there in less than forty minutes."

Rusty checked his watch; it was still only twenty-five minutes past ten. Time flies when you're enjoying yourself.

"Have you prepared a history lesson for me about our destination, Phoenix?" asked Rusty.

"A thumbnail sketch," replied Phoenix. "What do you expect? I'm a past master at turning over every little detail in case it affects the outcome of my mission. If you're sitting comfortably, then I'll begin. Coatbridge lies ten miles east of Glasgow; it's a working-class town, twice the size of the place we've just left, and is called Little Ireland. It has great transport links via road and rail. In recent years it's become Scotland's inland container base."

"That sums the place up," said McLean. "The container aspect gave the town ample opportunity to develop the trafficking of drugs, women for the sex trade, and illegal workers. It wouldn't surprise me if those Vietnamese teenagers we uncovered didn't arrive through that route."

"It sounds just the place to settle down and raise a family," said Rusty.

"As if," scoffed Jimmy McLean. "I can never remember you chatting to a lassie, let alone having any intentions of getting settled."

"Times change," said Rusty. "I needed to find the right girl, and I did. We live together at Larcombe Manor."

"Good for you, mate," said McLean. "Jessie left me while I was in Kosovo. There were no kids. When I threw my lot in with Olympus up here, I didn't think it fair to lumber a woman with the worry of whether I'd be coming home at night. Jessie had enough of that to bear while I was in the SAS."

"There's still time, Jimmy," said Rusty, "and it's good to

have someone to come home to after a mission. It makes the fight worthwhile, believe me."

"You'll get no argument from me," said Phoenix. "My wife and daughter keep me sane. If I had nothing else to occupy my mind except the criminals out there and the depraved nonsense they get up to, I'd go crazy."

"I'll bear it in mind, Rusty," said Jimmy. "If you find a girl looking for a vertically challenged Scotsman, the wrong side of forty-five, tell her to call me. Right, lads, this is your stop."

Jimmy had turned off the motorway and was nearing the ubiquitous industrial estate. Phoenix thought their footprints were so similar these days that you could be anywhere in Europe. Only the local road signs and the weather set one place apart from the next. Truckers from every corner of Europe used the motorway systems these days, and the estate they were entering had vehicles from Germany, Norway, Poland, Netherlands, and Spain, parked up overnight.

"Who are we meeting here?" asked Rusty.

"The Edinburgh team Greg was talking to when you met us at the airport. Their leader is Hugh Fraser, an ex-Captain in the Scots Guards. Hugh earned a reputation as the Army's supreme logistics man. When Greg took us through tonight's small skirmish, he showed us the floor plan, issued basic instructions, and then relied on our training to know what to do when the action started. Fraser gives each agent under his command a detailed, colour-coded file containing every step of the mission. It's all rather anal if you ask me, but his success rate is off the chart, and his men never complain, not in public, at least."

Jimmy was soon driving onto the Monklands Industrial

Estate. In front of them was a single black van with tinted windows. It was facing the estate road exit.

"I think that's Fraser's crew," said Jimmy. "Hard to tell whether they're inside the van or already on the ground."

"Did Laidlaw say what time Fraser was hitting the warehouse?" asked Phoenix.

"There's something you need to know about Fraser," chuckled Jimmy. "When he thinks he has the same window of opportunity, he's off like a rat up a drainpipe. He likes to lead from the front and isn't one for waiting around for backup. When I got out of the van to talk to Rusty earlier, Greg had a few words with our Hughie. Unfortunately, he never did fill me in on the outcome of that conversation. We were too busy with our work after that."

"I'll walk over and have a word," said Phoenix, "you two cover me in case it's a trap."

"No problem, Phoenix," said Rusty.

He and Jimmy got out of the van and collected their weapons. They watched as Phoenix wandered across the lorry park towards the van. As he drew near, the passenger door opened, and a tall, distinguished-looking man stepped out.

"Phoenix, I presume?"

"You must be Fraser?"

"I have something for you," said Fraser, handing a blue folder to Phoenix.

"What's this?"

"My report on tonight's direct action. In brief, my four agents and I entered the building at 21.50 hours. We overpowered the four criminals we found. They're in the warehouse's canteen, for now. I've indicated where the relevant documentation was so it could go to the police. We found information on the entire trafficking network from Asia through Central Africa, Southern Europe and beyond. I think you'll find the report comprehensive enough for the authorities to take immediate action to cripple this damnable human trade."

"There's little to do, then?" smiled Phoenix.

"Sorry I didn't wait for you. Time was of the essence. The criminals could have left by ten o'clock. Instead, they used this building as a transit site after the human cargo arrived. Men, women, and children were shuttled through here overnight, with none staying long. Then transport arrived to distribute them throughout Scotland. On the outside, the firm looked like a building trades supplier. But it held a far darker secret."

"Does your report suggest how we proceed regarding your prisoners?" asked Phoenix.

"Of course," said Fraser, somewhat surprised at the question, "it's unlikely the police will rouse themselves tonight. So I'll arrange a call in the morning. One of my men is standing guard. Once the police are on their way on the approach road, I'll tell him to get off home. He knows the escape route."

"He has a blue folder, too?" asked Rusty.

"Naturally," replied Fraser. "Look, if there's nothing more, I'd prefer to get off home. I suggest you read the report at leisure, and then you can head back south. Our work here is as good as done. We'll tie a neat bow on matters first thing tomorrow."

"Right," said Phoenix, "well, thank you, and good to meet you."

Fraser turned on his heel and got back in the van.

"White was the colour in Glasgow," said Phoenix, "blue seems to be popular in Edinburgh."

Phoenix and Rusty stood and watched as Fraser's driver

pulled away. Jimmy's van was now the only vehicle in the lorry park.

"Back to the airport, guys?" he asked.

"We might as well get some shut-eye with Biggles and then head home at first light," said Phoenix. "I can't help feeling cheated. I was looking forward to the action."

Rusty smiled. That was typical of Phoenix. He liked to take the troubles of the world on his shoulders. So much so that he had been stressed in recent months. When someone gave a helping hand, he took umbrage.

Jimmy McLean dropped the two agents at the airport building.

"It was grand to meet up with you again, Rusty," he said, "keep in touch. A pleasure working with you, Phoenix."

"Thanks, Jimmy; I'm sure we'll be back this way before too long."

They heard loud snoring from the room's far end as they walked through the building door. Phoenix sat in the nearest chair and read the report Fraser had handed him. Rusty found a comfortable chair and hoped to get some sleep before sunrise.

Biggles never stirred.

Phoenix reckoned it would be a long night.

The upside was that Fraser was everything Jimmy McLean had said. The man was meticulous; never a bad thing as far as Phoenix was concerned.

# Revenge Comes in Many Colours: Chapter Two

**Wednesday, 2nd July 2014**

The journey back from Glasgow had been uneventful. Les Biggar had woken up at four o'clock without an alarm. Finally, he was ready to fly after a cold shower and changing clothes. Phoenix and Rusty were tired, dirty, and uncomfortable.

"A good morning for it," Biggles had shouted as they took off.

"If you say so," Rusty had replied.

"Everything went to plan last night, I suppose? I didn't hear you return."

"I'm not surprised with the racket you were making. Yes, our involvement was limited, and both crews will apply the finishing touches in an hour or two."

"We could have stayed at home," Phoenix had said. "By the way, I've asked for someone from Larcombe to collect the van from Bristol airport. I hope you don't mind?"

"Not a problem."

Biggles had then taken them straight home to Larcombe Manor, touching down on the lawns at the far end of the grounds. Long enough for them to gather up their kit and jump out. Phoenix and Rusty had run at a crouch towards the ice-house and watched as Biggles lifted and powered away. He signed off with a swish of the helicopter's tail as he flew over the manor house and back to base. Several people sleeping in the main building, and the staff quarters, were now wide awake. It was a few minutes before seven,

"That will go down like a lead balloon," Rusty had said.

"I didn't fancy driving through the morning traffic from Filton back to Bath. I need a shower and a decent breakfast before I start work. There's plenty to get done."

"Artemis is already at work in the ice-house. I doubt she realises we're back. I might grab a bite, too, before the nine o'clock meeting. See you there later."

The pair had crossed the lawns to the house and gone their separate ways to their apartments.

The next forty-eight hours had seen activity, both north and south of the border. An anonymous call about the illegal immigrants working in the warehouse in Barrhead offered the Glasgow police a terrific start to the week. The paperwork they found opened several lines of enquiry, and the elaborate production set-up raised eyebrows but brought a rare smile from the Chief Constable. At last, they had good news to deliver to the public.

In Edinburgh, the police were also seeing a more positive future, as news from Coatbridge filtered through from their Glasgow colleagues. They found four men with known links to organised crime at premises on the Monklands Industrial Estate.

Data gathered from the offices showed a well-established global trafficking network, with items offering them the chance to identify how this warehouse linked to one of the most famous gangsters in Scotland. A man who had been untouchable for decades and known to be involved in drug supply the length and breadth of the Central Lowlands.

It was early in July and seasonably warm, but there would have been no cold hands in police headquarters even if it had been January. Every senior police officer in Fettes Avenue was rubbing his hands with glee.

Further south, in Manchester, enquiries remained ongoing. Activity had been high since the night of the incidents in Beswick, Hulme, and Cheetham Hill. The news from Scotland only added extra fuel to the frequent requests for overtime. There were smiling faces everywhere.

Except in the home of Gregor McGrath and those of his fellow gang members. They were trying to stem the flow of damaging information. Scapegoats were selected. There was an inevitability this would end with somebody ending up in prison.

McGrath and his senior colleagues determined it wouldn't be them.

Within every organisation, some are expendable. In the criminal underworld, it's no different. If your name came up, you hoped the gang looked after your family while you were inside taking one for the team.

Two things bothered Gregor McGrath. First, who had notified the authorities of the Vietnamese workers in the first place, and then where had the police taken the men running the drug operation in Barrhead? The guys arrested in Coatbridge assured him they weren't in Glasgow. He was awaiting news from Edinburgh. Inevitably, someone there knew their whereabouts. McGrath planned to call a Grid colleague in Manchester to check whether they had gone there if all else failed.

Gregor McGrath needn't have worried about the Barrhead gang members. The police also wondered where they were. They couldn't imagine the Asian teenagers running the show alone, but they were clueless about who their bosses had been. Or why they left their workers alone without supervision.

Greg Laidlaw could have told them both not to worry. The gangsters enjoyed the rural views from the forested hillsides in several country parks between Glasgow and Edinburgh.

At Larcombe Manor, Athena had been full of admiration for the success of the Scottish missions.

"Apart from giving Hope and me a rude awakening when you returned on Monday morning without warning," she had said to Phoenix, "we couldn't have hoped for more."

"Everything went as planned," Phoenix had replied.

"Do you think we've got the Grid on the run now?"

"Let's not count our chickens yet,"

"Resources are thin at present," Athena had said, "but our meeting on Wednesday will be a happier one now despite that. It's always good to report successes to Zeus and the others rather than excuses for lack of progress."

At dawn on Wednesday, Phoenix and Athena had driven north to Manchester. They arrived at the conference centre in Fountain Street at a quarter to nine.

"Maria Elena was half-asleep when she arrived, wasn't she?" asked Athena as they took the lift to the second floor.

"Hope won't have woken up for at least two hours. Maria Elena will be wide awake by now. I expect Hope is wondering where her parents have gone, though.

"I don't enjoy leaving her," sighed Athena, "but we both must attend these get-togethers."

The lift doors opened, and the two senior Olympus agents walked along the corridor to the conference room reserved for their meeting.

"I agree," replied Phoenix. "Look who's here before us. Zeus, and Hera, there's never any question of either of those two taking a holiday."

They exchanged greetings. Hera was keen to take Athena to one side to ask how little Hope was progressing. Phoenix and Zeus discussed the weather and the latest news headlines. It didn't take them long to exhaust those topics. Zeus knew Phoenix wasn't a great conversationalist. He was more interested in action than words; he switched focus to Olympus-related matters.

"You might imagine we have enough on our plates, Phoenix, but you can rely on the authorities to give us even more work. An announcement of a major review of allegations of historical sex abuse across every area of UK society is imminent. The Home Office's failure to act on allegations that a paedophile ring operated at Westminster in the Eighties prompted this decision."

"Another review into a cover-up, you mean; will it have any teeth, or is it destined to be another whitewash?"

"Well, the police are to get emergency powers to access phone and internet records, as I understand. But, unfortunately, the government have had to rush them through after the European Court of Justice overturned the existing legislation."

"Worst day's work we ever did, throwing our lot in with Europe," muttered Phoenix.

"You'll get no argument from us on that one," said Hera as she and Athena re-joined their husbands.

"Is there a specific time frame for this review, Zeus?" asked Phoenix.

"It will take a while to set terms of reference and choose a figurehead to lead it," replied Zeus. "Experience tells me the former will take many months, and the latter will be such a poisoned chalice the list of people they will need to approach will grow and grow."

"So, the finished report will be due some time, never."

"Ever the optimist," said Athena.

"I believe we should check what the review uncovers and take direct action without delay. One thing is vital. If Westminster figures still alive today were guilty of offences thirty years ago, they must be dealt with immediately. There's nothing to gain by wasting valuable resources on dead men."

"I agree," said Athena. "Ah, here come the others."

As usual these days, Heracles and Aphrodite entered the room together. It wasn't long before the eagle-eyed Hera spotted the Duchess's left hand as she brushed her ash-blonde fringe from her forehead.

"Elizabeth, darling," Hera cried, "congratulations. James, you old romantic. Congratulations to you both. What wonderful news."

Phoenix strolled across to the side table to fetch himself a soft drink. He knew he might as well make himself comfortable for a while. This meeting would get nothing done until the women had gushed over the size and quality of the ring Heracles had bought.

Although he wouldn't admit it, he was pleased for Heracles. Sir James Grant-Nicholls was one of the Olympus hierarchy for whom Phoenix had a lot of time. Aphrodite was from the nobility, extremely wealthy, and with her big heart in the right place. Phoenix accepted her as a staunch supporter of the Olympus Project and its ideals. But he could never imagine inviting Elizabeth to Larcombe Manor and chilling out on the patio with her over a few beers. The gulf between their social standing would always be far too wide.

Phoenix sat and watched as Zeus, Hera, and Athena surrounded the happy couple. Apollo and Dionysus had arrived, had a brief chat with Zeus, and came across the room to join him.

The newcomers, Achilles, Daedalus, and Ambrosia, were present today, ready for their first meeting. They looked uncomfortable as they stood to one side, confused by what they saw.

"Good morning, Phoenix," said Apollo, "it's good to see you again."

Dionysus nodded a greeting. Sir Malcolm Dunseith had earned respect through his civil service career and his role on the Privy Council. He was as eager as Phoenix to cut this pantomime short and get into the meat of the meeting.

"Let's make the three new gods welcome," said Phoenix. "I checked the seating arrangements as I collected my orange juice. Each of us has one of them sitting next to us. If we introduce ourselves and usher them to their seats, it might persuade the others we need to start."

Phoenix had recognised Achilles at once. Ludovic Tremayne's bearing showed him to be every inch the military man he had been before leaving the British Army to create a successful business empire. He offered his hand.

"Welcome, Achilles; I'm Phoenix."

"Ah, Phoenix, I look forward to working with you."

Phoenix guided the ex-soldier to the oval table.

"We're here," he said and sat next to where he hoped his wife would be very soon.

His companions had joined them, and all six were now

seated. Zeus spotted the flurry of movement around him and realised it was time to move.

"Right," he said, "perhaps we can begin," and he took his place at the head of the table. Hera sat on his right-hand side; Athena sat on his left, next to Phoenix, as the others filled the remaining seats. Phoenix glanced towards the vacant twelfth chair. There would be no place for Aurora, not now nor in the future. They had avenged Dawn Prentice's death even if her position within Olympus had never materialised.

As he reflected on the events leading up to her death and the subsequent action he and Rusty had taken, he sensed somebody watching him. At the far end of the table, next to Dionysus, sat the diminutive Piya Adani, now known as Ambrosia.

Phoenix smiled. Ambrosia gave no sign she had noticed; her eyes had shifted to Athena.

"Ah, she's giving each of us the once-over," thought Phoenix, "weighing up the opposition."

The successful young businesswoman had great ambition. She hadn't transformed her father's modest family business into a global phenomenon by being afraid to make tough decisions.

Phoenix anticipated her having designs on reaching the summit of the Project. Zeus would step aside one day. Athena was next in line for the top job, with Phoenix by her side. How long before Ambrosia mounted a challenge against that eventuality, he wondered?

Zeus checked everyone had switched off their mobile phones and confirmed that the venue had been swept for bugs by Olympus staff before the gods arrived. Security was essential.

"Today marks the start of a new era as we progress to

regaining our optimum number of twelve gods. Our three newcomers provide us with far more than the money they have agreed to commit to the Project. They bring valuable commercial experience, military intelligence, and in Ambrosia's case, youth. These qualities will be essential to Olympus's future."

Over the next ninety minutes, he gave them an update on the Project's progress in many countries worldwide. He described the significant commitment of agents in hot spots on four continents and the drain on financial resources this represented. Athena and Phoenix listened as Zeus praised them for their successful actions at home since the last meeting.

"The Grid is far from being beaten," he cautioned, "but, week by week, we have dealt telling blows on their network, thanks to Phoenix and his teams. We removed their leading figures, and as the summer ends, we will receive a welcome addition to the number of agents at our disposal. Perhaps, you can expand on that, Athena?"

"The first intake of new operatives will finish their training at Larcombe Manor by September," Athena said. "The first batch of agents withdrawn from duty overseas are four weeks into their six-week reassessment programme. Our two teams of trainers have been superb. They have proved to be an excellent choice. The speed of training and re-training may be slower than we wish, but when the agents start active duty, they will be ready."

"How many agents will that be?" asked Ambrosia.

"We can only train fifty new agents yearly," replied Phoenix. "The re-training exercise is for the one hundred agents we repatriated. We are handling a dozen agents on this course. So far, their physical and psychological tests haven't eliminated anyone as unfit for active duty. That may not be the case with later batches. We hoped for an eighty per cent success rate. Early signs are good for bettering that, but it's impossible to predict."

"Will a twenty-five per cent increase in UK-based agents be enough for Olympus to carry out the missions we need?" asked Achilles.

"With only five hundred agents available, it stretches our resources," said Athena. "An extra one hundred and thirty will not be unwelcome."

"Recent events have shown that as we step up the direct action against the Grid, we will experience losses," Phoenix added. "Two men were injured on Sunday night in Scotland, as you have heard. When the 2015 intakes take up their posts, they might only replace men and women who have lost their lives in the fight against the Grid. Unless there's a sudden cut in the number of volatile spots around the globe, then we cannot count on any agents arriving for re-training for the foreseeable future. If we lose people in actions abroad, we will need to replace them. So, we must understand that not everyone training at Larcombe will end up on assignment to a UK-based team."

"Maybe, we need to think outside the box," said Ambrosia, "because operating from hand-to-mouth could lead to cutbacks in the services we offer. One only has to look at every other organisation in the country at present to see what damage that does."

"If you have any suggestions on how to do things better during this period of austerity, then please, share them," said Athena.

Phoenix could feel the tension in the room as the two younger women crossed swords for the first time. He was not alone; Mother Hen came to the rescue.

"I think it's time we took a break for refreshments," said

Hera. "There's much for everyone to take in. Our newcomers haven't met everyone around the table yet. I suggest we relax, socialise for thirty minutes, and then tackle the second half of the agenda."

**Grab your copy...**
**vinci-books.com/revenge-in-colours**

## About the Author

Ted Tayler is the international best-selling indie author of the Freeman Files and Phoenix series. Ted lives in the English West country, where his stories are based. He was born in 1945 and has been married to Lynne since 1971. They have three children and four grandchildren.

His thought-provoking mysteries appeal to readers of Sally Rigby, Joy Ellis, Pauline Rowson, and Faith Martin. His action-packed thrillers are a must for fans of Mark Dawson and J C Ryan.

Gus Freeman's cold case investigations are carried out with reasoned deduction rather than bursts of frantic action. In each of the 24 books, unsolved murders are accompanied by romance, humour, and country life. The core message in the 12 Phoenix novels is that criminals should pay for their crimes. Unfortunately, the current system fails to deliver the correct punishment, so Phoenix helps redress the balance.

# Acknowledgments

The love and support of my family; without them, this would have been impossible.